BATTLESHIP

BATTLESHIP

PETER DAVID

BASED ON THE SCREENPLAY BY
ERICH HOEBER AND JON HOEBER

BALLANTINE BOOKS • NEW YORK

Battleship is a work of fiction. Names, characters, places, and incidents either are products of the author's imagination or are used fictitiously. Any resemblance to actual events, locales, or persons, living or dead, is entirely coincidental.

A Del Rey Mass Market Original

Copyright © 2012 by Hasbro, Inc. All rights reserved.
BATTLESHIP motion picture copyright © 2012 by Universal Pictures, All rights reserved.

All rights reserved.

Published in the United States by Del Rey, an imprint of The Random House Publishing Group, a division of Random House, Inc., New York.

BATTLESHIP is a trademark of Hasbro, Inc. and is used with permission.

DEL REY is a registered trademark and the Del Rey colophon is a trademark of Random House, Inc.

Based on Hasbro's Battleship® Board Game

ISBN 978-0-345-53537-5
eBook ISBN 978-0-345-53538-2

Cover design: Susan Schultz
Cover illustration: HASBRO and its logo and BATTLESHIP are trademarks of Hasbro and are used with permission. Copyright © 2012 Hasbro. BATTLESHIP motion picture © 2012 Universal Studios.

Printed in the United States of America

www.delreybooks.com
www.hasbro.com

9 8 7 6 5 4 3 2 1

Del Rey mass market edition: May 2012

*"I wish to have no connection
with any ship that does not sail fast;
for I intend to go in Harm's Way."*

—JOHN PAUL JONES

BATTLESHIP

SOME YEARS AGO

"Miss."

The two brothers are in the forest near their house, sitting opposite each other. They are both quite young, although the big brother has felt very old for a long time— because he is the older brother, and as such has many important responsibilities. The most vital of these, as far as he is concerned, is to make sure that his kid brother remembers who's boss.

It is the younger brother's greatest failing that he never seems to remember that.

The older brother is sitting on a log, allowing him to look down upon his brother. This is, as far as he is concerned, what should be the natural state of things, the proper order of the universe. The younger brother is seated across from him, cross-legged on the ground, getting his pants filthy from sitting in the dirt and not caring about it. It is a crisp day and they're both wearing light hoodies: the older brother's is white, the younger's is red.

They both have pads of lined paper on their laps, playing a game their father taught them called "Broadsides." They've used pencils to draw vertical lines intersecting with the horizontal ones and thus created grids, which they've then numbered. They're using the pads to have a simulated naval battle. It's natural that their father, a Navy man himself, would teach them how to play it, and claims to have played it when he himself was young.

It is the older brother who has just said "Miss," and the younger brother's eyebrows both leap up on his forehead as if they've come loose and are endeavoring to make a run for it.

"Whattaya mean, 'miss,'" says the younger brother in irritation.

"It's like a hit, but the opposite," the older brother says.

"It can't be a miss!"

"Well, it was. D-7 . . ."

"No, wait, shut up." The younger brother stares at his smaller grid where he's keeping track of his hits. "I said G-1."

"And I said miss."

"It can't be! That was the fifth hit on your aircraft carrier! Game over!"

"It wasn't and it isn't. D-7 . . ."

"You're cheating."

The back of the older brother's neck starts to get red. "I am not. You just can't stand that I'm going to win a game—"

"No," says the younger brother, getting into the elder's face in that way that he has. "You just can't stand that I'm going to win AGAIN. You can't stand that I always win and that you always lose. Loser. Looooooser. Looooser loooooser looooser!" He forms an L-shape from his thumb and forefinger and puts it against his head.

"Shut up!" The older brother's fury is rising. "G-1 wasn't a hit. Live with it."

"I don't believe you. Lemme see." He is up on his knees and he grabs for the older brother's pad of paper.

The older brother yanks it away. "Forget it! If you look at it, the game's over!"

"The game's already over, loser."

The worst thing of all is that the older brother knows that this is true. He looks at G-1, where the prow of his *theoretical aircraft carrier is sitting. He looks at the smug expression on his stupid little brother.*

And suddenly long-simmering resentment boils up and over, and before his younger brother can get to him, the older brother tears apart the lined notepad in a paroxysm of fury. "This game is stupid and you're stupid!"

"You're stupid, loser!"

The older brother doesn't want to run back to the house because he feels hot tears of mortification streaming down his face. And the last thing he needs is his father standing over him and demanding to know what's wrong. So instead he swings his legs over the log, gets to his feet, and starts running, shouting, "Leave me alone!"

"Will not!" *says the younger brother—the little idiot, the brainless turd.*

The older brother is running through the woods now, and the younger is right after him, shouting at him, taunting him. He keeps moving, but the little brat is pacing him easily. How the hell does he do that when his legs are shorter? It should be impossible.

There is a river running through the forest just up ahead. It's too wide to ford, the boundary of their property. He cuts right, moving quickly along it. His younger brother is in pursuit, still taunting, still calling him names, and at that moment he has never hated anyone in his life more than he does his younger brother.

Suddenly he hears an alarmed shriek, and a skidding of feet on dirt. He spins just in time to see his younger brother tumble down an embankment, a section of dirt apparently having given way beneath his feet. His younger brother's head strikes a rock that's projecting sideways from the embankment, and the sound it makes when it hits is nauseating. The older brother sees, in horror, that there is fresh blood on the rock, and then his younger brother splashes into the river. It's not especially deep, but the current is quite strong lately thanks to the heavy rain. All the older brother can see now is a brief image of the back of his kid brother's sweat jacket—a flash of red in the speeding waters—and then his tormentor is washed away.

With a shriek of pure horror, he calls out his younger brother's name, "Alex!" and practically vaults down the embankment to the edge of the river. He sprints along it frantically, trying to catch up, hoping that on foot he's faster than the speed of the water. He closes the gap a little and then a massive fallen tree is blocking his path along the shoreline.

He has no choice.

He throws himself into the water and starts swimming for both his brother's life and his own.

THE HIMALAYAS—2006

The Himalayas? Are you serious? Are you kidding me? That had been Doctor Abraham Nogrady's original thought when he had first been approached about the Beacon International Project.

Nogrady was middle-aged, lean, with a perpetual stoop that had come from a lifetime of leaning over equipment and studying it with an almost demented intensity. He had a prominent nose and a head of curly black hair, with a bald spot developing like an island of flesh in the back of his head.

From Nogrady's personal situation, the offer could not have come at a better time. His work at SETI had been defunded, thanks to the shortsighted fools in Congress who couldn't see the fundamental necessity of searching for extraterrestrial life. Bad enough that they had gutted NASA, woefully sighing that there was simply no point in focusing on building moon stations and such when we had so many problems right here. But they had literally laughed his SETI work right out of existence, with many snide comments and even a few reactionaries stating that the only way they'd fund searches for extraterrestrials was if Will Smith was put in charge so he would be able to fend off any resulting alien attacks.

Nogrady had wanted to get right into the faces of those smug bastards during the congressional budget hearing. Were they at all aware of the amount of modern technology, which they took for granted, that was a direct result of the space program? Did they ever consider that watching the skies would enable scientists to pick up on objects in space heading toward Earth on a collision course, enabling them to sound the alarm and—with any luck—see that countermeasures were taken? Did it occur to them that, on the off chance humanity managed to beat the odds and actually make contact with extraterrestrial life, it would be the single most important development for mankind since the discovery of fire and the invention of the wheel? *How could you be so blind?* That was what he had wanted to jump up and shout. But he had held his tongue, and the result had been his job flushed away by idiots and buffoons.

When Beacon had been offered him two months later, it had been a godsend. However the prospect of relocating to the Himalayas, of all places, had been less than attractive.

And the *Greater* Himalayas, just to make it worse. At least there were some sections of the Himalayas that were livable. The Shilawik Hills, for instance, were supposed to be quite nice. The Midlands were said to have over sixty species of rhododendrons alone in the subalpine conifer forests.

But the Greater Himalayas were . . . well, they were exactly what one pictured when one heard the name "Himalayas." Mountain ranges nearly three miles high, cloaked in an endless blanket of ice and snow. The facility itself was buried—almost literally—in Tibet, and the howling of the wind never stopped so much as it sometimes grew and sometimes diminished. On occasion the sunlight filtered through, but routinely they would go for days shrouded in darkness, like an entire facility of people who were slowly going blind.

And yes, Nogrady understood the need to operate under the radar. He understood the desire for secrecy. The funding for this endeavor was coming through governments working with private sources, and that was always a touchy subject because nosy politicians would then start demanding investigations and wanting to know what were the sources' motivations.

When Nogrady had finally made the trek up to the site, what he saw on the outside didn't seem especially promising. In fact, it looked downright unprepossessing. Short and squat, two stories tall, fashioned of white brick, with antennae arrays and satellite dishes on the roof and massive generators next to it. There was already a layer of permafrost on the building and Nogrady was concerned that within two weeks he'd go stir-crazy.

That hadn't been the case, as it turned out. Instead he had found a dedicated group of scientists who were familiar with Nogrady's work and were thrilled to have him on board as the project director. What he hadn't accounted for in his initial trepidation was that this sort of environment tended to cause people to bond in a way that wasn't possible under less claustrophobic circumstances. The team had quickly formed a smooth, cohesive unit as they had worked together to develop and fine-tune the equipment necessary to accomplishing their collective goal.

Most intriguingly, they had been doing so in tandem with several other locations. Nogrady had never been to them, but he had seen pictures of the cinder-block building in Morocco, isolated in the Sahara—hidden in plain sight, as it were—and a third on a mountaintop in Hawaii. The respective staffs had shared information, engaged in lengthy intercontinental brainstorming sessions, and ultimately come up with designs and equipment together that no individual group could have developed fully.

And when they hadn't been working, there had been plenty of late-night parties to blow off steam. Curiously, some of the best ideas had resulted from those gatherings, as idle talk and occasionally drunken inspiration had sent the group sprinting back to the lab to try implementing them.

Now, finally, all of that had come to a head. Approaching the moment with what seemed appropriate pomp and circumstance, Nogrady had arranged a full-blown ribbon-cutting ceremony. His colleagues had suspended a long, red ribbon across the middle of their now state-of-the-art facility and Nogrady had sliced through it with a replica samurai sword he'd borrowed from Doctor Okuda. This had been met with a burst of cheers, followed by the scientists settling down to work. There was growing excitement in the air for this moment toward which they had been building for two years.

"Synch with Morocco and Oahu," Nogrady said briskly. He was trying to keep his voice flat and even. He needed to remain professional, and chortling with unconcealed delight would certainly not be in keeping with his desired demeanor.

"Synched," said Carlson, a young technician who was so fresh out of grad school that sometimes he was jokingly referred to as still having that "new scientist smell."

There had been a constant buzz of motion and activity, but all that somehow quieted to a hush when Carlson said that. Everyone stopped in anticipation of Nogrady's next words.

He tried to think of something that wouldn't sound too pretentious and he failed utterly. "People . . . get ready to make history."

Doctor Calvin Zapata rolled his eyes when Nogrady spoke about making history. Zapata thought that Nogrady was brilliant, but—even for a scientist—he could be kind of a dork on occasion. This was one of those occasions.

Not to mention the fact that Zapata had his own issues with what they were doing there that he had to deal with. Issues that he wasn't hesitating to voice to one of his coworkers, Rachel Dorn. It didn't hurt, of course, that Rachel was also the best-looking woman in the place: several years younger than Zapata, with thick red hair, a charming array of freckles across her nose that had faded during her time there (but were still slightly visible), and horn-rimmed glasses that were perpetually perched on the edge of that same nose.

He was seated next to Dorn, both of them on rolling chairs, studying the readouts to make sure that—as the energy levels increased—the climb was slow and steady and didn't spike. In a low voice he muttered, in regards to Nogrady's pronouncement, "I think that's what Napoleon said right before Waterloo."

She shook her head. "Cal . . ." she said scoldingly, knowing what was coming next.

She was absolutely right. Zapata was on a roll, and faint recriminations from Dorn weren't about to stop him. "Everyone here still believes that if there's life out there, it's kind and good and all that *Kumbaya* crap."

Dorn had been keeping her attention fully on the

monitoring devices in front of her, but she risked a side-long glance at Zapata. "Your conspiracy disorder is activating again."

He rolled in closer to her under the guise of wanting to speak confidentially. In point of fact, he just liked being near her. She smelled incredible. He had no idea how the hell she was getting a supply of whatever that scent she wore was, considering they were in the middle of nowhere. It took him a moment to get focused back on what he'd just been talking about, but he managed. "We need to worry about what happens *after* we get a response, because believe me, it's not gonna be—"

"All Kumbaya? Cal, do you even know what 'Kumbaya' means?"

He paused, looking confused. "It means everybody gets along and toasts marshmallows around a campfire and stuff. Doesn't it?"

"It means 'come by here.' It's asking for God to come by and smile on his creations. And if there *is* a God," she added, smiling, "then he created whatever's out there, and maybe he'd like us all to meet and hold hands."

If she hadn't been so charming, Zapata would have been appalled by her naïveté. "If there really *is* intelligent life out there and they 'come by here,'" he said sourly, "it'll be like Columbus and the Indians. Only *we're* the Indians."

"Most of the time he traded peacefully with the Indians, except for one time in the Dominican Republic when the Indians attacked and drove him away. So what's your point?"

He stared at her. "You're just a fount of information today, aren't 'cha."

"Look, Cal," she said patiently, "if you don't believe in the mission, why are you here?"

It wasn't an unreasonable question. "J. Robert Oppenheimer never believed in using atomic weapons. But he's the guy who built the bomb. The Manhattan Project was where the smartest guys in the world were. And the smartest women, too," and he winked at her.

She shushed him and pointed toward the other side of the room. They turned their attention there as Nogrady, standing behind Carlson, rested a hand on the young technician's shoulder. "Send it," he said.

Carlson inputted the codes that would bring the entire facility online. There was a pause, no more than half a heartbeat, but enough time for Zapata to realize that if everything suddenly short-circuited and went dark, he wouldn't be the least bit choked up about it.

Instead all the instrumentation came online perfectly. The project had gone live.

The next sound they heard was a hollow popping noise. One of the scientists had opened a bottle of champagne. The cork flew, ricocheted off a far wall and bounced off Zapata's forehead as if it had eyes. Nobody except Dorn noticed, and she put up a hand to suppress a laugh. Zapata forced a smile.

The very first glass to be filled with champagne was handed over to Nogrady. He held it up and announced, "And that's how it starts."

Similar scenes were simultaneously being enacted in Morocco and Hawaii. In both those locations, as well as this one, the radar dishes pinged to life and began sending out a steady signal. Thousands of miles over the planet, satellites were orbiting, their panels adjusting to receive the transmissions and beam them into the depths of space.

It was the astronomical equivalent of a message in a bottle, but at least it was something.

Zapata watched all the relays, the steady pulsing lines moving with perfect synchronization across the screens, indicating that everything was processing correctly. Everyone else, even the enticing Dorn, was part of the celebration, Dorn clapping her hands and "whooping" as if she were at a football game. Only he remained at his station, watching the results of the initial pulses with cold, hard eyes.

Get ready to make history.

Nogrady's words came back to Zapata. *Yeah. That's all well and good. But there's a thin line between making history, and being made history. And I hope to God we haven't crossed it.*

HONOLULU, 2006

The Hideaway was kind of a dump. The patrons liked it that way. It meant that the idiot tourists tended to stay the hell away from it, and it could be someplace for people who were in the know to hang out.

It was a hotel bar, attached to a hotel that was somewhat of a fleabag itself. But it was cheap, which was something you couldn't say about a lot of hotels in Honolulu, and that was enough to prompt a few tourists— who didn't care that the neighborhood was run-down—to book rooms there. Not a lot, but enough to keep the place in business. It was also a popular hangout for the U.S. Navy, for reasons that no one could quite determine. The general suspicion was that the tradition had its roots somewhere back in the days of the Pearl Harbor bombing. Supposedly key Navy personnel had snuck off the base and were drinking at the Hideaway when the Japanese attacked. Consequently they survived, and the place had maintained a charmed existence ever since.

At least that was how the story went.

The cocktail waitress looked worn and haggard, as she tended to be when she was approaching the end of her shift. Her straight black hair was tied back in a bun, but there were random strands hanging in her face. She wore a blue flowered sarong—since that was what the tourists expected—but she moved like someone who wasn't particularly comfortable in it. She'd rather be wearing a T-shirt and shorts any day.

Pouring whiskey into two shot glasses, she placed them onto a tray and headed over toward a table where a couple of brothers, the Hoppers, were seated. They'd both already had more alcohol than they really should have, but they didn't care in the least. All that mattered to them was that the whiskey arrived in time, because the clock was ticking down. There were a few other customers in the Hideaway, but most of them were pretty much drunk anyway, oblivious of one another's existence. "I love my life," she muttered unconvincingly.

The Hopper brothers were waiting for her, a bedraggled-looking cupcake sitting in front of them, a single pathetic candle sticking lopsidedly out of it, like the Leaning Tower of Pisa.

Stone Hopper was tall and lean, with a head of thick blond hair, a wide nose and plain, open eyes that seemed incapable of hiding a lie. His default expression, indeed his entire attitude, was one of patient understanding. But that could, at a moment's notice, harden into a look of total command. Considering he was an officer in the U.S. Navy, it was a capability that served him in good stead.

His brother, Alex, was a different story. Barrel-chested and well-muscled, he maintained a look of permanent party-boy dishevelment. On any given day he had at least three days' growth of beard, with his overlong brown hair frequently hanging in front of his round face. A T-shirt that read *Burnt Demolition Co.* was stretched across a ripped chest that had gotten that way mostly because he had formerly worked at the place emblazoned on his shirt. The job was gone, but the shirt remained. He had long ago disdained his first name, embracing his surname and preferring to be addressed simply as "Hopper" or "Hopps." When asked, he would cavalierly explain that "Alex" was a lame-assed name compared to "Stone" and he would leave it at that. If asked to explain beyond that, all he'd give you was a stare equal to Stone's look of command.

Stone was squinting, watching as best he could—considering his inebriated state—the second hand sweeping around on his wristwatch until it finally hit midnight. Then, very portentously, he announced, "This year, Hopps, I'm quoting from—and this one took me awhile—the great, late Coach John Wooden."

"Who?" said Hopper.

"John Wooden!" Stone sounded surprised, even a bit hurt that he had to explain it further. "Great college basketball coach! Maybe the greatest coach ever!"

"Greatest coach?" Hopper regarded him with a raised eyebrow that was pretty much all the dubiousness that he could muster at the moment.

"One of 'em," said Stone.

Hopper considered that, clearly not accepting the proposition. "If he was the greatest coach, why'd he coach college? Couldn't cut it in the big show?"

Stone was offended at the notion that his younger brother would challenge him on this point. "'Cause he was a purist and an educator. And," he added as if this was the slam dunk of his claim, "a man of honor."

"So he was broke," said Hopper.

Stone raised his voice to drive home his assertion. Because when one is having trouble convincing someone of the rightness of one's belief—and facts are being thrown in one's face that would seem to undercut those beliefs— it was always best to up the volume. "He was one of the *greatest* men who ever *lived*."

"Broke."

Stone was both offended and dismayed at his brother's attitude. "No, actually, Hopper, *you're* broke," he said pointedly. "John Wooden died rich in respect, and golden in reputation."

Hopper snorted, as if Stone's extolling of Wooden's virtues was simply proof of what Hopper was saying. "But real low in cash."

"For someone who only cares about how inflated a person's wallet is, you've done a pretty piss poor job of living up to—" He stopped himself and shook his head. This was clearly a pointless discussion. Hopper was never going to get it; all he'd do was dig in to the notion that nothing mattered but money, failing to realize that holding that up as an indicator of a man's value reflected rather poorly on his own sense of worth. "Light your cupcake and raise your glass," he said with grudging acknowledgment that it was time to move on.

Hopper wasn't looking at him. He was staring in his general direction, but not actually paying attention to his brother. Stone turned in his seat, and when he saw the subject of his brother's scrutiny, he moaned inwardly. *Oh God. Not* her. *Anyone but her.*

A gorgeous young woman was seated at the bar, arguing with the bartender, a big Hawaiian named Akau. The woman was a knockout of a blonde, with sculpted features and piercing blue eyes that a man could take a headfirst dive into and never want to emerge. Add to that the fact that she not only had a body that wouldn't quit, but a body that no one would ever think of firing once it was in their employ. A couple of island boys were standing off to the side, eyeing her with a drunken longing, although it was impossible to determine whether they would wind up hitting on her or just admiring her from afar.

She was pointing at a sign hanging just beyond the bartender's head. "Sign says 'food till close,'" she said with the triumphant air of a lawyer who had just proven her point in a court of law. She gestured around the still-active bar. "This is not closed. I want a chicken burrito. I just drove from North Shore."

"Kitchen closed," said Akau, regarding her with a bored expression, clearly not the least bit interested in diving into her eyes or any other part of her. He just wanted to be left the hell alone.

Like a dog with a bone in her teeth, the blonde wasn't about to let it go. "You can't stick a burrito in a microwave?"

"No," he said flatly. He picked up a glass that was already clean and started wiping it.

Stone was determined to drag Hopper's attention, kicking and screaming, back to their underwhelming—but still sincere—birthday celebration. He made an effort to straighten the candle and then lit it. He snapped his fingers in Hopper's face, startling his brother back to the real world, a world that the gorgeous blonde was not, in any way, shape or form, going to be a part of. "So," Stone said before his brother could refocus on the girl. He had removed a small folded piece of paper from his shirt pocket and was reading from it. "In the great Hopper family tradition, I, on the day now of your twenty-sixth birthday—"

"Twenty-fifth," Hopper corrected him.

Stone lowered the paper and stared at his brother incredulously. They were going to argue about *this* now? Was there anything the kid *wouldn't* argue about? "Twenty-sixth," said Stone.

"I'm twenty-five."

God, give me strength. Speaking very slowly, as if to

an idiot, Stone said, "You were born on March 11, 1980."

"I know when I was born."

"You're just on a power trip," the girl's voice came from the bar. She was dripping with sarcasm. "The keeper of the food. Power trip. Would it *really* crush your little world to break the big rule and fire me up a burrito?"

Hopper was starting to lose focus on his brother, something that Stone was determined to avert, because there was no way that any involvement between Hopper and that particular girl could end in anything but disaster. "You are twenty-six years old," Stone said with determination. "It's March 11, 2006. So, 1980 to 2006. Twenty-six-year difference. Makes you twenty-six years old. I'm twenty-nine. You are twenty-six. That's never changed. Impossible to change."

The fact that Stone was right shouldn't have deterred Hopper in the least. All that was required for him to become intransigent was for Stone to make an assertion, and Hopper would promptly dig in to a contrary position. He was perfectly capable of claiming that it was, in fact, 2005, just to keep the argument going.

In this instance, Hopper quickly said, "Okay." Stone should have been pleased that his brother was willing to drop it. Instead he was concerned that the only reason Hopper conceded the point was because he wanted to go back to looking at the girl. Determined to make certain that Hopps didn't do something stupid like follow the impulse, Stone raised his glass to keep the celebration on track.

"From John Wooden," he said with great solemnity. "'Adversity is the state in which man most easily becomes acquainted with himself, being especially free of admirers then.'"

Hopper stared at him blankly. "What's your point with that one?"

"My point is: happy birthday. I love you, and I'm wishing you growth and success. May this be a great year for you."

They both downed the shots. It wasn't the world's greatest whiskey, or even the tenth greatest whiskey. But it still caused a pleasant heat as it went down, and Stone briefly allowed it to dull his brain and take some of the edge off his normally edgy personality. Then he saw that, once again, he might as well not have been there insofar as his brother was concerned. Hopper was watching the damned girl, who was still locked in battle with Akau. At least *she* was locked in battle. Akau was ignoring her, so it was more or less a one-way fight.

"Don't you dare," said Stone, knowing what was going through his brother's mind.

"What?" Hopper gazed at him with that patented look of disingenuous innocence.

Stone pointed at the candle, indicating the flickering flame. "You actually need some wishes to come true. Some *real* wishes, big life wishes."

"It's my wish," he said defensively.

"Don't you waste it."

Hopper was smiling at the girl. "*My* wish."

"Do not waste your wish on a girl," Stone warned him. "Not now. Especially not on a girl who is way, way above your pay grade. Wish for a job. A family, children. A job."

"You already said a job."

Stone wasn't going to be distracted from the central theme of his premise. "Don't waste it."

Hopper blew out the candle, never once removing his gaze from the girl.

His brother sighed heavily. "You wasted your wish, didn't you."

"Let's find out."

Hopper slid off his seat . . . and nearly kept going,

heading to an inevitable date with the floor. As far as Stone was concerned, that would have been far preferable. Having Hopper sprawled unconscious on the floor was definitely a better outcome than the certain train wreck that was going to result from him hitting on the blonde.

Unfortunately Hopper managed to catch himself at the last moment and keep his feet. Very carefully, he stood up to his full height and began to half saunter, half stagger toward the bar.

Stop him. For God's sake, stop him. Stone began to rise from his seat and then, with a resigned sigh, sank back down. His brother was twenty-six (not, as rumored, twenty-five). Sooner or later, Stone had to stop working overtime to keep him out of trouble. Perhaps if Hopper got his nose good and bloodied, he might wind up listening to Stone instead of disregarding his counsel.

Besides, he was sitting in a run-down bar at just past midnight. One had to find entertainment where one could.

"Policy change," said Akau in his same, flat, disinterested voice.

"Policy? *Really?*" The calmer the bartender got, the more agitated she became. "A policy is something that you have on immigration, education, invading a country."

He was not remotely persuaded. "Policy change," he repeated monotonously.

Hopper had a self-image of being smooth and charming. The reality would not remotely have matched up with what was in his head, had he been able to see it. Fortunately for the tattered remains of his self-esteem, he couldn't. He slid in next to the blonde and said, in his best imitation of the guy from *Friends*, "How *you* doing?"

"Hungry. Starving." She wasn't addressing her comments to him. Instead she was lobbing them like poison spears at the bartender. Akau continued not to react in the slightest.

"I've got a cupcake. It's my birthday cupcake."

She still wasn't even deigning to look at him. Instead she closed her eyes in annoyance, as if wishing she could open them and find herself someplace else, where eats were plentiful and available in an inverse proportion to the availability of drunken idiots. "I don't want a cupcake. I want food."

"Can I buy you a drink?"

With a sigh she finally turned and looked at him with those gorgeous blue eyes that a man could just get lost in. She didn't seem to be losing herself in his, however. Instead she looked vaguely bored. "What's your name?"

"Hopper," he said eagerly.

With overstated, weary patience, she informed him, "I don't want a drink, Hopper. I don't want a cupcake. I want a chicken burrito. That's *all* I want. A chicken burrito, and this jackass won't give me one. You want to buy me a drink? Get me some food."

It was obvious that she wasn't expecting him to do anything of the kind. It was just the simplest and most expedient means of getting rid of him. That, however, did not deter Hopper. If anything, it only provided him with incentive. "Done. I give you my word. Two minutes. Will you give me two minutes?"

In spite of herself, she smiled ever so slightly. He was amusing to her. "You're on the clock," she warned.

Hopper quickly headed out, his total focus on his quest burning away some of the haze that had settled in his brain. As he passed Stone he said hurriedly, by way of explanation, "Girl's hungry."

His brother moaned when he heard that, shaking his head. "It's like a factory fire. You know you're witnessing a disaster, but you can't look away."

Hopper wasn't listening. Instead his mind was racing and his body was hurrying to catch up.

The fortunate thing was that Hopper knew the area very well. He'd hung out around there enough that at this point he could be leaning against a lamppost, going nowhere and doing nothing. If the cops should happen to cruise past—instead of rousting him and telling him to move along—they'd wave, greet him by name and keep going.

Best of all, he knew that there was a convenience store less than thirty seconds away. He would be able to beat the two-minute deadline with time to spare.

He sprinted out the back of the hotel, across the block, toward the convenience store. But as he approached, he was dismayed to see the proprietor, an Asian woman of indeterminate age—somewhere between forty and a hundred and forty, as near as he could tell—was pulling a rattling gate across the door. There was a heavy padlock on it. Before she could reach for it, he ran up to her. The world was spinning around him as he tried to shake away the buzzing in his head. "Excuse me, ma'am . . ."

"Closed," she said brusquely. She reached for the padlock.

"No, wait!" He gestured toward the padlock desperately, trying his best to sound charming . . . or at least as charming as he could considering he was fighting to remain conscious. "Don't lock it. You're not closed until you lock it."

This seemed to him to be irrefutable logic. Unfortunately she managed to refute it through the simple means of snapping the padlock shut. "Closed."

"Yeah, yeah, but this is important. I need a chicken burrito."

"No chicken burrito." The woman couldn't have been more than five feet tall, and yet she loomed like a colossus in the path of true happiness.

"Yes, chicken burrito. I see them right there." He pointed toward the darkened window.

"Chicken burrito, 9 a.m."

There seemed to be no arguing with her. Yet that didn't deter him from doing so all the same. "That sign in there says chicken burrito, $2.99. I'll give you . . ." He shoved his hands into his pockets and yanked out the first bill he found. It was a ten, all wadded up, and he smoothed it as best he could. "Ten dollars if you let me in."

She maintained her indifferent attitude. "Closed. Go away."

"Twenty." He was pulling more money out of his pockets, trying to figure out how much he had on him. All the bills were crumpled. It was like carrying an assortment of spitballs in his pockets. He pulled them apart frantically.

The Asian woman started moving toward her car, an ancient Toyota with rust spots on the roof. Hopper paced her, counting the money he had on him, hoping that it would be enough.

"Fifty. *Fifty dollars* for a chicken burrito." He waved the money in her face. "That's my spending money for the *month* and I'm going to give it to you." He tried desperately to drive home the importance of his offering, not even mentioning that—for crying out loud—it was nearly twenty times the cost of the damned burrito. She managed a store. Her whole thing was about making money. With this kind of offer in front of her, there was simply no way that she would walk away from it.

She walked away.

He ran around her, interposing himself between her and the car. This finally stopped her and she glared fiercely up at him.

"Ma'am. Ma'am, please." He spoke rapidly, the subsequent words tumbling over each other, and he had to fight not to slur them. "If it was for me, I'd go away. But it's not. There's this girl over there," and he pointed in the general direction of the hotel. "She's incredible." *Establish human contact. The way that waiters do right before they bring the bill, in order to get a bigger tip. Touch her. But not in a threatening way; do it in a socially acceptable way.* He put a hand on her arm. "You don't understand. She's my future. And she's hungry." His voice was throbbing with emotion. "My future depends on a chicken burrito."

Apparently he would have made a lousy waiter, because the woman lifted the small can of Mace dangling from her key chain and assumed a vicious karate stance. "Your future's gonna be pepper spray."

Immediately he removed his hand from her arm. Brushing him aside, she climbed into her car. He made no move to stop her because he had finally admitted to himself that this wasn't going to get him anywhere. It was time for Plan B, and the first part of Plan B was having this obstructionist store manager get out of here as quickly as possible. In this action, at least, she accommodated him, because apparently she couldn't wait to get away from him. The Toyota peeled out with a screeching of tires.

Time was ticking down for Hopper. He'd already wasted a minute pleading with the useless store manager. In his mind's eye, he could see Stone sitting at the table, sipping another whiskey or maybe a beer, with that knowing smirk he always had during times when Hopper was embarking on some disastrous course of action. And then there was the girl, sitting at the bar, waiting for her future husband to get the job done.

All this and more went through Hopper's mind even as he clambered up the side of the building. It wasn't all that difficult. The windows may have had bars over them, but the bars themselves provided toeholds, and his natural athleticism—not to mention single-minded drive—enabled him to reach the flat roof in no time. It was unconscionably thin. "How the hell does this thing even keep water out?" he said as he stomped on it. He looked around and, to his dismay, didn't see any sort of roof access door. Hopper moaned softly. "Now what the hell am I—?"

The roof answered the question before he could finish articulating it, giving way beneath his feet. Hopper crashed through.

Fortunately enough, since he was still pretty drunk, he was also very loose-limbed and didn't tense up. As a result, he didn't hurt himself too much when he slammed to the floor. Mostly it just knocked the wind out of him. Pieces of acoustical tile and insulation fell all around him and he threw his arms over his head to shield himself from it. Once the rain of debris had stopped, Hopper staggered to his feet and moved toward the stack of chicken burritos sitting in a refrigerated compartment. They were individually wrapped in red and white paper. Hopper selected one at random, tossed it in the microwave, and pushed "Start." As the burrito cooked, he moved over toward the register and dropped a few bucks next to it. He briefly considered leaving the fifty he'd originally offered but then decided against it. She'd passed on it. In fact, she'd threatened to pepper spray him. *Fine. Be that way, lady. You get the money for the burrito. Let your insurance company deal with the crappy ceiling. In fact, the whole roof was so shoddily made, I probably did you a favor. Take the insurance money and get a decent roof.*

The microwave dinged and he snatched the burrito out of it. He let out a yelp and tossed it from one hand to the other as he waited for it to become cool enough to handle. As he did so, he glanced around, looking for a means of exit. There was a stepladder propped against the far wall that she probably used for mundane things like changing lightbulbs. He set it under the hole in the roof and quickly clambered up and out. He felt heady with excitement and triumph. *I'm gonna make it,* he thought deliriously, right before another section of the roof gave way. Seconds later he was back inside the store, lying atop a rack of condiments that had exploded all over him from the impact.

As he lay there, trying to shake off the pain, he noticed a back door with a hand-scrawled sign that read "Emergency Exit" on it.

"Yeah . . . that would have been easier," he said with a low moan.

He got slowly to his feet, looking in disgust at the condiments that were all over him, and that was when he heard the police sirens in the distance.

"Oh, that's not good."

He banged through the door and hoped he would be well clear of the convenience store before the cops were close enough to get a bead on him. This hope was quickly dashed when he saw two police cars pulling up, their lights flashing, illuminating the darkened street like a Christmas tree. There were two cops in one and a single cop in the other. The doors were flung open and they spilled out, shouting over one another such useless orders as "Stop!" "Halt!" "Don't move!"

Hopper had never been much when it came to following orders.

The remaining haze of near drunkenness burned away as he sprinted toward the hotel. He figured they weren't going to shoot if he didn't draw a weapon or in some way threaten them. That was his theory, at any rate. If nothing else, he knew that there was a whole lot of extra paperwork cops had to go through if they discharged their weapons and took down a fleeing felon, and he hoped they'd figure he wasn't worth the time.

Felon? Is that what I am? Screw that. I'm not a felon. I'm just a guy who's fighting for his future.

That's what she was. His future. He sprinted toward where he'd left her, picking up speed with every second.

If he were of a fanciful mind, he would have felt love was lending wings to his feet.

He dashed around the back of the hotel, where the bar was situated out on the broad patio. Stone had gotten up from the table and was heading right toward him, probably in response to the police sirens and the shouting. He had a quick glimpse of Stone's face, and his thought process was right there, writ large upon his expression: *Please don't let it be Alex, please don't let it be Alex, please don't . . . oh, crap, it's Alex, I knew it, I knew it.*

But Stone was only a momentary diversion. Hopper's real interest was the girl. No, not just the girl. The Girl. She was The Girl, capitalized, and over time she would become *The Girl* and then THE GIRL and then THE WIFE and eventually *The Wife* and then the wife . . .

Maybe this wasn't such a great idea after all . . .

Instantly he dismissed the doubts. There was no room for doubts. All that mattered was they were meant to be. Except none of it was going to mean a damned thing if she had already left. He'd taken longer than two minutes, and if she had gone . . .

No! There she was! She had been sitting on a bar stool but now she was half off it, her purse in her hand, and she was gaping at him. She looked as if she had no idea how to react. That was hardly surprising. He must have looked insane, his face and clothes covered with mustard, ketchup, mayonnaise, and whatever the hell else had splattered all over him. Not to mention plaster and random bits of debris from the roof he'd fallen through.

He ran right up to her and extended the burrito. She wasn't even looking at it. Instead she was staring straight at him, a dozen different emotions warring on her face.

He tried to catch his breath so he could form words. He was giving no more thought to the cops; as far as he was concerned, the chase was over.

Unfortunately no one had bothered to tell the police. Hopper had just enough time to feel something jammed into his back before his body was jolted by electricity. He tried to say, *I give up* but the only thing to come out of his mouth was "Urkh." As he fell, he flipped the burrito to The Girl. It wasn't so much a toss as it was a spasm, but it was enough to send the burrito angling toward her in an arc. She caught it on the fly, but did so more out of reflex than anything else. If she was still hungry, the feeling was very likely forgotten in the wake of the insanity she was witnessing.

Hopper fell to his knees. The cops had his hands pinned behind his back and were busily applying cuffs to them. *All right. Old school. Not those stupid twist ties, like I'm a plastic garbage bag. Real-life handcuffs. Makes me proud to be an American.*

He managed sufficient breath to get out two words, directed to The Girl: *"Bon appétit."*

One of the cops was busy rattling out Hopper's "right to an attorney," and Stone was shouting that this wasn't necessary, certainly it was just some big misunderstanding, and one of the cops was telling him to step back, this wasn't his business, and Stone was saying, like hell, this was his kid brother, so it sure as hell was his business . . .

And none of it mattered to Hopper. None of it. Only one thing mattered, and that was the reaction of The Girl as she stared down at him being hog-tied like a bull at a rodeo.

A long moment hung there, stretching out into eternity, and one of the cops was saying with increasing irritation, "Do you understand these rights as I have just read them to you?"

Then The Girl said two words. Two magic words.

"Thank you."

And she smiled.

It wasn't just with her mouth. When she smiled, her whole face lit up. And not merely her face either. She lit up the night, like a beam from a lighthouse showing the way to safety and salvation.

Totally worth it.

"Oh yeah," he said, which was all the cops needed to hear before they dragged him away. The last thing he saw was her waving to him, still smiling, as she bit into the burrito.

I can't wait to tell our kids this story . . .

It helped that Stone knew everyone.

He knew Stan, the desk sergeant. He knew Tony, the local sheriff. He hadn't known the three arresting officers, but they were new, and within a few hours of encountering him, Howie, Bob, and Mike were pals of his, too. He also knew the cranky Asian woman, whose named turned out to be Maxine, rather than what Hopper's best guess had been: Medusa.

Now, sitting in front of the television in the living room of his apartment, sunlight filtering through the blinds, Stone watched a copy of the surveillance tape that had caught every moment of his brother's stupidity in the convenience store. It was hot as hell, what with the air-conditioning having broken, so he was wearing only his boxer shorts and an undershirt. Sweat dripped off the Navy anchor he had on his right bicep, the one he'd had tattooed when his carrier had been stationed for a week off San Diego. The way the perspiration was rolling off it, the tattoo was doing a nice impression of having just been weighed.

He winced as he witnessed Hopper crashing through the ceiling a second time. Sometimes he couldn't determine whether the gods protected Hopper from his own stupidity or just enjoyed using his life as a Hacky Sack for their personal amusement. Hopper had been given not one, but two opportunities to break his neck and all he'd wound up with were bumps and bruises.

Slowly Stone looked around the apartment, surveying the visual record of his and Hopper's life together. The living room was lined with photographs that sent such a distinct message to what their futures would be that it was hard to believe the current situation was anything other than inevitable. There were the young Hoppers, ready to go trick-or-treating. Stone was dressed as a cop; Alex was a burglar. There they were as teens, standing on either side of their father, who was dressed in his crisp Navy whites. Stone Hopper was standing at proud attention; Alex Hopper was standing with his shoulders slumped, looking vaguely bored. There was Stone, having just graduated Annapolis, his arm around Hopper. Alex was smiling, but not into the camera. Instead he was looking off to the side and Stone remembered that a gorgeous redhead had been walking past.

It was literally the story of their lives, ever since they were kids.

What was it that Einstein said? The definition of "insanity" was doing the same thing over and over and expecting a different result.

Something had to change. And it had to change immediately.

Stone heard the sloshing of water in the bathroom. Hopper was soaking in an ice bath, trying to prevent swelling and numb the pain.

He called to Hopper, "I told Tony that you're gonna pay Maxine double for all the damage. *Double.*"

"The little witch," Hopper's muttered response came back to him. "Mean . . . nasty . . ."

"Hey!" Stone bounded up from the couch and headed toward the bathroom.

Hopper gazed at him through bleary eyes. His lips were starting to turn blue. If he stayed in there another ten minutes, he'd look like a Smurf. "It was her fault in the first place," he said defensively. "I was a paying customer. She threatened to pepper spray me. What kind of business model is that? If she'd just—"

"She was within her rights to go home! You were not within your rights to break into her store! Let me say that again: You *broke into* her *store!*" Stone was amazed at his brother's attitude. "She presses charges and you're in jail for at least six months! I talked her out of it, and all you can do is blame her? Are you *kidding* me?"

"I'm sorry." Hopper winced in response to Stone's escalating volume. "But could you please talk a little quieter?"

If there was one thing that Stone had no patience for at that moment, it was his brother's hangover. He fought to keep his voice steady. "That girl you were trying to impress—her father runs the whole damned fleet. Rear Admiral Shane. So now you're messing with my job."

Instantly all his aches and pains were forgotten. Hopper looked up at Stone with renewed interest. "The burrito girl?" He could not have sounded more excited if Stone had told him that the secrets of the universe had been revealed to him. Actually he probably would have been less excited over that prospect. "You *know* the *burrito girl*?"

"Y'know, Hopper, you can be so freaking single-minded . . ." He shook his head. "If you could just, for once, devote that single-mindedness to something worthwhile . . . God, you could go anywhere. Do anything. Instead . . ."

"Sorry to be such a disappointment," said Hopper. Which would have annoyed the hell out of his older brother except, somewhat to Stone's surprise, Hopper really did sound somewhat contrite. More so than he ever had before, at any rate.

Something has to change . . .

Naked and bruised, Hopper pulled himself out of the

ice bath. He moaned softly as he reached for a large towel and wrapped it around his middle. Every step he took was an exercise in agony, his body screaming at him over the way he'd abused it in the past twenty-four hours.

Hopper stumbled into the living room and then flopped onto the couch that doubled as his bed. "Pants," he said groggily.

Stone ignored the request. If Hopper put on pants, there was nothing to impede his departing, and he needed to hear what Stone had to say. He stood over his younger brother, his arms folded across his chest. "Here's the deal, Hopper. I've stayed out of your business for the last five years. I've watched you throw away every opportunity, every job, every break. You've got sixty-five dollars to your name, a car that does not start, you're living on my couch . . ."

Hopper pulled a pillow over his head. From beneath it, his muffled voice said, "You know where I can find that girl? That admiral's daughter?"

This was a typical Hopper approach to situations that he didn't want to deal with. He would try to change the subject, or send Stone completely off track. *Not this time.* Stone summoned his best impression of their father, adopting the tone with which he would speak to his sons when he'd become completely fed up with whatever stupidity they'd gotten themselves into. *Something has to change.* "As of now," he said sharply, "as of right this second, there's a new dynamic at play. This dynamic is the following." He held up his hand and started ticking off the points on his fingers. "From here on out, until I state otherwise, there is no more debate. No more discussion. No more compromise. There is, from here on out, me speaking and you listening. Me saying and you doing. It's time for a new course of action. A new direction. A game change."

Slowly Hopper emerged from under the pillow. He

looked wearily at his brother. "What did you have in mind?"

Without a word Stone pointed at the tattoo on his arm.

"You're kidding," said Hopper.

"Do I *look* like I'm kidding? First we get you a proper haircut because, as much as enlistments may be down, I'm not entirely sure they'd take you looking like the slob that you are."

"Thanks, bro."

"Second, we get you inked up."

Hopper looked uncertainly at his brother's anchor. "Navy requires tattoos these days?"

"No, *I'm* requiring it. Think of it as a promissory note. Or a reaffirmation of brotherhood. Or proof that you're serious about making changes."

"Who said I'm serious about it?"

"*I* did. Because this is it, Hopps. This is the bottom line for you. One way or the other, you're out of here. And it's either into the arms of the Navy or it's out into the street."

"You'd do that to your own brother?"

"That's nothing compared to what you've done to yourself."

Hopper seemed as if he was about to fire off a response, but then he gave it a moment's thought. "Touché," he said reluctantly. Slowly he sat up and stared wearily at Stone. It was as if the fight had been knocked out of him.

Still, Stone felt uncomfortable. If all he did was force Hopper into doing this, then how much commitment was his brother likely to have to it? He could easily go AWOL, try to desert. Considering how he routinely screwed up everything, there was a tremendous likelihood that he'd wind up getting caught and sent to prison. How much good would Stone be doing his brother if his actions led to Alex being incarcerated?

It couldn't be all one way. There had to be motivation

for Alex beyond doing things because his brother told him to. Stone knew exactly what that motivation would be, and reluctantly decided it was pretty much the only card he had left to play.

"Sam," he said.

Hopper looked confused.

"Burrito girl. Her name is Sam. Samantha. She's studying to be a physical therapist. And she told me she was impressed by you."

"She . . . She did?" *Physical therapy. Jackpot.*

"Well, actually what she said was that she thought you were nuts, but in a good way. But she said that if she went out with a guy who wasn't in the Navy, her father would go ballistic. It's a family thing. Can't argue with family."

Hopper slowly got to his feet, grunting in pain only once. "You're making that up."

"I swear on my life, I'm not. Hell, you can ask her yourself when I introduce you . . ."

"You . . . you'd do that?"

"Yeah."

Hopper crossed the living room and threw his arms around his brother. Stone felt vaguely uncomfortable. "Dude . . . being hugged by a mostly naked brother . . . could you, y'know . . . not?"

"Sorry, sorry." Hopper stepped back. "Yeah, that wasn't cool. So . . . so when do I meet . . ." His voice trailed off as it sank in. "You're introducing me after I enlist, aren't you." It wasn't really a question.

"They say you never get a second chance to make a good first impression. But as it turns out, that's exactly what you have," said Stone. "You're going to get spiffed up. You're going to get enlisted. You're going to get your life headed in a direction we can all be proud of. And then you're going to get your second chance to make a good first impression." He spit in the palm of his hand and held it out. "Deal?"

Hopper sighed heavily. "Y'know . . . if it were just my own future, I'd tell you to shove it. But we're talking about the future of my unborn kids, so . . ." He spit in his own palm and they clasped hands firmly.

KAPI'OLANI PARK, 2012

It was a cloudless day, the sky an achingly perfect blue. The shouts of "Here! Over here!" and "Watch your back!" filled the field at Kapi'olani Park, a three-hundred-acre expanse named after Queen Kapi'olani, the 19th-century consort to a Hawaiian king. In the distance, Diamond Head loomed, and the more fanciful might imagine gods perched atop it, looking down at the foolish mortals engaging in their meaningless pursuits.

There was an all-purpose expanse of lawn that had been used variously for competitions ranging from football to baseball to just a few kids tossing around a Frisbee. On this particular day, it was host to a soccer game being played so intensely, so brutally, that one might think lives depended upon it.

Instead it was something of far greater import to the players involved: pride.

Over the sideline of the field fluttered a banner that read, "Navies of the Pacific Rim, Welcome to RIMPAC 2012." No one was paying attention to it, however. Instead the several hundred fans were focused entirely on the game being played, screaming themselves raw with encouragement as two teams squared off for personal and national glory, not to mention bragging rights.

Ten countries. Over one hundred players. This was the third day of a three-day tournament, with more than half the field of competitors eliminated in the round-robin group play of the previous two days. This morning, two of the remaining four countries—Australia and South Korea—had fallen. Unlike the previous day's losers—who were off in the local bars drowning their sorrow and frustration—this day's failed champions had hung around, mostly so they could respectively root against whichever of the remaining two countries had managed to knock them out. Thus it was fairly evenly split, with half the sidelined players cheering the United States and the other half rooting for Japan. The rest of the hundreds of spectators were likewise a mix of competing loyalties. There were a couple of scuffles as waved arms led to elbows accidentally striking heads, but for the most part everyone's attention was upon the activities on the field.

Alex Hopper was currently in possession of the ball, moving it deftly downfield. Running alongside him was Walter Lynch, a man with a build so formidable and a body so hirsute that he had picked up the fairly obvious nickname of "Beast," even though in his usual day-to-day deportment, he was as mild as they came—except when he needed to be otherwise.

This was one of those occasions, and Beast was not hesitant to throw his weight around. Japanese defenders were doing everything they could to try to get within range of Hopper in order to take the ball away, and Beast was running interference that an NFL linebacker would have envied. He stopped short of knocking people aside with a sweep of his heavily muscled arms, but he was fast enough on his feet to body block anyone who came near, sending more than a few of them falling on their asses.

However, even Beast couldn't be everywhere. As he was distracted to the right, Hopper saw a player coming in fast from the left. *"Beast!"* he shouted over the bellowing of the crowd and quickly passed the ball over to him. Beast wasn't as quick as Hopper, but once he had the ball, all bets were off. An opposing player came in too close and Beast simply knocked him aside, sending him flying off his feet. No one bothered to mount a protest with the referees; the refs—one American, one Japanese—had proven consistently and deliberately blind to anything on the field short of one player trying to rip out another's throat with his teeth . . . and even that might have passed uncommented upon.

The Japanese were leading three to two and the time was ticking down.

"Go, go, go!" shouted Stone, who was playing goalie for the Americans and was moving up and down the line.

On the sidelines, Beast's wife, Vera, was cheering wildly. She was renowned for her easy smile and out-sized personality. She was cradling one of their five-year-old twin boys in either arm. Facially they were dead ringers for their dad. The joke was that they'd probably be sprouting hair on their backs before they hit their eighth birthday.

On one side of Vera was weapons specialist and petty officer Cora Raikes. Copper-skinned, with hazel-green eyes, fiery red hair and a Bajan accent, she was shouting instructions and strategies even though no one on the field could possibly pick out her words. Next to her, matching her enthusiasm, was Seaman William Ord. He was a fairly recent arrival to Hawaii. Wide-shouldered and solidly built, Ord looked exactly like what he was: a farm boy who had spent autumn Friday nights in high school playing football. He was a big believer in the axiom of hoping for the best and expecting the worst.

"Tie it up! Tie it up! We're definitely going into extra time!" he shouted, right after which he muttered under his breath, "This isn't gonna end well."

Beast shoved the last defender clear. The Japanese goalie looked ashen, seeing the man-sized equivalent of a locomotive bearing down on him, and then Beast took the shot.

At the last second it was blocked, bouncing off the chest of a defender who appeared to have come out of absolutely nowhere. He deftly took control of it and moved around Beast as if the larger man were standing still.

"Nagata again," Hopper said with a snarl. Hopper and Captain Yugi Nagata had been going at each other constantly from the first minute of the game. Nagata was the tallest Japanese player—nearly five-eleven—and it gave him reach and speed that most of his teammates couldn't begin to approach. His black hair was close-cropped, as befit a Navy man, and he wore an expression of perpetual, unflappable superiority no matter what he was doing. It was this, more than anything, that infuriated Hopper.

It didn't help that Nagata was also a hell of a soccer player.

He started bringing the ball back up the field. Other defenders came in from either side, but Nagata—never taking his eyes off Hopper—shouted an order in Japanese. They immediately peeled off.

So that's how it's gonna be? Fine. I get it.

"Back off! I got 'im!" Hopper called out to his teammates. He saw a quick flash of amusement in Nagata's eyes and knew that he had correctly intuited the captain's mind-set. With a minute remaining, it was time to square off, *mano a mano*.

Bring it, jackass.

Hopper came straight at Nagata with no hesitation. Nagata faked left, moved right. Hopper swung in tight, trying to get the ball, but it wasn't there. The move to the right had been another feint and Nagata darted around Hopper. Hopper muttered a string of profanities as he spun on his heel and went in pursuit.

He sprinted up the field, one step behind Nagata the entire way. The crowd was shouting, everyone going berserk. Hopper, his heart pounding, managed to bring himself up alongside, and he tried to knock the ball away from the captain. Nagata didn't slow, keeping the ball away even as the two men slammed into each other repeatedly, side against side. The referees apparently couldn't overlook this and they started throwing around yellow cards. The two men ignored them.

Hopper went for a full-body slam, banging into Nagata, almost causing him to stumble. He collided with him a second time and was about to go for a third when Nagata suddenly stopped, throwing his right arm straight to the side. The move clotheslined Hopper, knocking the wind out of him, and he tripped over his own feet and went down. With a clear shot at the goal, Nagata sped forward and slammed the ball with all his strength.

It hurtled straight toward the goal . . . and a hole in Stone's defense.

Stone lunged for it and, an instant before it could roll across the white line, he smothered it like a hero landing atop a hand grenade.

An approving roar went up from the crowd, but Stone had no time for accolades. He never stopped rolling as he came up with the ball, looking for someone in whose direction he could throw it.

His brother, having regained his feet, ran up to him as Nagata retreated downfield, anticipating the throw. "Kick it deep. Hit me deep," said Hopper.

Stone saw that Nagata was already positioning himself. "He's been owning you all day," said Stone, and Hopper didn't need to ask his brother which "he" was being referred to. "We need to tie this thing up quick."

"Deep, me, Stone."

Stone looked at Hopper. Hopper was only partly look-ing at him. His attention seemed more focused on Nagata, who was already halfway downfield.

"This isn't about you and him," said Stone. "Don't make this personal . . ."

"It's sure as hell personal. That doesn't mean I can't do it. Deep. Me."

Stone paused a second that felt like an hour. Then he nodded. "Be there."

The words were like the firing of a starter's pistol. The instant he said them, Hopper was off. He sprinted downfield, his arms pumping. He saw that Nagata was watching him with that same arrogant confidence as be-fore. Hopper dashed to the right and Nagata started after him—then, the moment Nagata committed to the move, Hopper quickly broke left. *You're not the only one who can do fake-outs,* he thought smugly.

There was one American player near Hopper, Tomp-kins, which was—as far as Alex was concerned—more than enough. From a distance he heard the thud of Stone's foot coming into contact with the soccer ball and he turned, looked, panicked for half a second because the sun was in his eyes and he couldn't pick up the ball's location.

Then he saw it, coming in fast, straight up the middle of the field. It was a beautiful shot, arcing through the sky, turning slowly and lazily in the air. Hopper took a few steps to the left to line himself up and didn't even have to look to know that the opposing goal was di-rectly behind him.

They figure I'll play it off my chest, bounce it to Tomp-kins, who'll try to drive it in. No one would be insane enough to try and head it directly into the goal from this angle. At least that's what they figure. I'm about to show 'em they figure wrong.

The ball descended toward him, and he braced himself,

ready to propel the ball at the goal and himself into glory, or at the very least his team into overtime. Suddenly he heard a grunt, though, and a body hit the ground. He barely had time to register that it was Tompkins before Nagata was suddenly in front of him, facing him with a grim smile.

With a roar, Hopper came at him, but Nagata didn't wait. Instead he performed an astounding backflip with the intention of catching the ball in midair and kicking it downfield.

Because of Hopper's lunge, however, Nagata's foot didn't quite come into contact with the ball. Instead his foot struck Hopper full in the face.

One moment Hopper had been preparing for the ball, and the next he was hurtling through the air, landing with a heavy *thud* some feet away. There was a collective gasp from the crowd of onlookers. Even for the level of violence to which this hard-fought game had escalated, this was pretty bad.

And in the startled, momentary silence that followed, Hopper heard a familiar female voice cry out, *"Hopper! Oh my God!"*

Hey, he thought happily, *Sam came. She said she wouldn't be able to make it but she came. How nice.*

Then he started to black out.

No. Oh hell no. You are not *going to give that son of a bitch the satisfaction.*

He fought his way back to consciousness before the darkness could completely overwhelm him. The world came back into focus, one piece at a time. First the concerned muttering of his teammates who were standing above him, and then the brightness of the sky overhead against his closed eyelids. From the things they were saying—"Should we get him a doctor?" "Do you think he's dead?"—he gathered that only moments had passed since he'd gone down.

He also became aware of the throbbing in his shoulder. He'd landed on it fairly hard when he'd hit the ground. It was hard to decide which hurt more: that or his face. Hopper decided to push himself all the way back to wakefulness and sort it out later.

His eyes snapped open, taking in the concerned expressions of his teammates. "Didn't hurt at all," he said, lying through his teeth.

They must have known he was full of crap, but no one was about to call him on it, although Stone was slowly shaking his head in disbelief. His older brother looked inclined to leave Hopper lying right where he was, presumably while he went to get a medic for his prone brother. Beast, however, kept his priorities firmly in order and reached down to Hopper, gripping him tightly by the arm. Unfortunately it was the arm with the injured shoulder, and it was all Hopper could do not to scream at the top of his lungs as Beast hauled him to his feet. His face went white as a sheet, and he gasped repeatedly in order to get enough air into his lungs.

"Alex, you sure—?" Stone said.

Hopper managed a nod and forced a wry smile. Preferring to double down on the lie rather than admit to it, he said, "Never better."

Apparently this latest overaggressiveness had been the final straw for the refs. Or at least it was for the American ref. The Japanese ref was angrily protesting, but his counterpart was shaking his head as he shoved his way through the crowd of onlooking American sailors. "Penalty kick. End of injury time. This is it." He leaned in and looked into Hopper's eyes. "You in shape to take it, son?"

"Oh, I can take it." He raised his voice to make damned sure the Japanese players heard him. "I can take whatever they dish out!"

This was all that was required to get the Americans psyched up. Shouts of "U.S.A! U.S.A!" rose from the onlookers, mixed with chants of "Hopper! Hopper!" The Japanese, meanwhile, were trying their best to keep their expressions carefully neutral. But Hopper was sure that he saw growing nervousness in their eyes. They were aware that the tide was shifting against them, and that Hopper could single-handedly tie the game and force them into overtime. Furthermore Hopper was convinced that when that happened, the Americans would have the momentum to run roughshod over them.

He took a few steps forward on his own and then pain ripped through him. It wasn't his head or his legs; instead it was his shoulder, which was hurt worse than he'd thought. His arm was hanging at an odd angle; it had been dislocated.

He looked toward the sidelines to see if Sam had noticed, since she was the one he was most concerned with. She knew his body better than anyone except himself, so if anybody was going to be aware of the level of damage he had sustained . . .

Yup. She sees it. I'm boned. She was standing next to Vera, pointing to her own shoulder as an example, and Vera's gaze shifted from Sam's demonstration to Hopper's actual right shoulder. She saw the damage that Sam was indicating and there was real concern on her face. Sam started gesturing for Hopper to remove himself from the game, but he simply shook his head and turned away from her. She wouldn't understand. It was a guy thing.

"You want someone to take it for you?" said Stone, referring to the penalty shot.

"I got it," said Hopper.

The ref flipped the ball to him and Hopper fortunately caught it with his left hand. He brought the ball over to the penalty line and dropped it at his foot. The goalie was watching steadily. He slapped his gloved hands together and then spread his arms wide in a defensive posture. Hopper could see the sweat beading on his forehead.

"You ready to kiss the donkey? Kiss. Kiss. Kiss," Hopper muttered.

No reason to hurry. That's what the goalie wanted him to do. He wanted him to rush the shot, and Hopper had no intention of accommodating him. Instead he stretched his legs, buying a few more moments to get his head together.

As he did so, Nagata took a moment to cruise past him. Hopper didn't bother to ask if he was there to apologize for his cheap attack. There was no quarter being asked or given.

"Two kinds of idiots, Hopper," said Nagata in a low voice. "One looks where he kicks. Other looks where he doesn't kick. Which idiot are you?"

Hopper had no idea what he was talking about. Nagata was trying to get into his head and Hopper wasn't about to let him. "I'm the idiot who's gonna kick the ball through his face."

Nagata simply gave him one more contemptuous look and moved on.

It had all come down to him. He closed his eyes, took a deep, cleansing breath. Then he backed up several steps, preparing to make his final charge at the ball. People were screaming themselves into a tizzy from the sidelines, shouting encouragement. Pain continued to throb in his shoulder and he pushed it away so it wouldn't distract him.

The goalie was slowly drifting from side to side, looking at Hopper challengingly. He was practically daring Hopper to drive the ball past him.

Hopper was more than happy to oblige.

He took one more breath, and then charged. The ball was sitting there waiting for him, inviting him. The goalie was prepared to obstruct him, expecting Hopper to try to get the ball to one side of him or the other.

Screw that. Hopper knew exactly what was going to

work. Why go to one side or the other of an obstruction when you can go through it, and exact a bit of revenge at the same time? Send Nagata and his people a message that they couldn't get away with that kind of crap.

The kick was perfect. He sent the ball spiraling directly, and with full force, at the goalie's face. In Hopper's mind, the goalie stood there with a stunned expression, caught completely flat-footed. The ball smashed directly into the target, knocked him flat and sent him sprawling to the ground. It rolled past him into the net. The crowd went wild, the game went into overtime, the Americans won, and a triumphant Hopper was hoisted onto his teammates' shoulders and paraded around the field.

In reality, however, the goalie judged the ball perfectly. Rather than flinch, he reached up and caught it on the fly. The solid *thump* of the soccer ball into his hands was the death knell of the Americans' hopes as the game ended with the victorious Japanese swarming onto the field, pounding one another on the back in triumph.

Hopper stood there, staring, his jaw twitching as his mental image of what would happen crashed up against what had actually transpired. Nagata, of course, chose that moment to step in near him and say, just softly enough for only Hopper to hear, "So predictable."

Hopper had never wanted to punch someone in the face as much as he did Nagata at that moment. The fist of his left hand curled up tightly and he turned to face him. But the Japanese captain was no longer there; he was crossing the field and, projecting dignity and control, joining his teammates in celebration. Instead there was Beast, patting him on the back, and Tompkins, and Stone shaking his head consolingly, saying "Good shot," "Good try," and all the other useless condolences that are typically offered when things simply don't go the way you wanted them to.

Nor did it help that they were patting him on the

shoulder, which was throbbing like a son of a bitch. He tried not to wince from it and didn't even come close to succeeding. *Just like you didn't come close to succeeding in tying the game.*

Stone stepped closer to his brother. "At least you demonstrated mild self-control," said Stone. "You didn't beat up the Japanese officer. Well done."

Hopper wondered if Stone knew that he'd nearly lost control and belted Nagata into the middle of next week. *In my defense, he had it coming.* Somehow he didn't think that that excuse would have flown with his brother—or, for that matter, with anybody else.

It didn't matter, though. Nothing mattered as far as Hopper was concerned, because there was Sam, his beautiful Sam. *His* beautiful Sam. She would comfort him, she would speak kind words to him, she would say all the right things. She would—

All business, Sam skipped over sweet nothings and instead inspected his right shoulder with practiced confidence. "On your back," she said briskly.

"Right here? In front of everybody?" He lay down slowly. "All right, honey, I'm game . . ." As a couple of his teammates snickered, he gestured for her to lie on top of him while he moved his pelvis in a suggestive manner.

Sam was clearly not amused. She reached down, grabbed his wrist, and put a foot in his armpit. "It's gonna hurt," she warned him.

"You always hurt the one you—" He didn't get the rest of the sentence out. Instead he let out a startled shriek that was higher-pitched than he would have liked as Sam pulled hard and snapped the shoulder back into place. He lay there for a moment, gasping in pain. Then slowly he sat up, growling as he flexed his arm. It was still sore as spit, but the agony was subsiding.

"Damn, that's fun." Sam sounded far more entertained by it than he thought she had any right to be.

He rubbed his shoulder, making as big a show of it as possible, his face twisted into a mask of exaggerated pain. As he got to his feet, he said with a growl, "Evil woman."

Then he charged her.

With a delighted shriek, she turned and ran, Hopper chasing her off the field. She was running as fast as she could. He wasn't. He caught up with her anyway.

KUHIO BEACH, LATER THAT EVENING

The throbbing in Hopper's shoulder had more or less faded to nothing as he sat on the beach next to Sam, the water gently lapping against the shore. Kuhio Beach was adjacent to Kapi'olani Beach Park, and this late at night, the beach was largely deserted. The Pacific Ocean was smooth as glass, and the full moon reflected down upon it, making it seem as if a giant yellow eye was staring up at them from the depths of the waters.

Sam was holding a bottle of wine and was sipping from it. A blanket was spread out beneath them and a gentle breeze was causing her long hair to flutter. They had forgone glasses from which to drink the wine and instead were simply passing the bottle back and forth.

Handing the bottle to Hopper, Sam said, "So . . . big day tomorrow."

Slowly he lowered it and tried to smile. Unfortunately, all he could manage was a grimace. Sam noticed it and her expression darkened. "Hopper . . . are you ready for this? I mean, are you *sure* you're ready for this?"

"I'm ready," he said, a little faster than he really needed to. As a result he didn't sound quite as confident as she would have liked and he would have wanted.

She rested her hand on his shoulder and the concern upon her face was palpable. "You *suuuure*?"

Hopper heard the challenge in her voice. She wanted the truth, and he had to take a long, hard look into himself. As it turned out, he liked what he saw. More specifically, he liked it in relation to her. "Never more sure," he said with growing confidence.

She studied him, not looking totally convinced. "What are you going to say?"

There was a long pause as his mind raced. Truthfully he didn't have the faintest idea. The fact was that he had been trying to put off the conversation even in his mind, opting for that oldest of strategies: if you ignore something, it will go away.

It didn't seem to be working this time. Instead Sam was becoming increasingly annoyed. It was clear she was having serious doubts that he was intending to follow through on what they'd discussed. *Well, she discussed it, for the most part. You just listened.* Finally he said, "I'm just gonna ask him. Man to man."

"With *what* words?"

"*My* words: 'Sir, I love your daughter. More than anything in this world, and I'm asking you for your permission . . .'" Then his voice sputtered and died, like a deflating balloon running out of air.

Sam prompted him to continue. "Permission . . . ?"

"He's gonna knock me out." *Oh yeah. Man to man. That sounded . . . manly.*

"Permission . . . ?" she said again.

"Can we go swimming?"

She was relentless, though. At least she gave him the next word. "Permission *to* . . . ?"

Hopper desperately wanted to be anywhere else than

where he was at that moment. He was wearing a light shirt
and his bathing trunks, and Sam had on her bikini beneath
a loose T-shirt and shorts. Why were they sitting here,
dwelling on a dead-end conversation, when the ocean was
beckoning? "*Please* can we go swimming?"

"Finish the question. Then we can go swimming."

Clearly she wasn't about to let up and—his back against
the metaphorical wall—he was forced to admit what was
truly on his mind. Very softly, so much so that she could
scarcely hear him, Hopper looked down at the blanket on
which he was sitting. "I think he's gonna say no."

"Hopper." She sounded so disappointed in him. "Don't
you think he wants me to be happy?"

"Yeah, but I'm pretty sure he's not gonna give a crap
about *my* happiness."

"He's going to have to, because you're what makes me
happy."

He took that in, and even though there was a cool
breeze coming off the Pacific, he still felt suffused with
warmth. He stared fixedly forward, as if her father were
standing directly in front of them and, with a formal tilt
of his head, said, "May I please have permission to marry
your daughter. The most beautiful and the best thing to
ever happen to me." He turned back to her, waiting for
approval, hoping it would be forthcoming.

She took his chin in her hand and kissed him. "I love
you."

"Can we *please* go swimming?"

As an answer, she jumped to her feet and started shed-
ding her clothing, stripping down to her bikini. She then
sprinted into the ocean, with Hopper bounding in right
behind her.

He's gonna kill me. That certain conviction went
through Hopper's mind, taking some of the fun out of
splashing about in the water with his intended, the love
of his life, the woman he'd nearly wound up in jail for.

From that day to this one, he'd never been able to look at a chicken burrito again. But what did burritos matter when he had a beautiful woman like this in his arms?

Besides which, there were always tacos. And enchiladas.

They swam and kissed under the full moon, and concerns about her father departed from his mind to become problems for another day.

"Hopper." It was Sam's voice, and there was a shaking. She was shaking him. He didn't want to be shaken. He wanted to sleep some more. *"Hopper!"* she said, more insistently this time, shoving him around so violently that he felt as if there was an earthquake underneath the sand . . .

The sand? We're still on the beach? If we're on the beach, why is it so bright out . . . ?

That was when his mind began to piece together the truth. They had fallen asleep on the beach, wrapped in the overlarge blanket. Night was gone and the sun was much higher in the morning sky than it had any right to be, considering he was supposed to be elsewhere at this very moment.

"This is bad," he said.

Instantly they scrambled to their feet, gathering their belongings, stumbling in the sand as they did so. At one point Hopper lost his footing, tumbled against Sam, and they both wound up falling down onto the sand again.

"You better get it together, Hopper!"

He nodded in hurried agreement as he pulled on his shirt. Sam was hastening to get into her shorts and succeeded in shoving both of her legs into the same pants leg, cursing like—appropriately enough—a sailor as she extracted her left leg and started over, bouncing on her right foot as she endeavored to maintain her balance.

With all this frantic hurrying and the fact that he was probably going to be late as a result, Hopper had to think that perhaps the timing of the intended request for the hand of the admiral's daughter might leave something to be desired. "Maybe we should put it off till next month?" he ventured.

He didn't have to explain to her which "it" he meant. "No way," she said. By this point she had managed to get all her body parts into the proper sections of her clothing and was sprinting toward the Jeep they'd driven out there. He caught up with her and then passed her effortlessly. Hopper leaped into the driver's seat, yanked out his keys, fumbled for a moment with them before shoving the right key into the ignition and turning it. For a moment the engine failed to catch. *Dead, dead, I am so dead.* Then it miraculously turned over. He gunned it, tearing out of the parking lot so quickly he nearly left Sam behind. As it was she barely had time to leap into the passenger's side before the Jeep took off.

Just another day in Paradise, he thought.

PEARL HARBOR

It was unusual for a Navy band to preform a full version of "To the Colors," the haunting bugle piece that was typically played at times such as the flag being lowered at the end of the day on a base. However, it was occasionally played in circumstances where there were going to be honors to the nation more than once. At least Hopper supposed that would be the case here as the Jeep Hopper was driving hurtled into the parking lot adjacent to the USS *Missouri.* The Jeep screeched to a halt and Sam and Hopper clambered out. One would never have guessed that, barely two hours ago, they'd been two disheveled people on a beach. Yet now here they were, one hasty plane ride from Honolulu to Oahu later, after changing and primping en route while squished into the island jumper, much to the amusement and entertainment of the pilot.

Hopper was looking every inch the Navy officer, attired in his crisp white uniform. As for Sam, she was exquisitely attired in a black Chanel dress, her hair as coifed as she could make it under the circumstances.

The *Missouri*, sometimes referred to as "Mighty Mo" or "Big Mo," was a proud Iowa-class battleship with an impressive history stretching back to the Second World War. She had been involved in such naval endeavors as the battles of Iwo Jima and Okinawa before eventually being decommissioned in the 1990s and transformed into a museum ship. She overlooked the remains of a vessel that hadn't been fortunate enough to serve in the Allied efforts—the *Arizona,* a Pennsylvania-class battleship that had performed ably during World War I, but was sunk years later during the Japanese attack on Pearl Harbor. When the vessel went down, she took eleven hundred lives with her. Her remains were still at the bottom of the harbor, but a memorial had been built in her stead, straddling her hulls.

As Hopper and Sam moved as quickly as her high heels would let her, they passed a cheesy gift shop outside the entryway to the *Missouri,* selling every battleship-themed souvenir that anyone could imagine. Hopper considered the fact that before joining up—even with the Navy background of both his father and brother—he wouldn't have given a crap about the relentless merchandising of a proud vessel. Now it bugged the hell out of him, but there wasn't much of anything he could do about it.

There was a skinny, bespectacled tour guide lecturing a group of tourists who were studying the various gifts, some of them expressing annoyance that they weren't being allowed to take the usual tour on the vessel, arguing that—after all—that's what it had been built for. The tour guide, who was wearing an unspeakably tacky hat in the shape of a foam battleship (available for $5.99 in the gift shop), was busy explaining that, first of all, the Mighty Mo was reserved today for a special ceremony, and second, yes, the ship was now a museum, but that wasn't what it had been built for. Hopper rolled his eyes at the stupidity of some people. He started to slow and, as if she were reading his mind, Sam pulled on his hand to make sure he didn't get dragged into the middle of something.

"The USS *Missouri* was the final battleship to be completed by the United States," the guide was telling them, "before being decommissioned and replaced by a more modern fleet of vessels, known as *destroyers*."

"What's the difference between the two?" asked a kid.

"Well, destroyers are lighter and faster and fire different weapons."

Whoa, what—?!

Hopper stopped short, jerking Sam to a halt as well. Before she could do anything such as, for instance, talk sense into him, Hopper pulled away from her and turned to the guide. "That's what you're telling 'em? That's bullshit!"

Sam visibly blanched, as did a couple of old women. The men looked surprised, and a grin split the face of the kid, probably because he liked hearing grown-ups curse.

"Hopper—!" said Sam warningly.

"I'm coming," he said, but it was perfunctory, his attention entirely on the boy. "Battleships: dinosaurs. Destroyers: *awesome!*"

Sam put her hands on her hips in a manner that indicated he wasn't going to be getting any anytime soon . . . if ever. "Are you kidding me right now?"

"I'm coming." He didn't mean it any more the second time than he had the first, and he continued addressing the kid, grabbing tiny gray plastic models of the two types of boats from the souvenir stand. He held up a little battleship in his left hand. "Battleships: designed to take hits like a floating punching bag." Then he held up the right. "Destroyers: designed to dish it out like a frea-kin' Terminator!" He thrust the small destroyer toward the kid, whose eyes were round and goggled. "We've got Tomahawk cruise missiles, sea-skimming Harpoons, torpedoes like there's no tomorrow . . ."

"Awe-*some* . . . !" said the kid.

"Yeah," said Hopper, nodding, feeling much like a kid himself. "That's what I'm talking about."

"*Hopper!*"

The kid glanced toward the annoyed Sam. "Your girl-friend's hot."

"Get your own," said Hopper. "Gotta go."

He hurried over to Sam, who glared at him as they started running. "Everyone's waiting and you're talking about boats?"

"We were also talking about how hot you were."

"You were not!"

"Swear to God."

"Oh. Well . . . okay, then," she said, slightly mollified.

The deck of the *Missouri* was filled with naval officers from an assortment of countries. The United States, Japan, Great Britain, Australia, South Korea, India and more were all represented, and flags from each of the nations were fluttering in the morning breeze. Having left Sam to find a spot in the audience with the families and other guests, he threaded his way through the assemblage of naval officers, looking to find his friends while trying to make sure he didn't draw any attention to himself.

He finally located Stone and slid in next to him. His brother kept his attention focused on the podium up front, but said out the side of his mouth, "Nice of you to show up, lieutenant commander." He was big on invoking Hopper's rank and getting formal when he was pissed off with him. It was Stone's way of letting Hopper know that he was annoyed, not to mention underscore their difference in rank and reminding him who was in charge. "You ready for this? Or would you like to sleep in and we'll just do the war games without you?"

"Hey, at least I'm here. I made pretty good time considering I woke up on the wrong island this morning," he whispered back.

"The wrong *island?* Which one? Gilligan's?"

"Ha-ha. Think the Jedi Master noticed?" It was the nickname that the officers had for Admiral Terrance Shane behind his back, because of his knack for saying things that his subordinates somehow felt compelled to repeat word for word, as if he were controlling their minds.

"Considering he's glaring right at you, I'd say yeah."

Hopper turned his attention to the podium and felt his heart sink to somewhere around his shoes. Sure enough, the admiral was staring down at him with clear disapproval. He was a towering presence, well over six feet, with aquiline features that made him appear like a cross between a hawk and a Roman senator. He spoke with a gravelly voice that had a lyrical Irish lilt to it.

"First off, I'd like to welcome all of you to the RIMPAC International Naval War Games," said Shane. The way he was looking at Hopper, Alex had a feeling he personally wasn't all that welcome. Shane then turned his attention back to the rest of the assemblage. "And I'd like to welcome you on board the greatest fighting ship in American naval history. The Mighty Mo. The USS *Missouri*, where, in Tokyo Bay, on September 2, 1945, Japan surrendered to General Douglas McArthur."

There was applause throughout, although Hopper couldn't help but notice that the response from the Japanese officers was, to put it mildly, muted. Either Admiral Shane didn't notice or else he simply didn't care. More likely the latter. He was going to say what he had to say, and obviously he didn't give a damn who he pissed off.

Which pretty much guaranteed that he would have no difficulty whatsoever—when Hopper asked for Sam's hand—of providing a detailed list of every single one of Hopper's shortcomings, verbally making mincemeat out of him before showing him the door and telling him never to utter Sam's name in his presence again.

We should just elope. It would run contrary to Sam's fantasy of having her father perform the ceremony at sea, standing on the bridge of a ship in his capacity as captain. But hell, at least they'd be married and there wouldn't be a damned thing the admiral would be able to do about it. *What am I saying? Of course he could. He could have me court-martialed for . . . for any reason at all. Or just throw me overboard late one night. Hell, he could probably order Stone to do it, and depending on Stone's mood that day, he just might be happy to obey. Oh God . . . I think my chest is tightening up. Is this what a heart attack feels like—?*

Stone reached over and straightened Hopper's ribbon bar, looking at him with genuine concern. "Jesus, man, you look like death warmed over," he said softly. "You're a mess."

"Can't breathe."

"Relax."

That was easy for Stone to say. He wasn't the one who was preparing to walk into the lion's den, hand the lion a knife and fork, expose his chest to him and say "Chow down." Still, Hopper tried to do as Stone said and get his breathing under control.

"He hates me," said Hopper.

"It's gonna be fine. Just keep your distance from him today."

Which was, of course, exactly what Hopper wanted to hear. Stone didn't know about Hopper's plan to approach his potential father-in-law today. Still: *Stone ordered me to stay away from the admiral.* He's the ranking officer. I can't disobey a direct order. Sorry, babe, it'll have to wait. *Sounds like a plan. A crap plan, but a plan.*

Oblivious, or perhaps simply indifferent, to the turmoil that Hopper was going through, Shane said, "We have with us today veterans, some going back to World War II. Examples of the finest men to have ever served in any Navy." Shane gestured to the vets, and applause rippled through the audience. Hopper clapped his hands purely as a response to everyone else; he wasn't consciously thinking about it. Instead he was turning around to see if Sam had maybe, perhaps, been making out with some other officer, having completely forgotten about Hopper and deciding that she could do better. That would get him off the hook. But no, there she was, off to the side, looking at him with that same mixture of confidence and adoration. It was the way he'd dreamed of her looking at him when he'd first seen her at the bar.

"And now," Shane was saying, "as we prepare to embark on this outstanding exercise of global cooperation and competition, I would like the commanding officers of every surface warfare ship involved in this year's game to come to the stage."

Stone stood up in response to the summons, patting his brother on the shoulder as he did so. "Stay out of trouble while I'm gone," he said. It had become a running joke, one of those things that wasn't funny to anyone outside of the family. It provided comfort and continuity to Hopper, or it irritated the hell out of him, depending on how he felt at any given moment. This was one of those occasions when he didn't think about it at all, since he was so distracted by the emotions roiling within him.

Stone and the other commanding officers lined up be-

hind the admiral. As they did so, a huge cake in the shape
of the *Missouri* was wheeled up in front of them. Hopper
saw it being brought forward and didn't feel the least bit
interested in eating any of it. That alone was more than
enough to tell him he was off his game, if he hadn't
known already.

Admiral Shane turned and offered a rare smile to
Hopper's brother. "A special acknowledgment to American Stone Hopper, who—along with his outstanding
crew and ship, the USS *Sampson*—had the highest overall rating last year and will be looking to repeat that
terrific performance this year."

Hopper felt momentary chagrin, as he frequently did
whenever he heard the name of Stone's ship. He remembered as if it were yesterday the first time he'd seen the
name emblazoned on the side of the *Arleigh Burke*–class
destroyer and airily informed his brother that some idiot
had misspelled the name "Samson." Stone had then patiently, and with an air of condescension that put Hopper's teeth on edge, informed him that the vessel was
named after Rear Admiral William T. Sampson and not
the biblical judge and strong man.

Admiral Shane handed Stone a saber. Tragically it was
a regular sword rather than a Jedi light sabre. It was a
bit more weather-beaten than Navy swords typically
were since it was reserved for ceremonies such as this,
and cutting cakes weren't exactly good for the blade. Yet
Stone displayed great care as he took it from the admiral
with a small bow, and then turned to face the audience.

"Welcome everybody," said Stone. "It's great to see
you here. Your ships look outstanding and your men
look ready. Good luck to you all, be safe, fight hard."

He nodded once more as if affirming everything he'd
just said and then sliced into the cake. The moment he
did, the band launched into a stirring rendition of "Anchors Aweigh." This disappointed Hopper, who was of

the firm opinion that once, *just once,* the band should play the Village People's "In the Navy." *Yeah. Opinions like that are why Stone's up there and you're down here.*

"Hopper. What's wrong?"

Raikes had come up beside him and was looking at him with genuine concern. "Seriously, Hopps. You look terrible. What's on your mind?"

His mouth moved before he could stop it and the words all came out in a rush. "I was going to ask the admiral for permission to marry Sam except he totally hates me and you can't tell anyone, okay. Please?"

She was clearly startled by the confession spilling from him. "Wow," was all she could say.

"Seriously. Don't tell anyone. None of the guys, and definitely not Stone."

"Absolutely. Not a soul."

"I had to hear it from Ord? *Ord?* From *freaking Ord?*" Stone said in disbelief. Then he paused and turned to Ord. "No offense."

"Oh, none taken," said Ord. "I'm right there with you. Who wants to hear something like that from me? Hell, I couldn't believe it when Beast told me."

"Color me shocked," said Beast.

His closest friends and his astounded brother were grouped around Hopper at the far end of the deck. Hopper was glaring at Raikes, who was standing there shifting uncomfortably from one foot to the other and trying to look at anyone except Hopper. She was eating a slice of cake with great concentration. " 'Absolutely not a soul,' Raikes?" said Hopper. "Really?"

Her response was a shrug.

"I have no soul, if that helps, so technically she kept her word," Beast said helpfully. "I'm actually a robot sent back in time to kill John Connor."

"Shut up," said Hopper.

"Roger, I copy that."

Stone circled the group, but his attention never left his brother. Clearly he didn't give a damn about Raikes breaking her word; he was more focused on other aspects of the news. "Why did you keep it from me? From your own brother?"

Hopper was inclined to spend some more time being pissed off with Raikes, but that pretty much seemed to be a dead-end path. So he said in frustration, "Because there's only so much humiliation I want to handle, okay?"

"What are you talking about? Why would you think I'd humiliate you?" Stone was clearly astounded at Hopper's attitude. "I want nothing but the best for you and Sam! You guys are a great couple. Right?" He addressed the question to the others.

"Yes, absolutely," said Beast.

Raikes nodded, her mouth still full of cake, and she gave a thumbs-up.

"I'd totally do her," said Ord. Then, when he saw that everyone was glaring at him, he said defensively, "Hey, I'm new here. Gimme a break."

Raikes swallowed the piece of cake. "I'll give you a broken nose is what I'll give you."

Hopper shifted his attention to Sam. She was standing next to her father, the admiral. She was holding a glass of champagne and laughing in that marvelous way she had. That laugh that, no matter what manner of gloom had settled on Hopper at any given moment, always made things right somehow. Officers from Japan, England, and South Korea were grouped around her, hanging on every word she said, every movement, every toss of her head. They adored her. Everyone adored her. Especially her father, who had an arm around her shoulders and was clearly bristling with pride over the splendid young woman he'd raised.

And he couldn't stand Hopper.

"It doesn't matter what a great couple we are," Hopper said. "There's no way the admiral's gonna approve. And when that happens—or doesn't, I should say—at least none of you would have had to know about it. There wouldn't be a whole 'So how'd it go?' thing. I could keep my humiliation hidden and my guts would tear themselves apart in private instead of you guys knowing what was going on."

The others exchanged looks. "Are you serious?" said Stone. "C'mon, Hopps. You're selling yourself short."

"You absolutely are," said Beast. Raikes, having shoveled another forkful of cake into her mouth, nodded.

"I'd totally do you," said Ord. The others stared at him. He looked defensive. "Boy, try to lighten things up around here . . ."

Hopper stared forlornly at Sam. She might as well have been standing on the other side of the Pacific for all that he could see of their life together. "Her father's gonna smash me."

"He's not," said Stone. His earlier irritation with his brother had subsided, replaced by sympathy for Hopper's obvious turmoil.

"I really think he is."

Stone shook his head. "He loves his daughter. She loves you. He's gonna respect that. Stop worrying about what hasn't happened and get it done." He paused and then said, "You want me to come with? Would that help?"

"There's no need I can absolutely do it myself yeah would'ja, please?"

Releasing a brotherly chuckle, Stone clapped Hopper on the shoulder and with an inclination of his head indicated Hopper should follow him.

"Want us to come, too?" said Ord cheerfully.

"Actually, I'd like you, Ord, to jump overboard," said Stone. "Raikes, Beast—you two go fish him out once he's splashed around for a while."

As Stone and Hopper walked away, Ord looked nervously at Beast and Raikes. "He was kidding, right? That . . . wasn't an actual order, was it?"

"Sounded pretty official to me," Beast said sternly. Raikes, wiping cake from her mouth with the back of her hand, shrugged.

Stone and Hopper walked toward the admiral's group. As they did so, Hopper was busy running through all the possible scenarios he could employ to casually get Shane away from the other officers. Perhaps Sam and Stone could somehow pitch in. Offer to take the others around the ship, leaving Hopper with the admiral for a few minutes.

That could work. Maybe this whole thing could work. All I need is for things to go my way . . .

"Nagata," said Stone in a tone of formal greeting.

The name snapped Hopper from his musings and he looked dead ahead of them. Sure enough, there was Nagata—along with one of his men—having approached from the side and come up to them just before they arrived within range of Admiral Shane's group.

Instantly Sam, her father and proposals were forgotten. His world was now filled with nothing but Nagata, standing there in his crisp uniform, oozing smug superiority. Nagata was regarding Hopper with his usual cool contempt even as he said to Hopper's brother, "Stone. Good weather for our exercise."

"Yes, it is, and good luck to you."

"And to you," said Nagata. He tilted his head toward Hopper. "Your brother could use a lesson in tactics from you." He threw Hopper a cold smile.

Hopper shoved his hands into his pockets, trying to look casual even as he fought to resist the impulse of smashing in Nagata's smug face. "We were doing fine last go around," said Hopper, "till you tried to ram me in open water."

"Ships never touched," said Nagata. "Accident."

"Says who?"

"The independent naval inquiry."

Working quickly to avert catastrophe, Stone said, "Hopper, back out of this. Don't you have something much more interesting to be doing *right now*?"

Hopper took a deep breath to steady himself, and then looked over to the admiral and Sam. "Roger that," he said.

He quickly hurried away, as Stone turned back to Nagata and said, with as much charm as he could muster, "Beautiful day for sailing, isn't it, gentlemen?"

From a short distance away, Hopper's crewmates were watching with growing interest the altercation that appeared to be shaping up. "This is going to be sweet," said Raikes, who had finished the cake and was stuffing the crumpled napkin into her pocket.

"He walked away, though," Beast pointed out.

"Come on, Beast. You should know better than that. That was just round one. Round two'll come up before you know it."

"What's going on?" said Ord, relieved that the conversation had shifted away from the notion that tossing him off the ship was somehow a good idea.

"Last year Hopper's and Nagata's ships nearly rubbed paint. Nagata blamed it on 'wind shear,'" she said, putting air quotes around the latter two words to underscore just how seriously she took that excuse. "Hopper blames Nagata. Hates the man."

"Why?"

She smiled. "Hopper likes to find people to hate. It's how he motivates himself."

"Really." Ord was unimpressed by that. "Sounds a bit juvenile."

That was exactly the wrong thing to say. "Go mess with him," Raikes said challengingly. "See what happens."

Ord might have been new to his surroundings, but he'd been around long enough to know when he was being set up. "No."

"Do it," she dared him.

"No."

"Do it," said Raikes. She nudged him between the shoulder blades.

"Leave me alone," he said, and quickly backed away. This prompted a hearty laugh from Raikes and a low rumble of amused approval from Beast.

Initially Hopper had been heading straight toward the admiral. That worked right up until the admiral happened to glance in his direction and give him one of those patented scowls of his. This promptly sent Hopper off on a sharp left turn and his feet brought him, almost of their own accord, to the nearest head. Or, as civilians termed it, the bathroom.

He stood in there for a time, staring at himself in the mirror. *You look like a scared little girl. Pull it together, for God's sake.*

He turned the spigot and watched the cold water splash and swirl in the sink for a few moments, trying to avoid thinking of himself as swirling down the drain along with the water. He cupped some of it in his hands and splashed it on his face. He looked back up into the mirror and tried to ignore that water was dripping from his eyebrows. He forced what he imagined was an expression that exuded confidence onto his face. "Sir, it would be my great honor . . . my great privilege, for your daughter's hand . . ." *Honor? Privilege? You sound like you're getting a bump up in rank. Let him know how you feel, dammit.* "My joy . . ."

The creaking of the door was so unexpected that Hopper nearly jumped two feet in the air. He turned and saw, to his anger and dismay, Nagata standing there. Nagata was studying him with open curiosity. "Talking to yourself?"

Not now. Don't do this now. "Just leaving."

He started to head for the door. Nagata had stepped through and now he allowed it to swing shut, making no move to get out of Hopper's way. "Practicing all the things you wish you'd said to me?" said Nagata.

Hopper felt the familiar rage starting to surge through him, and he did everything he could to contain it. "I don't know how things work in Nagata land, where you're utterly blameless in all things, but in the real world, not everything is about you."

"You have something to say, why not say it to my face?"

Hopper took a step toward him, his fists trembling. "If I'm going to do something to your face, Sparky, it isn't going to involve words."

"Big talk. Big talk from a little m—"

He didn't manage to finish the sentence because Hopper chose that moment to drive a fist squarely into Nagata's gut. It caught Nagata completely by surprise, doubling him over and bringing his face close enough to Hopper that the American was able to punch Nagata in the eye. *Probably thought I didn't have the nerve.*

Nagata staggered and Hopper closed in for the kill. But he was too slow. Even in the confined area, Nagata was able to sidestep him and he brought the base of his hand slamming up into Hopper's mouth. Hopper's head snapped back and he tasted his own blood in his mouth. Nagata's hand thrust forward once more. Hopper was able to block it, just barely. He grabbed Nagata's wrist and slammed him back up against the wall, which shuddered under the impact. They grappled for a few moments and then Nagata—bigger and stronger than Hopper—shoved him back. But Hopper didn't let go and together the two of them crashed into the nearest stall, the wall collapsing under their combined weight.

Hopper lost track of time after that, the world transforming into a vast haze of red. All he knew was that one minute he was snarling in Nagata's face—the two of them slamming each other around and rolling on the bathroom floor—and the next they were being separated by masters-at-arms. As the MAs pulled the two of them apart, Hopper had a brief glimpse of a tall figure standing in the corridor, looking on in disgust. It was Admiral Shane.

Terrific, he thought, as he came to the realization that trying to distinguish between the subtleties of words like "honor" and "joy" had suddenly become woefully, painfully moot.

WARDROOM, USS MISSOURI

The wardroom was filled with the remainders of all the material that had been used in the food preparation for the celebration. There were trays and large serving plates everywhere, either empty or with crumbs and scraps of food remaining on them. The catering crew had been in the midst of cleaning up, but when an assembly of high-ranking officers had walked in and told them that they needed the room, they did not hesitate to make themselves scarce. It was obvious from the attitude of the officers that being anywhere other than the wardroom at that moment was an incredibly good idea.

Hopper and Nagata were both standing stiff-backed,

accomplishing the impressive task of staring straight forward without actually making eye contact with any of the officers arrayed in front of them. Hopper didn't feel much like speaking anyway, since his mouth was swollen to such a degree that he was going to sound stupid trying to form words. The only positive aspect of all this was that Nagata's right eye had swollen shut, although considering that the vice admiral of the Japanese Navy was standing there glaring at Hopper, perhaps it wasn't so wonderful after all. Admiral Shane was fuming . . . at Hopper. Standing to Hopper's left was Commander Sherman Brownley, his commanding officer aboard the *John Paul Jones,* a broad-shouldered, middle-aged man who was dyspeptic on his best days. He was glaring, too . . . at Hopper. To Hopper's right was Tony Mullenaro, Brownley's executive officer, a short, thick Italian who was glaring . . . at Hopper. Off to the side was the tall, dark-haired Commander Rivera, who was glaring at—big surprise—Hopper.

This is ridiculous. There were two of us in the fight. How come everyone is glaring at me? My COs. Nagata's COs. It's not freaking fair. Hell, he's the one who started it.

Somehow Hopper suspected that the famed "He started it" defense wasn't the best avenue to take.

"It was just a crazy accident, sir," Hopper said through his swollen lips. His words sounded slurred and thick, as if he were a boxer who had just gone five rounds. "The floor was wet. I started to fall. He reached out to help."

"Hogwash," said Mullenaro, clearly having none of it.

There was a moment of silence. Nagata and Hopper, for the first time since they'd been hauled off each other, exchanged looks. Then, very coolly, Nagata said, "It was an accident."

Hopper was momentarily surprised that Nagata was covering for him. Then he realized it shouldn't be a surprise at all. Nagata had as much at stake as Hopper did and was just covering his own ass. After all, the Japanese vice admiral clearly already blamed Hopper for everything. Why would Nagata say anything honest, like, "I started it," when there was no benefit in it for him?

"You're a lying mule hound, Hopper," said Mullenaro. "This is your fifth fight in three years."

I'm a lying mule hound? Nagata just backed me up! Why not call him *a lying mule hound?*

And what the hell is a "mule hound" anyway? And are they known for being liars?

Wisely, he didn't say any of that.

Without a word, the Japanese vice admiral gestured for Nagata to follow him out. Then he bowed slightly to the other officers, turned and walked from the room with stiff-backed precision. Nagata trailed behind him and Hopper didn't doubt for a moment that he'd receive a hero's welcome once he returned to his own ship. Either he'd be characterized as a man unfairly accused (if his cover story was believed), or he would be seen as an officer who had been unwilling to take lip from a bigmouthed, arrogant American and pounded the living crap out of him.

No one said anything in the wardroom for long moments after Nagata and the vice admiral departed. Then Mullenaro stepped forward, clearly prepared to fill the void, but he was stopped by the calm voice of Admiral Shane saying, "Gentlemen . . . a minute."

Well, this worked out perfectly. You were trying to figure out how you could get some time alone with the admiral, and now you've got it. Excellent plan, well thought out, well executed. And all you had to do to accomplish it was flush your entire career down the toilet by having a fight in the toilet. Great job there, Hopps, old boy. You really slam-dunked this one.

Soon they were alone. Shane stared at him with a face

that could have been carved out of marble for all the emotion he was displaying.

I wonder if he's happy about this. He never liked me anyway. This just makes everything easier for him.

Shane offered no preamble; he cut right to it. "I'm ordering a captain's mast, Navy court-martial for you immediately upon return to Pearl."

Even though Hopper had been expecting something exactly like this, it was still like being hit in the face with a brick. He even rocked on his heels slightly as if a genuine physical impact had been made.

Shane was standing there, clearly waiting for Hopper to say something, to acknowledge what he'd just been told. Hopper managed a nod and said, "Yes, sir."

Apparently desiring to twist the knife in Hopper's gut some more, Shane went on to state the obvious: "This could very well be it for you in the Navy, son."

Son. He's never called me "son" before. That time I came to his house, sat down, had dinner with the man, he said four words to me the whole time: "Pass the salt, Hopper." Now I get "son."

"Yes, sir."

Shane studied him, clearly perplexed. He looked like different emotions were at war within him. "What is wrong with you, son? You became an officer in five years. Fastest Mustang in the history of the U.S. Navy."

"Yes, sir." He kept his voice flat and uneven, as if they were discussing the fate of someone else.

The admiral slowly walked around him, apparently wanting to see if his actions made any more sense if he was being observed from a different angle. "You've got skills. I've never seen a man waste himself better than you." He paused and then intoned, as if speaking from a pulpit, "Keep the ship out of the surf and spray or you will plunge to destruction."

"That was Homer, sir," Hopper said. "From *The Odyssey*. Part of the instructions for getting around Scylla and Charybdis."

Shane stopped in his pacing and gawked at Hopper. Hopper felt a brief flash of triumph over having garnered such a reaction from the admiral. Then Shane quickly covered his astonishment as it dissolved into the expression he typically had when he interacted with Hopper: disappointment. "The fact that you know that chafes my butt more than anything. What my daughter sees in you is a great mystery to me. You're a very smart individual with very weak character, leadership, and decision-making skills."

Hopper nodded. "I understand, sir."

The admiral again seemed to be waiting for Hopper to fill in the gap of silence. When he didn't, probably more out of frustration than genuine interest in anything Hopper might tell him, Shane asked, "Do you have anything to say? *Anything?*"

A lot of things. A ton of things. But none of them are anything you'd care about. And, frankly, none of them are any of your damned business. Besides, why should you care? You've wanted me nowhere near your precious Sam ever since I can remember. I've given you what you want. Served it up on a silver platter. So let's not pretend like you give a crap about the whys and wherefores.

"Negative, sir," was all he said.

Shane sighed deeply. "Enjoy these games, Mr. Hopper. It's likely this will be the last time you spend in the U.S. Navy."

"Roger that, sir."

Shane saluted. Hopper returned it without hesitation and then Shane left the wardroom, leaving Hopper standing there at attention. As soon as he was gone, Hopper sagged against the table.

He said nothing, did nothing, made not the slightest sound. He simply stared off into space and watched the entirety of his life spinning away. He had never more desperately wanted to sink into a morass of his own self-pity.

There was only one thing left to do, and that was exactly what Shane had suggested. Except he was going to take it to an entirely different level. He wasn't simply going to enjoy the war games. He was going to do everything he could to aid in completely annihilating any opponents. Maybe he couldn't win on the soccer field. And maybe he was a loser on the field of love, since there was no doubt in his mind that he and Sam were finished.

But on the battlefield, all was clear and simple. Get the other guy before he gets you.

Would that all of life were that simple.

PEARL HARBOR

Like the *Sampson*, the *John Paul Jones* was an *Arleigh Burke*–class guided missile destroyer, docked in Pearl Harbor, a long way from her home port of San Diego. Her famed motto was "In Harm's Way," and she had certainly lived up to it, having endured four deployments to the Persian Gulf. Along with eleven other destroyers from an assortment of countries, right now she was taking on the last of her crew and making ready to set sail for the international war games. The weather was certainly perfect for it. Not a cloud in the sky, no prediction of rain or storms anywhere on the horizon.

Although with the mood Hopper was in, he was already seeing that as a drawback. Inclement weather could sometimes be tremendously useful and give you a leg up on your opponent if you could detect their ships before they could see yours. With a perfect sun beaming down, it meant that the playing field was level.

Fine. Bring 'em on. He was definitely in the mood to blow something up.

What he was not in the mood for was to listen to Sam tell him how monumentally he had screwed up. Worse, he was not in the weapons bay, out of sight from everyone else; instead he was on the dock, approaching the gangway that led up to the ship, and Sam was right next to him, letting him have it in no uncertain terms.

"You had one job. One simple, very specific job," she said.

"It was not a good time to ask," he told her, never more certain of anything in his entire life.

She kept talking as if he hadn't spoken. "Five words: 'May I marry your daughter?' You ask the question. He says 'yes,' and we're there. We're good." She gestured in frustration, "You hitting a Japanese officer was *not* part of the plan."

He stopped and turned to face her. "I'm really sorry."

There was nothing in her attitude that led Hopper to think that apologizing was going to get the job done. As it turned out, he was exactly right. "You think this is a joke? You don't think I'm *serious* about this? I love my father more than anyone in the world, Hopper. You don't have the respect . . ."

Her voice became so laden with emotion that she couldn't finish the sentence.

Hopper was still having trouble believing that they were having this conversation. He'd been sure that once Sam found out how badly everything had gone, it would be the end of them right there. That he'd find a break-up email waiting for him, or perhaps a curt "Nice knowing you" on his voice mail. The fact that she was still talking to him at all was nothing short of astounding to him.

He reached out to her, tried to take her hand, but she shook it away. So he folded his arms, looking uneasy as he said, "I do have the respect. And I . . . I'm sorry." It seemed a hopelessly inadequate thing for him to say, but it was all he could manage.

She took a moment to regain control of herself and then looked up at him. He could see the red rims of her eyes. She'd been crying before she ever came to see him. "Stone says there's going to be a captain's mast as soon as you get back."

"Yeah." It was all he said. There didn't really seem much of anything else for him *to* say.

There was such despair on Sam's face that Hopper was starting to feel as if he were some kind of sadist for even spending time with her. "What is *wrong* with you?" she said, and thumped her palm on his chest for good measure.

"I'm not sure."

She was starting to tear up again, and she wiped them away as quickly as she could. There were others around, sailors and officers and their spouses, and the last thing she needed was for the daughter of the admiral to look weak, as if she were all choked up over the notion of her boyfriend going off to war games. Sam spoke to him low and intensely: "Something is wrong, Hopper. Really wrong, and you have to make it right. I love you very much, but something has got to change. Make it right." She didn't wait for him to leave her. Instead she walked away from him as quickly as she could.

Hopper stood there for a moment, wrestling with the possibility of running after her, maybe even blowing off the war games completely. Let her know where his priorities were. But what would be the result of that? Desertion charges? Dishonorable discharge? Then again, wasn't that a foregone conclusion, with the captain's mast? If he was going to go down, why not just go down in flames?

Because if you wait till after the mast, you might still have a whisper of a breath of a prayer. Turn your back on the Navy and it's all over. You, Sam, all of it. You'll never be able to make it right the way she wants you to.

These were the thoughts that hung on him as he joined his shipmates aboard the *John Paul Jones.*

Later, as he stood leaning on the railing of the prow while the destroyer prepared to pull out, he wondered if it was indeed too late to fix things. Sam had talked of love, but she'd walked away from him. She'd spoken of his making things right, but hadn't suggested how he could possibly go about it.

Maybe she's already preparing emotionally to cut me loose, and who could blame her? Is there any point in . . . ?

Then he saw her. She was standing in the parking lot, leaning against the Jeep, her eyes clearly searching for some sign of Hopper. Then she spotted him, raised her arm, and waved.

She came back to see me off.

It was like a jolt of adrenaline to his heart. He gave her a salute and then did a double tap of his fist against his heart, followed by a V-for-Victory sign with his fingers. He was trying to tell her every way he knew that he still loved her and would try to find a way to fix things, for her. It was a great message and he was positive it was exactly what she needed to hear.

Now all he had to do was find a way to make it actually happen.

U.S. FLEET, OUT TO SEA

Stone Hopper was never more comfortable than when he was on the bridge of the *Sampson*. He considered it to be his place of power, and his authority flowed from there. All eyes of his bridge crew were upon him, and he addressed them in a calm, almost leisurely manner. They listened attentively to his every word.

"All right, everybody, that was a great under way from Pearl. Solid job all around." He nodded in approval and everyone was smiling. They knew they were the best damned crew in the fleet—no reason to pussyfoot around it. "And good job on liberty. No incidents."

The moment he said it, he knew what they were thinking. There were certainly no incidents involving the crew of the *Sampson*. But the elephant in the room was the awareness—which had become common knowledge by that point—of the trouble that Stone Hopper's idiot brother had gotten himself into.

He didn't bother to address it. What was there to say? Instead he told them briskly, "Now, let's get buttoned back up. We're gonna be close maneuvering with a lot of other nations. This exercise will allow us to put our training to a rigorous test. I'm excited to see what we learn."

They nodded, almost as one.

He regarded them sternly. "Teamwork is unity of purpose. All of us pulling together. Trust your fellow crewmen. Respect is earned. There is no greater feeling I know of than individual excellence forming teamwork that leads to victory. Victory through teamwork. Be safe out there. Look out for one another. And let's keep chargin'. Working together, supporting one another. Your voice counts. Speak up."

He straightened his shoulders and saluted them. They snapped off a sharp, perfectly coordinated response and then went to their assigned tasks. Stone watched them moving with smooth efficiency. He should be focusing completely on them and taking pride in their actions. Instead he was thinking about Alex's troubles. *Did you let him down somehow? Was this, in any way, your fault?* Ultimately he decided that it was not, and that sooner or later he was going to have to stop taking emotional responsibility for Alex's screwups. At some point Alex Hopper was going to have to grow the hell up, and if it took a full-blown court-martial and being drummed out of the Navy for that to happen, well . . .

At least he'd finally learn.

Either that or spiral downward faster than ever.

Every department head on a ship such as the *John Paul Jones* was utterly convinced that his little realm was the center of the vessel's universe. The bridge crew would have assured any visitors that the bridge was the ship's soul, while the engine crew would have declared that the engine room was the ship's heart.

Alex Hopper knew for a fact that the combat information center, typically abbreviated as CIC, was where it all went down. Engines, bridges, those were all fine for what they were, but a fishing trawler had a bridge and an AMC Gremlin had an engine. The *John Paul Jones* was a *destroyer,* designed for combat on the high seas. Without weapons, nothing else mattered, and the CIC was packed with a billion dollars' worth of *Aegis*-class weapons technology. Any battle that the *John Paul Jones* found itself in was going to be fought from this room, and Alex Hopper was making damned sure that everyone in his command knew that. As long as he was weapons officer, nothing was going to stop the *John Paul Jones* from being the best damned destroyer ever to have sailed the Pacific Rim.

There were nearly two dozen people populating the CIC. Most of them were manning an assortment of very sophisticated computers, capable of providing every single reading that could possibly be desired.

"I want this understood: we are not in this weapons room to learn, we are here to *crush* the other ships. Is that clear?"

Raikes was the gunnery officer. As Hopper spoke, she could actually be seen to caress the controls, as if Hopper's words amounted to foreplay and she was being turned on by them. It was entirely possible that was the case. Aside from Hopper, there was no one in the CIC who got more jazzed from blowing things up than Raikes.

He moved through the CIC, checking each system, one by one. "Let's remember," he reminded them, "all this technology was manufactured for the U.S. Navy by the lowest bidder, because that's the American way. So we stay on top of things now to make sure nothing fails us when we need it. Clear?"

"Yes sir," they chorused.

There was a hand-scrawled sign above the radar station. It was against ship's regs; the commander disliked people putting their own personal touches on the equipment. Hopper read the sign: *"In God We Trust. All Others, We Track."* He grinned and left it there. It was odd; there was something strangely liberating about being slated for court-martial. When they were going to put you on trial for punching out a Japanese officer, it seemed pretty unlikely they'd tack onto the list of your offenses *"Left a personalized sign above the radar station."* Nothing like a captain's mast to put things in perspective.

He passed the close-in weapon system, or CIWS, nodding in approval as a check was made on it to ascertain that it was functional. "Let me remind you," said Hopper, "this is a combat vessel and we will excel in our command and control, our communications capacity, our tactics, our fire control, navigation, our weapons capabilities. Clear?"

"Yes sir," said the team once more in unison.

"If we return to Pearl without having outperformed every other ship on this ocean then I will personally hold every man and woman in this room accountable."

Then he heard Raikes muttering in that way that she had, the way she liked to pretend wasn't going to be heard by anyone else, except she knew perfectly well she was audible. It was her passive-aggressive way of saying exactly what she wanted to say while maintaining at least a façade of respect for her superior officers.

"What was that, Raikes?" he said sharply.

She looked at him with wide, innocent eyes. "Nothing, sir."

"No, I'm pretty sure it was something."

"Nothing."

In point of fact he'd heard every word and they were etched in his mind: *We've ended up in a department run by some kind of Donald Trump–Mike Tyson mutant combo package. Imagine if they ever gave this lunatic command . . .*

"Sounded like . . ." He pretended to be having difficulty remembering the name. " 'Donald Trump.' "

"Only in that you are both great motivators, Lieutenant Hopper," she said.

"Did I hear 'Mike Tyson'?"

"If you did, it was only in reference to the fact that you both project great physical intensity, and—"

That was enough of the game as far as Hopper was concerned. He leaned in toward her and said sternly, "Watch yourself, Raikes."

"Watching myself, sir." A smile played across her lips but she resolutely focused on her weapons systems.

Raikes was a good officer. Scratch that: as a gunnery officer, she was the best. That being the case, Hopper was inclined to give her more latitude than he otherwise would, and probably somewhat more than he should.

Still . . . no harm in laying down the law.

"Teamwork is all of you doing what I say," said Hopper. "Trust no one. Respect is taken." He turned toward a young officer. "Lieutenant Cruz: make enemies or make friends?"

"Enemies, sir," said Cruz.

"Why?"

"An enemy's desire to prove his worth to you is stronger than a friend's desire to prove gratitude."

As Cruz spoke, Hopper mouthed the words along with him. Cruz had learned well. "Cultivate . . . ?"

"*Enemies,* sir."

Hopper nodded approvingly and then turned to the rest of his crew. "Victory through victory. Demolishing competition. Protecting what is ours."

Raikes started to open her mouth.

"Shut up," he said.

She closed it again.

There was a loud clearing of a throat, and Hopper turned to see Mullenaro standing in the doorway. He'd been giving Hopper the stink eye ever since the meeting in the wardroom. *Well, he'll be rid of me soon enough; he's probably happy about that.* "Get to the helo deck. *Sampson* wants you on the pronto. In person."

They want me over on the Sampson? *Why would they—?*

Then he realized. It was pretty self-evident, really. Stone hadn't seen him since the entire fiasco on the Big Mo, mostly because Hopper had taken great pains to avoid him. Obviously Stone was going to take advantage of his last opportunity to boss Hopper around in an official capacity. For a moment, Hopper considered telling Mullenaro that he couldn't make it. That he wasn't leaving the *John Paul Jones* and if the *Sampson* didn't like it, that was too damned bad. If Stone wanted to take the time to bitch out his younger brother, he could bloody well come over here and do it.

Yet all he said was, "Aye, sir."

Minutes later he was on a chopper heading toward the *Sampson,* chewing himself out mentally for his inability to say what was on his mind. Ultimately he decided that there simply hadn't been any point to it. Let Stone have his say. *You have it coming, and you know it.*

Stone was standing on the flight deck of the *Sampson,* displaying as much emotion as his name might suggest. As the chopper set down, Hopper emerged from it, holding his hat securely under his arm to make sure that the whipping blades didn't blow it away. He came to a halt several feet from his brother and, standing at attention, saluted. Normally such a move would have prompted Stone to smile, seeing Hopper display genuine respect for the uniform and rank. Now, though, all Stone could think was, *Too little, too late.* He returned the salute dispassionately and indicated, with a nod of his head, that Hopper should follow him.

They made their way down to Stone's quarters. Stone stood to one side as Hopper entered and then he shut the door behind him. He dispensed with any niceties. They were both busy men, and besides, there seemed no point in trying to candy coat a poison pill.

"Captain's mast is real," said Stone as he walked around to the far side of his desk and sat down. He gestured for Hopper to sit; Hopper remained standing, and Stone saw no reason to push the matter. "Just got off the phone with 3rd Fleet JAG. I can't get you out of this one."

"When?"

"The day we get back. Nagata is being charged, too."

Hopper took in this bit of news. Stone could tell from the look on his face that he was relieved. If he was going down, at least Nagata was going down with him. Then he realized his priorities were out of whack. He brought himself back to his own concerns. "What do I do?"

"I don't know what to tell you this time, Hopps. It's three strikes." Stone shook his head. "I don't get it. You have everything. You've got the skills. More talent than me. You've got a great girl. And you just keep shooting yourself in the foot. Why?"

"I don't know."

"Yeah, you do," Stone said impatiently. "You're not that oblivious to whatever's going on in your head. But you try to avoid it, and if someone really presses it, you make a joke about it. It isn't a joke anymore, Hopper. This time it's very real. So tell me what the hell's going on."

"I'm just not you," said Hopper. "You got the character and quality. I got the other stuff."

"Yeah. Except you're on the verge of losing all the other stuff, including Sam. Is that what you want?"

Hopper stared at him. "Honestly?"

"That'd be nice."

He sighed heavily. "I don't know what the hell I want."

It sounded trite, but Stone could feel his brother's pain. Hopper had been so lost for so long, and Stone had done everything he could to get him back on track. Instead they were here, in this situation, and Hopper's career—which had seemed so promising—might well have hit a dead end.

"I hope you find it, Hopps," Stone said with sincere concern for his brother. "And I hope you find it before you've completely sunk yourself."

DEEP SPACE

They have been moving at a steady velocity as they plummet through the emptiness of space, but now that emptiness is coming to an end. A solar system is hanging in front of them. Nine worlds, or eight if one doesn't count the planetoid in the outer rim. In any event, it does not matter, for the incoming vessels have no interest in any of the worlds save one.

They move toward the object of their attention.

They are fully aware that their target will know they are coming. There are likely to be some manner of early warning systems available to them.

Let them know. Let them be fully aware. It's not as if there is anything they'll be able to do about it.

THE HIMALAYAS

It had been six years for the scientists of the Beacon International Project. Six long years of watching space, of monitoring the equipment, of waiting and seeing whether their messages-in-a-bottle would ever garner some manner of response.

Yet even after all that time, once the moment that they had been waiting for finally arrived, at first they had no clue what it was they were looking at.

One of the main monitor screens was tuned to CNN, as it typically was, since that had become the major lifeline for the scientists to the outside world. No one was paying any attention to it, however. Instead they were glued to their individual monitors, trying to make sense out of the readings they were getting.

"Speed is consistent with meteors. Trajectory?" called out Carlson.

Doctor Abraham Nogrady, wearing the nice sweater of local weave that he'd been given for his birthday the previous week, was standing in front of a monitor, tracking the blue line that represented the incoming object. "Oh my." He leaned close to the monitor, typing on the keyboard. "Whatever this is, it's tracking our message path. Bring up Hawaii. Get me Cal on the line."

He'd never blamed Doctor Calvin Zapata for "abandoning him," as he had laughingly put it two years earlier. Who could blame the younger man, really? The Hawaii offer was too good for him to pass up. He would actually be in charge of the location, something that wouldn't happen in the Himalayas, since Nogrady wasn't planning on going anywhere. That alone had been something of a revelation to Nogrady, discovering how much he preferred the solitude of the mountains. *Who knew that I didn't actually like civilization all that much?*

It took long moments to raise the Hawaii location. A junior technician whose name Nogrady couldn't recall came on the communications screen. The reception wasn't the greatest. The general feeling was that for all the money that had been poured into the high-tech system that linked them visually with the other Beacon stations, they'd have done just as well with a couple of PCs and Skype. Still, for all the static on the screen, at least Nogrady could make out the technician on the other end and hear what he was saying. "Doctor Zapata's in the computer room!" the technician told him. "He's busy trying to recycle some parts from previous models because the money's not there for upgrading . . ."

"Yes, yes, I get that, uhm . . ." He took a stab at the name. "Rice."

"Royce, sir."

Dammit. "Yes, I meant to say 'Royce.' Royce, are you seeing what we're seeing . . . ?"

"Yes, sir. There's massive activity on all the screens. I was just about to get Doctor Zapata."

"I suggest you do so sooner rather than later, son. Tell him I have a moon trail for him."

"I'm on it. Don't go anywhere."

Nogrady exchanged amused looks with the other technicians at Royce's parting comment. Where the hell was he going to go?

Minutes later Zapata's face appeared on the screen. He had a bit less hair up top than the last time Nogrady had seen him, but had apparently decided to compensate for it by growing a rather scraggly beard. He was wearing a gaudy Hawaiian shirt, festooned with a print of yellow and green flowers. He looked like Royce had just dragged him from a luau. But he was holding some microtools that he'd obviously forgotten were in his hands when he'd come from the computer room. He was slightly out of breath, indicating he'd been running. "Cal. You're looking well," said Nogrady.

"You look terrible," Zapata replied. "You're all grainy and flickering . . . wait, that's the reception. Or is that actually you?"

"A little of both." Nogrady had never really "gotten" Zapata's sense of humor, but at least he was able to tell when the man was joking and had developed the knack of smiling tolerantly. He did so now, but then got down to business. "Cal, are you seeing what I'm seeing?"

Zapata nodded. "The incoming tracks."

"I've either been at this too long, or our outgoing message path—"

"I have the same thing, Doctor Nogrady. This could be a hoax, a meteor with a jet pack . . . or . . ." He paused, licking his lips, which had obviously become quite dry, ". . . some kind of answer to the beacon."

The fact that Cal was addressing him as "Doctor Nogrady" was more than sufficient to convey the gravity of the moment, considering that the younger man had typically called him "Abe" or even "Abie," usually just to annoy him.

The two men shared a moment of pure astonishment. It wasn't as if they'd ever stopped believing in the possibilities of their endeavor, but somehow neither of them had ever been quite prepared for the actuality of it reaching fruition.

An answer to the beacon. Someone found our bottle, read the message and is responding. Nogrady could scarcely process it. He felt as if his brain was on the verge of being overloaded. *We are standing on the cusp of what may be the most important day in the history of mankind since the first of our ancestors hauled himself out of the primordial ooze.*

Then Carlson, sitting practically at Nogrady's elbow, said, "We've got something splitting off from the main."

Nogrady looked down and saw that Carlson was right. A new track had peeled off from the one they were already recording. Best guess was that it was heading toward Asia.

Zapata was tracking the same thing. "Looks like entry problems in the LEO debris belt. It hit something."

Immediately Nogrady was seized with a sense of helpless frustration. He'd written entire papers on the hazards of just this: the massive amounts of debris that were hanging in low Earth orbit (LEO) that nobody seemed to have the slightest interest in doing a damned thing about. Bad enough that it posed a threat to people residing on the earth below. Now all that space junk might well have crippled someone trying to make contact. What an ignominious, not to mention tragic, beginning to what should have been a new and golden age in Earth's history.

"It's splintering," Carlson confirmed Zapata's readings.

"At least three pieces of this thing are going to rain down. And at the current velocity, I'd say they're going to hit in less than ninety seconds."

Less than ninety seconds . . .

It was only at that point that Nogrady started considering the possible human element of what he was witnessing. Debris had routinely fallen from the LEO belt, and yet never in the history of the space program had any of it ever struck a human being. There were zero fatalities from man-made space debris.

There were not, however, any statistics related to debris manufactured by something other than man. As Nogrady stood there helplessly watching the trajectory—knowing that there was no time to warn anyone about anything—he prayed to a God that he didn't quite believe in that the odds continued to hold in their favor.

AROUND THE WORLD IN EIGHTY SECONDS

They know they are being tracked. They do not care. The arrival is simply the opening salvo and the creatures that crawl around on the dirt below have no concept of it.

The crew of a fishing boat were the first ones to lay eyes upon it, although they didn't know what they were seeing.

The high-speed projectile descended with unimaginable force and velocity from on high, blazing red, the air exploding around it, giving off a deafening *crack* like thunder. It slammed into the water miles away, and yet did so with such force that seconds later the water was surging around the fishing boat, threatening to swamp it. It was all the crew could do to keep the boat righted and they watched in astonishment as a massive blast of steam roared up from the entry point, as if a volcano had detonated deep below the surface.

"*What the hell was that?*" screamed one of the younger sailors.

The boat's captain, a grizzled veteran of many a storm, had been chewing tobacco when the object had struck. He spat some out while holding firmly on to the wheel and said, "Y'ask me . . . looks like God just hocked a loogie."

Kowloon City in Hong Kong had a population of nearly half a million. It was overlooked by Lion Rock, a hill named for the rock formations that resembled a crouched lion prepared to leap upon its prey.

At the base of Lion Rock, a small group of worshippers had gathered at the temple to engage in daily prayers. A statue of Buddha sat on a wide pedestal at the far end, looking both protective and benevolent. People were just beginning to gather when the sky above Lion Rock lit up as if sheet lightning had erupted from behind the clouds. It caught everyone flat-footed, since there had been no sign of any sort of inclement weather.

Then something hit on the far side of the hill, and the concussion ripped through the temple. The Buddha was toppled from its perch, knocked off as if it weighed nothing, and shattered. The temple itself was blown apart, the very air ripping it asunder. The people themselves were blown backwards, the ferocity of the impact shattering their bones, causing cerebral hemorrhages, or just stopping their hearts outright. Men, women and children lay entangled with one another, nothing more than meat sacks where there had once been humble worshippers coming to express devotion to their god.

The concussive force didn't stop there. Seconds later, Kowloon City was feeling its impact. Shock waves rippled down over the city, blowing out windows from its skyscrapers, shaking buildings that weren't designed to withstand that degree of force. Most managed to hold on; some did not. Their foundations crumbled and people both within and without screamed as the buildings toppled over, brick, mortar and glass falling everywhere. People on the ground ran, stampeding one another to get clear. Many of them, looking over their shoulders and seeing the falling buildings bearing down on them, had just enough time to spot people inside the buildings, tumbling out of the now glassless windows or hanging on in desperation, praying for some last-second miracle that might spare their lives.

The miracles were not forthcoming.

In the Scots highlands, four youths slowly approached the smoking remains of something that had come spiraling down from the skies and had annihilated an entire swath of trees. They exchanged confused looks as they drew closer, not sure what it was they were seeing.

It looked like some sort of large, metal container. Or perhaps even some sort of coffin. But they had no idea what it could possibly contain.

"Should we get some help?" one of them, an older boy named Tom, asked.

"We dinna need help," said another boy, Sean.

Tom didn't respond, save to turn his back and run.

This drew disdainful sneers and shouts from the others. They then descended into the crater that the container had created and proceeded to smash away at it with sticks, trying to pound it open. All they managed to do was shatter every progressively larger branch that they brought, leaving the container unscathed.

"Try this."

Tom had returned and he was wielding a car jack proudly. "Muh dad'll kill me if he knows, so let's put it t'good use."

The others grinned as Sean, the largest of them, put his hand out. Tom tossed it to him and Sean, catching it effortlessly, wedged it into the lip of the large container and started working on levering it open.

Since they were more or less in the middle of nowhere, and the only thing that had been damaged was a grove of trees, there were no TV cameras around to record the landing.

There were, however, plenty of cameras elsewhere.

In the Beacon research center in Oahu, Calvin Zapata and his assistant, Royce, watched the chaos unfolding and being reported on via CNN. The destruction in Kowloon City in Hong Kong was being played and replayed from dozens of angles; apparently enough survivors had been recording the horror on their cell phones and were posting it on the Internet. The view wasn't getting any better no matter which way it was being watched.

A reporter from the Hong Kong bureau was on-site. Zapata could see bodies lying everywhere, some covered with blankets, most not. Arms and legs were visible from beneath piles of rubble that had, shortly before, been buildings. There was a child wandering around aimlessly in the background, screaming something that Zapata very much suspected was Chinese for "mother" and "father." The reporter—whose name, *Bernard Chen*, was superimposed on the screen—looked like it was taking all he had to keep himself together. The devastation had been too massive and unexpected for him to treat with journalistic detachment.

". . . as casualty reports come in, it's still unclear exactly what it was that hit," he was saying. "Some say earthquake. Others report seeing something come from the sky. A meteor? Skylab? At this point we still don't know. Whatever it was, the death toll is in the millions and a massive worldwide relief effort will be needed to . . ."

Zapata killed the volume as he shifted his attention back to Nogrady, who was still on the communications screen. Nogrady looked ashen. There was a dead silence between them, neither able to form words that summarized the horror of what they had witnessed.

Finally Zapata managed to speak. His thoughts were racing so fast that he couldn't even finish one sentence before another would overtake him. His voice hoarse, he said, "This could get even worse. Those little splinters that split off . . . by my calculations, a point zero-zero-two course variation over that distance . . . these things could end up all over the hemisphere . . ."

Images were now hurtling across the television flat screen fast and furious. It was as if CNN didn't know where to look first. An entire section of a Kansas cornfield had been flattened, and a vast plume of smoke was rising from the impact point. In Paris, the Arc de Triomphe was lying in shattered ruins. There appeared to be some unit of . . . something protruding from it. Zapata leaned forward, studying it. The words "Fallen Space Satellite?" were emblazoned on the TV screen, but Zapata was staring at what he could make out of the debris from outer space (*Debris from outer space? Had he just thought that?*) and it wasn't looking like anything to him that NASA would have produced.

"You seeing that wreckage, Cal?" said Nogrady over the viewscreen. "The one that annihilated the Arc?"

"Yeah, I am." Zapata was studying it carefully. "I think it resembles a solar panel or satellite face. How about you?"

Nogrady didn't answer immediately. He was stroking his chin thoughtfully. "I think it looks like a massive communications tower."

"Who? To communicate? Who to communicate what to whom?"

"I don't know. I don't know, Cal." Nogrady had been looking inward, as if scrutinizing his soul, and then he stared bleakly at Zapata. "I've been waiting for this moment my entire life, Cal. Since before you were born. And all I can think of is the old saying—"

"Be careful what you wish for, because you just might get it?"

Slowly Nogrady nodded. "You read my mind, Cal."

No. Actually it's what I was worried about when we first started this project. My mind was way ahead of you. I just couldn't get anyone to listen to me.

Cal Zapata typically took great pride in being right about everything. There had never been an occasion such as this, where he desperately wished he'd been wrong.

Hopper walked briskly onto the bridge of the *John Paul Jones*, summoned there by Commander Brownley. Minutes earlier, he would have assumed that Brownley wanted to talk to him about the court-martial. Perhaps lecture him on how badly he'd screwed up. Maybe ask him how the get-together with his brother had gone . . . and then ream him out.

But he'd heard, as had the rest of the ship, about the space debris that was falling all over the damned globe. In the grand scheme of things, the court-martial of a single officer was meaningless. There was no way that Brownley—whatever the differences he might have had with Hopper during the time the younger man had served under him—was going to be harping about it when the whole world was in a state of emergency.

Brownley took one look at him and it was clear from his grim expression that Hopper didn't even have to ask about the subject of the impromptu meeting. "Hong Kong got hit hard," said Brownley, getting right to it. "Total devastation, massive civilian casualties."

"What was it?"

Brownley shook his head. "No one knows for sure. Best guess: meteor shower or fallen satellites. And they've hit more than just Hong Kong. At least a dozen locations known, with reports of more strikes coming in every minute."

"Let me guess. One near us?"

"Yeah. We've got new orders. Hawkeyes report there's debris near our position. We've been commanded to check it out with *Sampson* and *Myoko*. Coordinates being fed into the navigation computers right now. I want your department on full alert."

This confused Hopper somewhat. "Are we expecting that some busted space debris is going to open fire on us?"

"I am expecting nothing, lieutenant commander. I am, however, anticipating everything. I expect you to do no less."

"Aye, sir." Hopper saluted stiffly and headed out of the bridge. As he did so, he heard Brownley call out, "Set material condition zebra. Right full rudder. Flank speed."

Moments later, the three vessels dispatched to inspect the crash area had peeled off from the rest of the fleet, the war games forgotten, wholly unaware of just what exactly was lurking under the water, waiting for them.

OAHU NAVAL REHAB CENTER

Samantha Shane—outfitted in exercise gear, a file folder tucked under her arm—nodded and waved to her coworkers as she moved through the large clinic gym that was filled with all manner of exercise equipment. Weights to work both the upper and lower body, rowing machines, treadmills . . . anything that could be utilized to help hammer a human body into shape. There were several naval officers and a midshipman engaged in various types of physical therapy, each of them working with an endlessly patient trainer who would smile and nod encouragement. Sam had actually practiced the type of smile she used while working with a client. When she'd been training for her current job, she had stared into the mirror for minutes at a time. She was trying to make sure that her smile radiated confidence; a certainty that whomever she was working with was going to overcome whatever problems that the hazards of war, or just pure rotten luck, had saddled them with.

Unfortunately she knew she had a serious challenge in front of her this time. It didn't take her long to find him. He was seated in a chair, staring despondently off into space. He was wearing a U.S. Army T-shirt and a pair of sweat shorts, which revealed the prosthetics he had instead of the legs he'd been born with. They were high tech, even state of the art: C-legs, with microprocessor-controlled knees. The popular term among the soldiers was "bionic legs," after the appliances worn by the Six Million Dollar Man. Those bionic legs, of course, were fictional; indistinguishable from human legs and capable of enabling him to sprint at sixty miles per hour (mysteriously without ever causing his hair to ruffle). The C-legs had a ways to go before they reached that level of perfection.

Her patient had a thick coat of dark beard stubble and

his hair, which had grown out somewhat from the standard crew cut, was disheveled. His expression seemed set into a permanent glower and his eyes were bloodshot. *He hasn't been sleeping well. Who can blame him? Probably wakes up constantly trying to scratch the itch of his lower legs, which aren't there anymore.*

He was glancing around at that moment and his eyes fell on her. "Looking for my physical therapist," he said.

She spread her arms in a *ta-daaa* manner. "You found her."

"Nooo," said the soldier with the air of someone who felt he was talking to an idiot. "Dean's a stocky guy with a mustache who benches four-fifty."

"I'm your new physical therapist. Dean quit. Said you burned him out, so you get me."

He looked at her askance. "They punishing you for something?"

"I volunteered."

"Why?" He appeared intrigued by her, which was certainly better than thinking she was an idiot or brushing her off. His face hadn't lost its general air of sourness, however. "You like abuse?"

"My father is an admiral," she said with easy confidence, "and my semi-fiancé is a weapons officer on a destroyer. I understand and can handle 'difficult men.'"

"What's a 'semi-fiancé'?"

She ignored the question, not feeling like explaining it. Besides, it was none of his damned business anyway. "I'm detecting a lot of anger."

"That's very perceptive of you," he said sarcastically.

"Is there anything in there besides anger . . ." She glanced at the name on the file. "Mick?"

"Not much." He stared at her defiantly.

He's challenging you to meet his stare. He's trying to turn this into a pissing match. Don't do it. Instead she read from his file in a no-nonsense, businesslike way. "Mick

Canales. Thirty-five years old. Army Special Forces. Lost both legs last July. IED Korengal Valley in Afghanistan. Depression. Unwilling to go home."

He stared at her as he scratched the underside of his chin, saying nothing. To her that meant that he wasn't hearing anything worth contradicting.

She continued to read. "Football coach, Colorado Springs. 'Pikes Peak issues.'"

Upon hearing that, his face immediately went from annoyance to full-blown irritation. He was acting as if some deep secret had been brought out into the open, a secret she had no business knowing. "Where'd you hear that?"

For response, Sam pointed at the obvious source: the file in her hand. "Says you're pissed off because you can't climb Pikes Peak anymore. Is that accurate?" He didn't seem inclined to answer immediately, and so she simply gazed at him with a single raised, questioning eyebrow, acting as if she knew it was only a matter of time before he responded to her question.

He glared at her for a full minute, not saying a word. She did nothing to fill in the silence. Instead she just remained there, unmoving. A brick wall would have had more to say on the subject. Finally, though, he said, "Every season I would lead the team on a hike up to the top of Pikes Peak. The fact of that hike not happening is contributing to my," and he mockingly made air quotations, "'anger problem.'"

"It's a little more than anger, though. Your last therapist said you've lost your will to fight. Is that right?"

"I lost my fight when I lost my legs."

"You know you're the same man inside. Same brain, same heart, same soul that made you," and she glanced down once more. "A Golden Gloves champ at twenty-two, Bronze Star recipient in Afghanistan. All that's still in there."

"Nah. I'm half a man, and half a man ain't enough to

be a soldier." He looked away from her then as he said under his breath, "Or to see anything."

She considered that for a moment and then said, "I'll be right back. Stay here."

She walked away from him as he called after her in a mocking tone, "Where the hell am I gonna go?"

Less than a minute later, she returned from the equipment room with a backpack that had the rehab center logo on it. She took it to the small kitchen area nearby and started loading it with bottled water, protein bars, bananas, and the like. He watched her in confused silence, apparently having no desire to give her the satisfaction of asking what she thought she was doing. Once she was done, she slung the backpack over her shoulder. "Let's go."

He stared at her blankly. "Go where?"

For answer, she gripped him by the arm. He had no particular inclination to stand up, and was visibly startled when Sam hauled him to his artificial feet with no problem. She knew that she was stronger than she looked and liked to surprise people with her physical capabilities every so often.

"We're going to take a little walk."

"Walk where?" He was clearly suspicious.

"We're climbing a mountain. Up to Saddle Ridge."

Mick looked as if he wasn't sure whether to laugh or just sit back down and dare her to get him on his feet again. "No, we are not."

"Yes, we are."

"No." He shook his head firmly as if that was the last word on the subject.

Sam completely ignored his reluctance. "Got sunscreen? Don't worry about it if you don't; I grabbed some. Come on, let's see if we've got any hiking shoes around here that'll do you better than what you've got now."

She headed down the hallway. *Please let him follow*

me, please, she thought desperately while making sure none of that desperation showed in her body language. The only way he was going to have confidence in himself was to have it first in her. If he stayed right where he was, asserting that he wouldn't be climbing a mountain, a hill—or anything, for that matter—there wasn't a damned thing she could do about it.

To her utter relief, she heard a *thump thump* behind her. He was following her. She glanced over her shoulder as if his obeying her had never been in doubt and said, "Step lively, soldier. We haven't got all day."

Sam trudged up the mountain, glad that she made a point of keeping in shape. They were surrounded by lush, green vegetation, and the air smelled thick and sweet.

She was in the lead, if for no other reason than she wanted to make sure the path in front of them was clear. Taking spills was part of the learning curve when it came to prosthetic legs, but it was one thing to stumble while working in the gym and quite another taking a header over a projecting tree root or a gaping hole in the path. That could be catastrophic. She was trying to build up Mick's confidence, not cause him to get banged up from sprawling in the dirt.

Mick pushed forward. He was concentrating, his brow wrinkled and covered with sweat.

She didn't want to get too far in front of him, but she also didn't want him to feel as if she was taking it easy on him. The man was five foot nine inches' worth of pride. So she stopped, pretending to catch her breath. "You're doing pretty good for a guy who doesn't want to be climbing."

"This isn't no Pike's Peak," he said disdainfully.

"It's a start."

"My grandmother could climb this hill."

"It's a start."

"I got a dog named Mustard. He could climb this damn hill."

"Good." She adjusted her backpack. "Then you and Mustard can spend some quality time together back in Colorado." She started to turn away in order to continue their ascent.

"Mustard got hit by a dump truck eight years ago. Mustard's dead." He sounded indifferent, although it was hard for her to determine whether he was just maintaining a macho act.

She stared at him. "I'm sorry."

He trudged past her, taking the lead. "I'm over it. And by the way, I'm a big boy. I can watch my path just fine."

Sam smiled to herself. *He doesn't miss a trick. Might be fake legs, but nothing's wrong with his mind.*

He called back to her, "What's a semi-fiancé?"

She moaned softly, and then thankfully, before he could press the question—which she was pretty sure he was going to do—her cell phone started ringing. *Saved by the bell.* She glanced at the caller ID and saw Hopper's name. *Please let it be good news. Maybe they've reconsidered the captain's mast.* She answered it, putting the phone to her ear and moving away from Mick to get some modicum of privacy. "I thought you'd be out of cell range by now."

"I've got about five minutes," Hopper's voice came back. He was popping in and out. "Five minutes" came across more like "ive in uts." But she had long practice in deciphering sentences during patchy cell phone calls.

"Yeah. How's it going?" She unslung her backpack since just standing in one place made it seem heavier.

"It's all right. Something crashed near us. We gotta go check it out."

Something crashed? This time the patchiness of their connection made her concerned. Had there been another brushing incident, like last year? Had Hopper gone off and punched out another officer? They might wind up skipping the court-martial and go straight to sentencing. "A ship?" she said tentatively.

"I don't know. Not one of ours."

She closed her eyes and let out a relieved sigh. Whatever was going on, Hopper wasn't in the middle. He didn't even sound especially worked up about it. *Thank God. One less thing for him to get himself in trouble over.*

There was a lengthy silence and Sam started to think that the connection had gone dead. But then she heard Hopper's voice say awkwardly, "I know that I messed up. I'm really sorry and I'm going to try really hard to make it right. I'll talk to your dad as soon as we get back."

She appreciated the fact that he wanted to try and make things right, but somehow she had to think his intended course of action might lead to even greater disaster . . . assuming such a thing was possible. "Maybe you should think hard on if you really want to talk to my dad."

"I don't have to think. I know."

She wasn't sure she liked the sound of that. "You know? You know what? What do you know?"

"What I want." He hesitated and then said firmly, "It's you."

Tears rolled down Sam's face. She spotted Mick out the corner of her eye, watching stoically. She lowered her voice and said, "Stop screwing things up."

"I will. I love you."

They were only hundreds of miles apart, but she felt as if there was a gulf of millions of miles between them. "I love *you*," she said across the span. "I—Hopper?" There was silence on the other end. The line had gone dead.

She pocketed her cell phone and looked at Mick.

"Semi-fiancés," he said slowly, "get in there and mess up your heart. Blow your concentration—stomach ulcers, gas, prolapsed bowels—"

"Got it. Thank you," she said impatiently. Shouldering her backpack once more, she stalked past Mick, shoving him as she did so. "I'm taking the lead. You got anything to say about it, keep it to yourself."

"Yes, ma'am," he said, tossing off a mocking salute and falling into step behind her.

PACIFIC OCEAN, IMPACT POINT

Seaman Ord stood on the observation deck of the *John Paul Jones,* studying the surrounding area with binoculars. They were flanked on either side by the other two vessels, each of them hanging back about a hundred yards, making sure to keep their distance. The last thing anyone needed was for the vessels to get in one another's way.

He didn't see it at first, the object that they were looking for. It was as if his eyes went right over it—as if it wasn't there one moment and then suddenly it was. A maze of some sort, projecting from the water. It was triangular and industrial—definitely man-made, not some sort of natural phenomenon, like a meteor—encrusted with strange panels and what appeared to be a jagged assembly that looked like an antenna. It was protruding from the water about five hundred yards ahead.

"Is this some kind of surprise part of the exercise . . . ?" Ord said to no one. "Like a big 'Okay, what do you do when this happens' kind of deal?" He paused and answered his own question. "Doesn't really feel like it." Then he grabbed the phone that immediately put him through to the bridge. "Contact at zero eight zero. Repeat, contact at zero eight zero."

Word quickly spread to the other two vessels, and immediately all three came to a full stop. Brownley was on the horn with Stone Hopper over on the *Sampson*, who was saying, "Officer of the watch confirms contact, six hundred yards. But . . ."

"But what?"

"Tactical has nothing. We're seeing it, but the computers aren't. The Slick 32s say there's no electronic signal."

That made zero sense to Brownley. "Hang tight," he said, and called down to the weapons room. "Hopper. We've got an unidentified contact dead ahead, six hundred yards."

There was a pause and then Hopper's voice came back. "We've got nothing on the screens."

"Bearing 272."

"I'm not seeing a thing, sir." Hopper sounded as confused as Brownley felt.

Out of frustration with both Hopper and the situation at hand, Brownley said, "I am looking at it with my own eyes."

"Instruments are blind down here, sir."

"Okay. Keep monitoring." He switched back to Stone. "Yeah, Commander, we got nothing on our scanners either."

He could hear the voice of one of Stone's radiomen in the background saying, "This is the USS *Sampson* on a heading 038, hailing unidentified vessel . . . or structure. We are a U.S. Navy warship. Identify yourself." Pause. "No response, sir."

"Okay," said Stone, and returned his attention to Brownley. "Let's get up close and personal. We need a recon."

"I agree. We'll handle it, Commander. I have just the man for the job."

* * *

A twenty-foot rigid-hulled inflatable boat, or RHIB, cut through the water, heading straight toward the unknown structure situated two hundred yards ahead of them. Hopper was perched at the prow, with Beast at the helm. The RHIB was outfitted with a .50 caliber machine gun, and Raikes was crouched behind it, stroking it eagerly. To Hopper, it seemed as if she were just itching for an excuse to cut loose at something. If the opportunity didn't present itself, he might wind up having to let her shoot down some passing seagulls just to keep her happy.

He loved the spray of the ocean around him as the RHIB hurtled forward. When it was just him and the water and a mission, all the other crap just seemed to fall away. It was like his life made sense once more. The certainty that this was going to be his last endeavor in the Navy continued to root around in the back of his mind, an itch that couldn't be scratched. But at least fate had arranged it so his final outing wasn't going to be business as usual. He would be seeing something he'd never seen before. He just wasn't sure if that was a good or a bad thing.

They cut speed and Beast slowly nosed the craft near the metal structure. Hopper leaned forward, trying to get a sense of what the hell was in front of them. He kept thinking about icebergs: that the stuff you saw above the water wasn't what would kill you. "Don't get too close," he said when they were about forty yards out. He studied the structure. "What do you make of that?"

"I'm not sure," said Beast. He looked at the navigation array in front of him and cocked a bushy eyebrow. He tapped the array in order to bring Hopper's attention to it. "Check out the compass. It says we're heading due north."

"We're heading east," said Raikes.

"That's correct," said Beast.

Hopper looked from the compass back to the metal

structure that towered above them. "Whatever it is, it's creating magnetic flux." *Let's hope we don't get fluxed while it's at it.* "Get the PA system online."

Beast flicked a switch and passed a microphone on a cord to Hopper. Raikes called over to him, "Just be aware, if you're going to sing 'My Way' again, I *am* armed."

What Hopper *was* aware of was that Stone and Brownley were both watching from their respective bridges, so he refrained from sticking out his tongue at her. It was clear that he was never going to live down that Fourth of July party where he'd had way too much to drink and sung an assortment of Sinatra's greatest hits, encouraged by shipmates who were only marginally more sober than he was.

Thumbing the mike to live, Hopper—all business—said, "This is the U.S. Navy. Identify yourself or prepare to be boarded."

He hadn't expected there to be any sort of response. He was right. The structure simply sat there, ignoring him. For all he knew, if there was someone inside, they probably didn't speak English. He switched to Spanish but likewise got no answer, which also wasn't much of a surprise, since he didn't really think the thing had its origins in Madrid. His knowledge of Russian was limited to "Hello, how are you," which he readily tried. Still no response. Finally he essayed some Japanese, but that likewise elicited no reply.

"What the hell was the last thing you said?" said Raikes.

"I asked if it knew where the restroom was."

Raikes snorted. "That was useful."

"It was damned useful in Tokyo six months ago, so shut up. Bring us alongside, Beast." He tapped Raikes on the shoulder. "It's your boat. You've got the gun."

"Not afraid to use it, sir."

"Just try not to shoot me."

"No promises, sir."

Beast angled the RHIB against the side of the structure. Mooring was tricky in the ocean swell, and everyone was soaked with spray before he managed to anchor the ship within reach of their target. The RHIB bobbed furiously, and Hopper timed the rise and fall of the ocean. *Don't fall in the drink. They don't need to spend extra time pulling me out.* He waited until he was sure he had the feel for the ship's bobbing and then he leaped the remaining distance. He landed on a projecting ledge that seemed to run the length of the structure, and almost slid off the slick metal before steadying himself.

A distance away, there seemed to be a path that would allow him to climb higher up, along with a series of smaller projections that he could use as handholds to gain some altitude. Perhaps there was some sort of access there, since the area around him didn't seem to be presenting anything. He made eye contact with Raikes, pointed upward and then at his buttocks. An onlooker would have interpreted it as some sort of obscene gesture, but Raikes immediately got the shorthand:

I'm going. Cover my ass.

Hopper returned his gaze to the array toward the top. At first he thought he was seeing some sort of trick of light, but then he realized that wasn't the case. What he was actually seeing was some sort of blue and red shimmering being emitted from the top of the array. *That has to be what's screwing with the magnetism. But what's it for? Why is it even here? I've never seen something that looks so alien to . . .*

Alien. Yeah, right. That's a laugh.

Hopper tested the support of the narrow ledge upon which he was perched. It seemed solid enough. Slowly he started making his way toward the tower, which appeared to be the center of this thing's activity. To an onlooker, he might have seemed to be walking on water, since the ledge along which he was moving wasn't visible from more than a few feet away.

He drew close enough to the tower that all he had to do was reach out, get a grip on it and climb up. The closer he drew to it, the more intrigued he became. It was a unique collection of shapes, materials and colors, which seemed to be shimmering in time to the blue and red pulses that were being emitted from the top.

"What the hell—?" he whispered as he reached out toward its surface. His fingers brushed against it . . .

The instant he made contact with it, an electromagnetic pulse ripped across the structure. As if it had a mind of its own, it zeroed in on Hopper in a split second and blasted him clear off the tower.

Hopper hurtled forty feet through the air. He would have been better served if he'd landed in the water. Instead the trajectory of his fall sent him slamming into the metal surface of the structure itself. He slid across it and barely managed to hang on. The world was spinning around him. He heard Raikes and Beast shouting from a distance, but he couldn't determine how far they were.

He could, however, make out the tower. Apparently it was just getting warmed up. The panels that ran along its height were starting to glow, and there was a building cascade of electronic noise. Most bizarrely, from high overhead in what had been a previously clear sky, dark and fearsome clouds were rolling in and lightning bolts were ripping through the heavens.

Well, this can't be good, thought Hopper, desperately trying not to pass out.

An F-18, dispatched from USS *Reagan,* had been sent to monitor the situation. The pilot observed the American Navy officer attempting a slow approach, and on his instrument board the monitor was broadcasting a live feed. "This is Rough Rider 404," said the pilot, whose actual

name was the far less intimidating "Kenny Johnson."
"Boarding crew from the *John Paul Jones* has made contact with the object . . ."

And then he watched in horror as the officer was
blasted backwards, sent tumbling off the whatever-it-
was. "Man down! Man down!"

The strange structure below him was starting to glow.
His instruments went haywire, and suddenly, inexplicably, he was flashing back to that moment in *Close En-
counters of the Third Kind* when vehicles went berserk
in the presence of alien technology. Rough Rider was no
big believer in UFOs, but he didn't like the way this was
shaping up. He endeavored to seize control of his F-18,
which was fighting him as if they were suddenly opponents. "*Reagan* control, Rough Rider 404. I don't know
what this is! There's some kind of energy field forming.
There's an incredible amount of turbu—"

That was when the F-18 abruptly angled downward,
all control lost. Desperate, Rough Rider punched "Eject,"
even though he was so close to the surface it was unlikely
the chute would deploy fast enough to save him.

It didn't matter. The eject ignored him. The canopy
didn't blow. Nor did the *Reagan* respond, which made
him think that nothing was getting through. Then his
frustration with his inability to carry out his mission
gave way to his realization that he was in a spiraling
death trap with no means of escape.

And he was no longer Rough Rider. Instead he was just
plain old Kenny Johnson, screaming at the top of his
lungs as the F-18 crashed into the side of the uncanny
structure and exploded into a ball of flame.

The bridge of the *Sampson* became a hive of activity as
Stone saw what was happening at the structure. "Condition Zebra!" he shouted. "Raise the fleet!"

The communications officer, Ron Sinclair, was already

on the horn. "This is the *Sampson*. Alert, alert. Condition Zebra. We're encountering something that appears to be of . . ." He hesitated, having trouble believing that the next words were about to emerge from his mouth. ". . . of alien origin. We advise all . . ."

Then he stopped talking as he noticed that the dials measuring the volume of his output were flatlined. He tried to up the amps and got nowhere. The entire array wasn't responding. "Crap. Sorry, sir. She went dead. All comms fully disabled."

It wasn't just the communications units. All the bridge screens had gone blank as well.

"Do you think it's happening on the other ships?" asked Stone.

"That would be my best guess, sir," said Sinclair. "If you like, I could get some string and a couple of tin cans and see if we can communicate with those."

"Let's save that for a last resort." Stone stared helplessly toward the array in the distance. *Alien origin?* That's what Sinclair had said. It seemed ridiculous. But the most ridiculous thing of all was that Stone Hopper wasn't in a position to rule it out.

The weather roils the ocean, ionizing the air, seizing control of the waters, using them as the natural resource that they are, in ways that the pathetic residents of Earth could not begin to imagine. How blind they have been to the possibilities that their own world presents them. How inept they have been at exploiting them.

The churning waves grow, higher and higher. They reach up toward the clouds, and the pouring rain stretches down to meet them. The result is a massive wall of water, encircling the island of Oahu for a three-hundred-mile radius. Fishermen, marine vessels and two-thirds of the array of naval destroyers gape in astonishment at the barrier that has sprung up out of nowhere, an impossible wall of water that cuts them off from the remainder of the fleet. One of the vessels tries to power forward, but the contrary thrust is too strong; it literally pushes them back, the great propellers churning the water behind them with utter futility.

The commanders of the Regents fleet look upon the work that their machinations have accomplished, and find it to be good.

Now . . . on to the game. A game to test the resilience and cleverness of the natives of this world. These are their best warriors, and the game will see what they have to offer in terms of resistance. Not that the outcome is in the slightest doubt. It is simply required in order to see the level of resources the Regents will need to devote to this world.

If the Regents are nothing else, they are efficient.

An order is issued. It is not spoken; Regents need not waste efforts on something as primitive as simple speech. Communications off-world require technology, but every member of the Regents who dwells on this sphere, within range of the jamming array, knows what needs to be done as soon as a commander desires it be carried out.

And the desire in this instance is quite simple:

"Bring attack ships online."

PACIFIC OCEAN, IMPACT POINT

Hopper was trying to pull himself together, keeping conscious being his top priority. *You won't do anyone any good if you pass out.* That was what kept going through his mind, right until he passed out and lost his grip, sliding backwards into the water. But he was jolted to wakefulness as Raikes caught him before he could hit it and submerge. "Hopps!" she shouted in his ear, snapping him back to full awareness. It was the only way she could make herself heard as the water churned around her as if someone had turned on a vast, unseen stove top and the ocean was being brought to a boil.

Raikes was as scared as she'd ever been; Hopper could see that in her eyes. But, being the professional that she was—not to mention priding herself on being a total badass—she was shoving that fear down and away so it didn't interfere with what she needed to do.

She hauled Hopper bodily onto the ship and shouted at Beast, *"Let's get the hell out of here!"*

Beast nodded and fired up the engine. It, however, didn't cooperate. All he got was a series of loud clicks; the ignition wouldn't fire. The RHIB simply floated there, having no more control over its fate than any piece of flotsam.

Suddenly the water churned even more violently and there was a distant roar from far below. Raikes and Beast exchanged looks and she mouthed a question: *Submarine?*

Beast shrugged helplessly. "Bigger," he said aloud. "Way bigger . . ."

The roar drew closer and closer, the water displacement causing the RHIB to bob so violently that it was nearly capsized. Hopper tried to get to his feet and fell over, still woozy. "Stay down!" Raikes called to him.

"Not a problem!" he said, and lay flat on his back as the RHIB was flung around helplessly in the water.

The roaring continued, like a vast behemoth was rising from below. His mind flashed to old stories by H. P. Lovecraft. Tales of a monstrous creature that had resided on the ocean floor, waiting to be summoned by its modern-day acolytes so it could surface and bring annihilation to the puny humans running around like insects. He wondered bleakly if there was any chance those stories were somehow based on ancient myths that were, in turn, based on truth. *This would be a sucky time to find out.*

The roar was deafening now, as if gigantic lions were about to rise up and swallow them. And then, a short distance from the three hapless officers, something began to emerge. They couldn't make it out at first, and when they could, they still didn't fully understand. Or at least they didn't want to, because no one knew better the man-made, oceangoing vessels of this world. Whatever the hell it was they were seeing, it wasn't remotely *man*-made.

As the water fell away in vast sheets, it quickly became clear it wasn't just one thing surfacing—it was three. Three monstrous ships, like nothing that any of the *John Paul Jones* crewmen had ever seen. Like nothing that any human had ever seen. They weren't identical; there were variations, with fins or other accoutrements projecting from them in different places. But they were all long and flat and lethal-looking—like scorpions—jagged, with industrial sheathing that was a combination of dark green and gunmetal gray. There were projections beneath them that were similar to pontoons one saw on planes designed for water landings. In this case, though, they were far more stylized and added to the overall look of these vessels—each of which was the length of two football fields—as being like gigantic insects poised to pounce.

They reminded Hopper of some prototype designs he'd seen some friends of his in R&D messing around with. They'd been designated STNGR-14s; the R&D boys called them "stingers." Seemed as good a name as any to use as reference.

The water displacement resulting from their emergence caused a massive maelstrom to circle beneath them. The sailors in the RHIB hung on desperately, hoping that the whirlpool would subside before they were drawn into it and sucked down to certain death.

* * *

There was stunned silence on the bridge of the *Sampson*. *Oh my God, oh my God, what the living hell, oh my God,* went through Stone's mind. None of the men on the bridge, however, were at all aware of his inner turmoil. His face impassive, his voice calm, he said, "Query them." When Sinclair at communications just sat there, frozen, staring uncomprehendingly at the sight before them, Stone added a sharp, no-nonsense prod of, *"Now!"*

But Sinclair was still having trouble wrapping his mind around what was being presented to him. "But . . . what the hell—?"

"I know, sailor," said Stone, allowing for his comm officer's obvious shock. It was the only indication Stone gave that he was as stunned by this unknown technology as anyone else on the bridge. "But we don't have the luxury. Do it how you've been trained to."

"Yes, sir," said Sinclair, nodding. He operated the controls before him, trying to boost the signal as he said, "Uh . . . craft . . . please identify. Repeat, craft, please identify. This is the USS *Sampson*, of the U.S. Navy, please identify your origin."

Stone braced himself, wondering what sort of language was going to come through the board. He was destined to be disappointed, as after long moments Sinclair looked toward Stone and shook his head. "I'm trying all channels, sir. Translating into all known codes and languages. But the transmitter is still down. They could be trying to talk our ears off right now and we wouldn't be hearing a thing."

Considering they were the source of the electromagnetic pulse, the EMP, that had crashed the communications network, Stone suspected that he was already reading their intentions loud and clear. "Sound general quarters." In response to his order, a klaxon immediately started to echo throughout the ship. *At least that's working,* he thought grimly, and then continued, "Have we got intraship?"

"I'm hoping to have it in a few min—"

"We don't have time. Grab a walkie-talkie so I can stay in touch with you and haul ass down to weapons. Tell them we're going hot."

Sinclair wanted to make sure that Stone had just said what he thought he said. "Sir? Did I hear you right—?"

"Yes, you did, Ensign. Heat up the guns."

"Which guns, sir?"

Stone considered it and then said grimly, "All of them."

The RHIB had not capsized. Hopper believed that alone to be something of a miracle considering the amount of chop they'd had to deal with. Once they managed to stay afloat, he braced himself for the huge ships to open fire the moment they surfaced. Nothing of the sort happened. Instead they simply floated there as if their presence was the most normal thing in the world. Hopper was grateful for that, since it gave him the few minutes he needed to pull himself together after the massive jolt he'd received.

Beast was elbow deep in the engines, trying to figure out how the hell to get them up and running. He was obviously having zero success on that score. He looked at Hopper, grease staining his face. "Whatever fried you must have got the electrical system too," said Beast.

Suddenly five long, sharp blasts sounded across the water. They looked toward the destroyers floating a distance away, and Raikes said grimly, "That was the *Sampson,* wasn't it?" It was hard to be sure since the echo effect across the open water made determining the source uncertain. But Hopper nodded, making no attempt to keep the concern off his face. "Yeah."

"They're warning these guys," she said, nodding toward the vessels positioned about a hundred yards away, "that they're going to open fire if they don't retreat or respond."

"Uh-huh."

"They *do* know we're not exactly at a safe distance if the missiles start flying, right?"

"I'm sure hoping so . . ."

That was when the alien ships responded.

As if they were dinosaurs bellowing a defiant challenge to an oncoming threat, the stingers shrieked back at the *Sampson,* unleashing an unholy noise that sounded primal and terrifying. Hopper and his crew grabbed their ears, collapsing to the deck of the RHIB and writhing in pain. Hopper was sure that if the noise kept up, his brains were going to liquefy and spill out his ears.

Then the sound abruptly stopped, as the foremost of the stingers leaped forward. It didn't glide across the water; it actually leaped, like an insect. It vaulted through the air and wound up landing between the *Sampson* and the vast, incomprehensible structure that Hopper and his crew had been sent to investigate.

It's protecting it. Whatever this thing is, the stinger's protecting it. And it'll do whatever it takes.

A sense of overwhelming dread was bearing down on Hopper like a freight train. Wild-eyed, desperate, he brought all his resources, all his analytical power to the forefront. He mentally dissected the stinger, breaking it down into what he perceived as its component parts. Weapons system, propulsion . . . it had to have a control center. A bridge of some sort. Even aliens had to—

They're not aliens. They're not freaking aliens. This structure did not come from outer space. It's some kind of spy thing that crashed and now these ships are here to run interference while they do their . . . their spy thing.

"Chinese or North Korean prototype? What is it, Beast?" said Hopper.

"No idea."

"Agreed," said Hopper.

Raikes tracked it with her machine gun. She would not

open fire unless Hopper ordered her to, but there was no reason she couldn't be ready when the moment came. "It looks very angry," she said, working to keep her voice even.

Then, through the sea spray, Hopper saw something moving in the upper section of the stinger. At first he couldn't quite make out what it was . . . and then he saw it. A single figure.

It was wearing armor of some sort. It was blue and segmented but it wasn't wearing a helmet.

Its face was round and squat, almost triangular. The skin was a sickly combination of blue and black, like a sky filled with pollution. It didn't look vaguely human.

It *wasn't* vaguely human.

Then there was another blast of ocean foam and the creature was gone.

"Did . . ." Hopper tried to find his voice. "Did you just . . . ?"

He managed to tear his gaze away from where he'd been staring and looked to his crewmates, certain he'd been the only one who spotted it. Certain he was now going to have to try and convince them of what his own mind was telling him couldn't possibly be.

He was incredibly relieved when he saw that their faces had gone ashen.

"What the . . . ?" said Beast. He could scarcely form those words, much less any others.

"I know my eyes were lying," said Raikes. Yet it was clear she didn't know any such thing, but rather knew perfectly what it was that she had just seen.

Beast finally recovered his voice. He turned to Hopper and said, in an awe-filled whisper, "First contact."

Raikes turned and punched him in the upper arm with such power that Beast yelped. "What the hell—?"

"We have three unknown vessels guarding some equally unknown structure," said Raikes with barely contained anger. "We have two fleets about to square off, our boat is dead in the water, and you're giving me *Star Trek* crap. *Fix the damned engine!*"

Beast looked speechlessly at Hopper. Hopper shrugged. "You heard her."

Beast got back to work.

It had been a slow and frustrating process, but the *Sampson* had managed to reroute some of its main systems. She now had communications back online, as well as some basic systems, including tracking. Now it was just a matter of getting the weapons systems up and running. That had proven to be a slower and more frustrating process. Having established contact with the two destroyers flanking them, Stone said, "Status on WEPS?" asking for the latest report from the weapons officer.

"CIWS up, sir," said Sinclair. "*John Paul Jones* five-inch is hot."

Stone weighed the options and then said briskly, "All right. Let's put a warning shot across their bow. Radio Brownley."

Sinclair sent the message through to the *John Paul Jones*. He paused a moment and then said, "Brownley says they'll have to use manual targeting."

"If it was good enough for the original John Paul Jones, it's good enough for them. Besides, we don't want them to actually hit anything."

"Roger that." Sinclair reaffirmed the orders. Then he smiled grimly. "Now we're gonna see something."

It was obvious that Beast was laboring with the engine; the amount of profanity coming from him was increasing in volume and floridness.

At that moment, a puff of smoke emerged from the five-inch gun on the *John Paul Jones*. Seconds later, they heard the sound of the gun actually being fired, noise following visual much like a baseball player being watched from the grandstands, with the sound of the hit ball following an instant after contact has already been made.

"They're attacking?" said Beast.

Raikes shook her head. "Warning shot. That's SOP for . . ."

Beast looked skeptical. "For what? Alien invasion?"

The shell landed in an explosion of water and spray within range of the lead stinger. A clear message had been sent.

Hopper said grimly, "*That's* gonna piss 'em off."

Nothing happened for several seconds. During that time, Hopper briefly prayed that the aliens/creatures/beings would emerge from the ships, hands in the air, eagerly trying to explain that they were simply there by mishap and meant no harm to anyone on Earth.

Instead there was a quiet sound, like a whisper of a breeze, and a single cylindrical object was fired from the lead stinger, blasted out of what appeared to be some sort of launch array. It hurtled lazily through the air, heading straight toward the *John Paul Jones*.

Hopper watched with a sinking heart. *That can't be good.*

USS *JOHN PAUL JONES*

In the destroyer's CIC, radar officer Benjamin Rush was watching his radar screen carefully. They'd only just managed to bring it back online, and it kept flickering in and out while the system's big brains continued to make corrections and adjustments. Around him a row of other young officers, wearing headphones, were monitoring large, complex screens and struggling to operate the elaborate consoles of the AEGIS weapons system that was, at that moment, extremely hit or miss.

Abruptly an incoming blip lit up his screen, cutting across the monitor with a trajectory that was taking it directly toward the ship. "Incoming track, zero-seven-three-six," he called out.

Over the intraship radio, Mullenaro's voice came back: "Acquire incoming. Kill with guns. Light 'em up, son."

The order was instantly relayed, and two seconds later the Phalanx CIWS, consisting of two anti-missile Gatling guns on the foredeck, sprang to life. The CIWS functioned exactly as it was supposed to, as the guns sprayed so many bullets that it created a virtual wall of metal. Before anyone even could get a clear look at it, the cylinder disintegrated against the ship's firepower.

In the *John Paul Jones* CIC, a moment of relief and triumph rippled through the officers, pleased that good, old-fashioned American technology had triumphed over whatever the hell it had been that this interloper was attempting to throw at them.

That sense of good feeling lasted right up until radar officer Rush suddenly called out, "Incoming tracks! Coordinating zero-niner-seven-three." He stopped for a moment, overwhelmed by what he was seeing, a harsh reality crashing down on him. "There's too many of them."

He was right. There were at least ten of the cylinders, maybe more, hurtling through the air, zeroing in on the destroyer with lethal accuracy.

The CIWS was employed yet again as the Gatling guns cut loose in a wide spread. One by one the cylinders were blown out of the sky as the big guns continued to cut a swath through the assault that was coming straight at them.

They almost managed to take out all of the cylinders. But they fell short of their goal by one.

A single cylinder landed on the deck not ten feet in front of the starboard observation deck. Brownley and Mullenaro were both there, and they stared down at it in utter bewilderment.

The narrow white cylinder, which had landed surprisingly noiselessly on the deck, was still quivering slightly from the impact. Rather than at an angle, as one would have expected from the trajectory, it was upright. It looked to Brownley to be about four feet tall and less than a foot in diameter. Other than presenting a threat that someone might trip over it, the cylinder appeared utterly harmless. It might well have been made of plastic.

Mullenaro was no less confused, but he was also more outwardly irritated. "What kind of jack wagon crap—is this somebody's idea of a game?"

Suddenly the cylinder transformed, within an eyeblink, from white to red.

Then it detonated. In an explosive flash, Brownley, Mullenaro and the entire starboard observation deck vaporized.

USS SAMPSON

The stinger turned its attentions to the *Sampson*. This time, though, they were firing the cylinders much faster, but one at a time instead of a barrage, as if whoever was shooting them at the destroyer was testing his marksmanship.

The *Sampson's* Gatling guns roared to life, but the speed of the cylinders made targeting them more problematic. Several were picked off in midair, but one landed on the foredeck, transformed from white to red, and detonated. The explosion ripped through the ship. The windows on the bridge, made from reinforced glass that should have held together, blew apart. It was specially treated so as to shatter into dull pieces should breakage occur, and it performed as it had been designed to do. As a result, no one had to worry about getting shards of glass in their eyes. Still, the officers dropped to the floor to avoid the large chunks that were flying every which way.

"We're hit!" shouted Sinclair.

"Signal all ships!" Stone shouted over the wailing klaxon. "Full reverse! We need battle space!"

The engine room responded immediately. The *Sampson* started to pull back. It wasn't much; a ship as large as the *Sampson* wasn't designed for quick maneuvers. But it was just barely enough to allow another cylinder to go screaming past them and land harmlessly in the water.

"Miss!" Sinclair called out.

The running narrative was beginning to annoy the crap out of Stone. "Save the play-by-play. Are we targeting this thing or not? Sling some MK 41s their way!"

His executive officer, Lieutenant Commander Leong, looked up from her instruments. "Sir, comm's down again," said the XO. "That thing that hit us . . . it scrambled everything that we had just gotten back online. Computers are down, radar's down. All we've got are the close-in weapon systems."

"All this hardware and we're down to throwing rocks?" said Stone. He grit his teeth, seeing that the *John Paul Jones* was still under assault. "We've got to get in there. They need cover."

"Five-inch was knocked off-line, but now is moments away," said the XO.

"We're not waiting," said Stone. "Rudder hard right, engines full. We've got to get in there and give them some shade. Don't tell me the gun's not up." Through his binoculars, he stared at the launcher on the opposing ship that had been firing those strange white cylinders at them. It had paused in its assault. They were probably reloading. He had no intention of sitting around waiting for them to finish the process. "Take that launcher out."

With that order, the *Sampson* reversed course and hurtled forward, straight into the teeth of the enemy.

PACIFIC OCEAN, IMPACT POINT

In the crippled RHIB, Hopper watched with growing horror as he saw the *Sampson* angling straight toward the stinger.

"Screw this helpless crap," he said, suddenly full of resolve. He shouted to Raikes as he pointed, "Where we saw that . . . that creature standing before! Shoot there! Maybe it's their bridge or whatever!"

Raikes needed no further urging. She swung the .50 cal around and opened fire.

At first the bullets didn't penetrate. Instead Hopper saw lights flashing in response to where the bullets would have been impacting. There was some sort of field there, invisible, impenetrable. *Well, sure, because they're freak-*

ing aliens, so naturally they have invisible shields and crap like that.

And then, all of a sudden, areas of the shield weren't flaring back into invisibility as they had been before. Instead patches seemed to be hanging there randomly, black pieces of light as opposed to the other, unseen sections of the field. Spiderweb cracks spread through them, and Hopper immediately realized that—unlike the movies—the alien force fields weren't limitless in their resistance. They might be pure energy, but they were no more invulnerable than "bulletproof" glass. Give it enough of a pounding, and it would eventually shatter and break.

"Pour it on, Raikes!"

He moved behind the .50, helping Raikes to pinpoint her assault, which she did with malicious glee. As that happened, though, something moving on the forward section of the stinger grabbed Hopper's attention. He recognized it as the launch array that had fired off whatever the hell those weapons were that had impacted on the destroyers. It was rotating. Worse, it was rotating in their direction.

"We've got to move," he said nervously.

"Want me to get out and push?" Raikes offered.

The engine abruptly roared to life. They looked around in delighted surprise. Beast was crouched over the engine, holding two wires that he had twisted together. He hurriedly wrapped them in electrical tape to keep the connection solid.

Hopper leaped over to the helm. He brought the RHIB around, but the cylinder launcher was swiveling to acquire him. There was no way he was going to be able to get enough distance between himself and the stinger before it unloaded its lethal charge upon him.

Then he heard the distant sound of a 5-inch gun being

deployed. Seconds later, the ordnance from the *Sampson,* fired with pinpoint accuracy, obliterated the launcher before it could fire at Hopper and the RHIB.

Hopper exhaled in relief, but that breath caught in his throat as the stinger, with the faint sound of something within it powering up, launched itself once more, much farther than it had before. It sailed through the air and landed no more than a hundred feet aft of the *Sampson,* practically right on top of them.

Oh God, thought Hopper.

USS SAMPSON

Oh God, thought Stone, realizing that he was seeing technology that simply did not exist anywhere on Earth, not that he knew of. *It's true. We're in the middle of an alien invasion.*

A young helmsman stumbled back from his post, eyes wide with terror. On some level, Stone couldn't blame him. These were the best and the brightest that the Navy had to offer, and they believed themselves to have been trained to handle anything that was thrown at them. But how the hell do you handle something that is completely outside the realm of anyone's experience?

But that was no excuse for deserting one's post. *"Back on the con, Behne!"* said Stone.

Seaman Behne nodded, retaking his position.

"Hard ahead, full," said Stone.

"Aye, sir," said Behne with determination, dialing up the throttle.

The powerful engines of the *Sampson* drove the vessel forward. The alien ship crouched low in the water. *Like a lion in the high weeds*, thought Stone bleakly, but once again he didn't allow any of that worry to show. "Steady, people. WEPS, all guns forward, maximum rate of fire."

The 5-inch guns of the *Sampson* were unleashed upon the alien ship. There were no more attempts at communication—they would do all their talking with their weaponry. Stone reasoned that since their guns had been able to take out that weird-ass missile launcher, they should likewise be able to inflict some serious damage on the rest of the ship.

His reasoning turned out to be severely faulty.

The alien vessel shuddered under the assault, little bursts of light erupting everywhere that the *Sampson*'s guns made contact. But it didn't seem to be doing any substantial damage—they had some manner of force field.

Stone's mind was already racing. *It must be a limited resource. Otherwise we'd never have been able to take out that launcher. Perhaps they have to deploy it in specific areas of the ship, selectively. Right now they must have all their shields concentrated on forward assault. If we deploy the other ships around, surround it . . .*

That was when he saw another barrage of those same bizarre cylinder weapons being fired their way. They were arcing straight toward Stone's ship. *Dammit! They must have a secondary launcher!*

"Kill tracks! Fire at will! All of it!"

PACIFIC OCEAN, IMPACT POINT

"Gun it! Gun it!" Hopper shouted to himself for encouragement as he opened up the throttle

The RHIB hurtled through the water as fast as Beast
could make it go, eating up the distance between them and
the immediate field of battle. He continued to nurse the
engine, though, making sure his patchwork job held together. Hopper steered straight toward the stinger, keeping
on a steady path, praying he would get there in time.

The stinger withstood the pounding that the *Sampson*
was unleashing upon it. It was as if the strange vessel was
sending a silent message: *Go ahead. Take your best shot.
Is that all you can do? Because we can do so much more.*

From his angle Hopper could see the second weapons
launcher rising from the side of the stinger. Raikes opened
fire on it without even having to be told. It made no difference. This time the bullets pinged away without having the slightest impact.

Hopper didn't hesitate. He brought the RHIB around
in an arc, determined to place himself between the
stinger and the *Sampson*. His hope was to distract it,
provide an immediate nuisance, pull its attention away
from the destroyer. Maybe even hurt it if he was close up
to it. All he knew was that he had to protect the *Sampson*. He had to protect his brother. With one hand he
had binoculars to his eyes, and he could actually make
out Stone in the bridge, shouting orders, pointing, never
losing control, never losing hope . . .

Then he heard a series of whooshing noises that he'd
already come to recognize. It was those damned white
cylinders. They were hurtling straight toward the *Sampson,* and Hopper could only watch in frustration and
fury. He saw Stone monitoring them, calling out orders
that Hopper couldn't hear, no doubt ordering the de-
ployment of the Phalanx CIWS. Hopper swung his bin-

oculars toward the ship's Gatling guns and, sure enough, they were blasting the incoming missiles away. But not enough of them.

Not remotely enough.

No less than ten hit their target, landing straight down all along the deck of the *Sampson,* from stem to stern. Ten white cylinders, in a row, and suddenly they transformed to red.

Hopper had just enough time to turn his binoculars back toward his brother. Stone wasn't looking at the cylinders. He wasn't even looking at the other men on the bridge. Instead he was staring straight toward Hopper, as if he could see him, as if he knew that Hopper had binoculars trained on him.

Stone had just enough time to mouth words that Hopper was actually able to make out. And they were: *Stay out of trouble while I'm gone.*

A massive explosion ripped through the *Sampson.* Hopper heard someone screaming. It was he himself. Something jolted him and he realized belatedly that he'd actually been trying to throw himself off the RHIB, as if he could leap through the air in a single bound, like Superman, and land at his brother's side.

Except there was no brother for him to fly to. Not anymore.

The *Sampson* blew apart, flame ripping it from one end to the other. The ship shuddered, and metal screeched like a dying whale. He saw what looked like lightning bugs tumbling from the ship and realized it was sailors burning alive, their arms pinwheeling, falling into the water. Seconds later the ship's spine cracked in two. It rolled, pitched, and then sank beneath the waves.

Its job apparently done, the stinger vaulted away, landing securely back in front of the towering metal array, a dutiful sentinel returned to its post.

The RHIB had ceased all forward motion. It bobbed in

the water, the engine reduced to a gentle idling. Beast was keeping Hopper steady, on his feet. Hopper leaned against the controls, stunned, staring at where the mighty destroyer had once been.

"Hopper," Beast said softly, "what do you . . . ?"

There was a sudden thud behind them, and before Hopper and Beast could turn to see what it was, Raikes screamed, *"Down!"*

Without the slightest hesitation, Beast yanked Hopper to the deck. Machine-gun fire chattered in the air. Standing only a few feet away from Hopper was the creature he'd spotted up on the stinger. It was wearing its helmet, was fully armored, and it held some sort of knife in its hand. The blade was curved and serrated. Despite all the high-tech armament, clearly these things sometimes liked to get up close and personal.

But it wasn't going to be getting close enough this time. Raikes unleashed the .50 cal on it, her fury over the fate of the *Sampson* causing her body to convulse—but doing nothing to deter her aim. *"Die, you son of a bitch, die!"* she shrieked. Bullets thudded all over its armor, and the alien trembled and shook. Hopper saw dark streaks of what he assumed to be the creature's blood seeping down sections of its armor where the bullets penetrated. Riddled, the alien staggered to the side, its arms outstretched as if it had been crucified, and then it tumbled over the side of the RHIB. Water fountained from where it went in and then there was no sound, no movement.

"Hah! How do you like that? You dumb sack of shit!" Raikes was gasping for air, and then she stepped back from the machine gun, her hands trembling, her eyes wide. She forced herself to steady her breath, to calm down, and then slowly she composed herself and looked levelly at Hopper. She was still bristling with fury, but she had no place to put it, and it looked as if it was be-

ginning to crash in on her. "What . . . what do we do now?" she asked, her voice shaking.

Never in his adult life had Hopper so felt like just curling up in a ball. Just going completely fetal, shutting the rest of the world out and maybe even going to sleep in the hope that—upon waking—he would discover matters had changed for the better.

Instead he thrust all of those feelings—all those emotions, all the grief and agony that threatened to crush him—down where they could be of no impediment to what he had to do now.

"Beast," he said, stepping away from the throttle, "get us to the *John Paul Jones.*"

Without a word, Beast took over the throttle and gunned it. The small craft moved away from the scene, heading toward the illusion of security that the *John Paul Jones* seemed to provide. But Hopper knew there would never be anyplace safe in the world, ever again.

THE WHITE HOUSE

The President could scarcely credit what he was seeing. If he'd been informed about it secondhand, he would have questioned the reliability—if not the sanity—of the source. Looking at it now, though, he almost started to wonder about his own sanity.

What he was staring at, being played back to him on a screen in the Situation Room, was nothing less than a barrier constructed of the very Pacific Ocean itself. He certainly had experience with what nature was capable of accomplishing in Hawaii. Storms, typhoons, the best and worst that God, in His acts, had to offer. But what he was witnessing now was beyond anything he had ever seen. It seemed instead like something out of a fantasy movie, cooked up by a wizard as a weapon against another wizard.

Arthur C. Clarke's oft-quoted statement ran through his head. *"Any sufficiently advanced form of technology will seem like magic."* Still, it was so beyond anything he'd ever experienced that he had to remind himself that no, this wasn't magic; just technology. *Extremely advanced. Science against which no Earth technology had any counter. We are so screwed . . .*

The film had been taken from a distance by a naval vessel and forwarded through channels—not only to him, but to heads of state from every country being represented in the war games, which were—at the moment—suspended. Apparently a real war had overtaken the games, fought against an enemy that was outside the experience of everyone involved.

Mountains of water, impassable, impenetrable, were arrayed around Oahu. From the latest intel on the President's desk, there were three ships—two Americans, one Japanese—within the perimeter. Everyone else was stuck outside, cut off as a localized storm kept them at bay. Sheets of lightning rippled up and down the water barrier.

The Joint Chiefs sat around the table, waiting for the President to absorb what he was seeing. Meanwhile on another screen, CNN was on, muted, but the closed captioning was activated:

"Little is known beyond the fact that all communication with the island state went down at 12:20 Eastern Standard Time. Extreme weather is now cutting off Hawaii from the outside world. A probable connection to events in Hong Kong is being investigated."

The President leaned back in his chair, studying the other screens, each depicting a site around the world that had also been damaged.

"Best guess?" said the President finally.

One of the Joint Chiefs sat forward, resting his forearms on the large table around which they were all grouped. "We don't have a best guess, Mr. President. Every single country that could possibly be behind this got hit themselves. No one was spared."

"Which only means," said another general, "it was no single country. Terrorists. It has to be terrorists . . ."

The chief of staff looked skeptical. "You're telling me that the people who couldn't even blow up a pair of sneakers coordinated something like this?"

"I'm saying the people who knocked down the Twin Towers coordinated something like this . . ."

The President shook his head. "No. No, I'm not buying it. Even on 9/11, they used standard Earth technology, Earth airplanes . . ."

"Mr. President," the vice-president put up a hand as if he were in second grade. "You keep saying 'Earth.' Are you implying . . . ?"

"I'm not implying anything. I'm saying it outright. I'm saying what Sherlock Holmes always said. That whenever you eliminate the impossible, whatever remains—however improbable—is the truth. Someone here want to try to sell me on the notion that that," he pointed at the wall of water, "is within the realm of possibility, based on what we know current science can produce? Because I'm looking at that giant water wall, with lightning flashing all around it, and I'm telling you this is either the result of extraterrestrial science, or somewhere right now Zeus is instructing that the Kraken be released."

"Sir," the vice-president started again, "you're talking about alien invasion. That's . . . that's the kind of thing you see in disaster movies. Not in real life."

"Perhaps. Except how many New York landmarks have we seen blown up in those same disaster movies? Plus there was an episode of a television series, *The Lone Gunmen,* that centered around a plot to fly airplanes into the World Trade Center. Life imitates art, gentlemen. How many of you," and he took in the entire table in a glance, "didn't watch the Twin Towers collapsing a decade ago and feel as if, just for a moment at least, the world had turned into a Michael Bay movie?"

There were silent, reluctant nods from several of them. As far as the President was concerned, those who didn't nod simply didn't want to cop to it. Then the chief of staff said slowly, "Sir . . . if what you're saying is true . . . we need to get you on Marine One and to a secure location. And we need to do it immediately."

"I don't see that as a necessary—"

"Sir," the chief of staff said more forcefully, "if we're going to operate under the assumption that what you're saying is true . . . and considering that whomever or whatever it is we're dealing with has hostile intent— which we have to believe considering they've made no attempt to engage us in any way other than those that have cost human lives . . ."

"I believe what the chief of staff is saying," said the vice-president, "is that if we're sticking with the whole 'life imitates art' theory, well . . . I think we all remember the poster for *Independence Day.* The big alien saucer blowing the living crap out of—"

"Yes," said the President. "Yes, I remember it." He drummed his fingers on the table. "I don't like it. It seems like running away."

"Think of it more as a strategic retreat," said one of the Joint Chiefs. Heads around the room nodded in agreement.

"Sir," said the chief of staff softly, "it's worth noting that there may well come a point where the Secret Service isn't going to give you the option. Better to walk out on your own while things are quiet than to be dragged out while the ceiling's caving in. Don't you think?"

The President slowly sagged back in his chair and looked bleakly around the room. *So this is what it's like to be the most powerful man in the world: you go to ground when danger threatens.*

"Inform Marine One and get my family together," said the President quietly in the hushed room.

USS *JOHN PAUL JONES*

The skipper will know what to do. The thought kept going through Hopper's mind as he cast an apprehensive glance at the repair crew trying to deal with the wreckage from the hit they'd taken. At least the ship wasn't listing, so obviously nothing fatally catastrophic had happened to it. Yet.

Once having returned to the ship, Beast really should have hastened to the engine room to make sure his beloved Rolls-Royce engines were continuing to function and hadn't sustained any damage during the assault. Raikes should have returned to weapons, where she doubtless would've taken comfort in having all the firepower of the *John Paul Jones* at her disposal, rather than just a single .50 cal machine gun. Instead, however, they followed Hopper, who was heading straight toward the bridge, to bring his commander up to speed and to find out what the next course of action was going to be.

The skipper will know what to do. The man may be an officious jerk, and he's never liked me, but he's forgotten more about strategy than most naval men ever learn. He's probably already got an entire plan in place. He's probably already figured out a weakness that went past the rest of us. He's got this covered; he'll be totally on top of it.

Hopper walked into the bridge, Beast and Raikes behind him, and glanced around, not finding the person he was most expecting to. "Where's the skipper?" he asked.

There was dead silence. All Hopper saw was an array of young, terrified faces, looking at him . . . no, looking *to* him. Lieutenant J. G. Raj Patel, a young and efficient officer of Indian descent, and Ensign Anthony Rice, still so wet behind the ears he was practically dripping, looked as if they had one frayed nerve between them. Ord was also there, staring at him expectantly. Expectantly? What in the world was he expecting?

Hopper heard explosions in the distance. He turned and saw that the Japanese vessel the *Myoko* was under attack from the stinger. The stinger was firing singles of the cylinders, rather than barrages, and the weapons were falling short of the destroyer. *Warning shots. They don't have an infinite number of the things.* The *Myoko* was backing off, taking the hint, and that seemed to satisfy the damned stinger, as it ceased fire. *Why the hell aren't we coordinating attacks? Why are we just sitting here? Why isn't the skipper giving—?*

"Orders, sir?" said Ord.

"Why are you asking me?" Deep down, he already knew the answer. Some part of him simply couldn't acknowledge it, though. Didn't want to acknowledge it. When he'd first entered the bridge, his voice had been brisk, no-nonsense. Now when he spoke, repeating his previous question, it was low and level and barely above a whisper: "Where's the skipper?"

"Dead, sir." Ord sounded as if he were talking from

somewhere just south of the Twilight Zone. A dead man walking, emotionlessly reporting on the fate of those who had already preceded him down that road.

"What did you say?" He knew what Ord had said. He just needed time to process it, time that none of them had.

"Skipper's dead," said Ord. Anticipating the next question, he continued, "XO's dead."

The debris. The debris from where we were hit. They're under the debris somewhere. Oh my God, they're not just trying to repair the ship; they're trying to dig out the bodies . . .

Focus. Focus.

"Who's in charge?" said Hopper.

For the first time, actual emotion flickered on the previously numb, expressionless face of Ord. Sounding utterly matter of fact, as if he couldn't quite believe he had to make it clear, he said, "You are, sir."

"No." Hopper shook his head. "I fight the ship."

"You're doing that, too. You're all of it, sir. You're in charge."

Hopper stared at him for a moment, not comprehending. He looked to Patel, who nodded.

Apparently Raikes had an easier time grasping it, or at least saying it aloud, than Hopper did. "It's your ship, sir," she said firmly. "You're senior officer. What are the orders?"

He couldn't look at her. He couldn't look at any of them, because they were all staring at him, waiting for him to come up with answers that he didn't have. Instead he looked out the shattered window and saw that the stinger was floating five hundred yards away.

"Orders, sir?" Ord prompted him again.

Slowly he shifted his gaze to Raikes. His eyes hardened and narrowed to slits. Rage began to fill him. *Don't give in to it. Channel it. Use it.* "Guns hot?"

"Aye, sir," said Raikes.

"Engines good?" he said to Beast.

Beast was on the horn to the engine room, getting updates, doubtless in anticipation of the question. He glanced toward Hopper. "Yes, sir."

He felt hot tears beginning to surge in his eyes: not from grief, but from pure fury. These bastards . . . they'd killed his brother, upended his life. And they sat there, smug in their anonymity, secure in their invincibility. *Sons of bitches will pay.* "Do we have ship to ship?"

"We're holding it together with spit and bailing wire, but yes, sir."

"Good. Raise Nagata. Tell him we're going to attack."

"Attack? Really?" That obviously wasn't what Ord had expected him to say.

"Those are the orders," affirmed Hopper. "Raikes, get your ass down to the CIC. Ready all guns."

For a moment, Raikes looked as if she was going to balk at that. But then she caught herself. This wasn't the usual give and take that she and Hopper typically enjoyed. This wasn't her busting on him under her breath. This was combat and he was the one in charge of the whole damned ship. "Roger that, Captain," said Raikes.

USS REAGAN

In his ready room, Admiral Shane watched in silent horror as he played and replayed the final images that had come in from the F-18.

There was always a sick feeling in the pit of his stomach

when someone under his command died as a direct result of one of his orders. Today he'd sent Kenny Johnson—one of their best pilots—to see what exactly the *Sampson* and the vessels near it were dealing with. Shane hadn't known he was sending Johnson into a combat situation. He'd thought it would be a simple reconnoitering . . . and it was, until it went horribly, horribly wrong. Now Johnson was dead and, although rationally Shane knew the unknown enemy had been responsible, in his mind it had in fact been he who'd killed Johnson.

And even worse was the matter of Hopper.

For it most definitely was Hopper who'd been blown backwards by the energy of that . . . whatever it was. Even from the height the F-18 had been flying, taking photos, Shane had recognized him. If nothing else, the massive officer nicknamed "Beast" being there had more or less assured Hopper's presence; Beast was big enough to be recognizable from orbit. If he was out there, then surely Hopper was commanding the boat, and that had probably been Raikes at the gun. *Man down!* Those had been the last words that he'd heard from Johnson before the pilot's horrified scream and image dissolved into a blast of static.

Sam's going to kill me . . .

"Admiral, you were saying . . . ?"

It was thoroughly unprofessional for Shane to let his mind wander during such a high-level briefing, even if the man he was talking with wasn't in the room. Shane pressed the phone tighter against his ear to focus himself and said, "Sorry, Mr. Secretary. I was just . . . reviewing the latest intel."

"So what's the situation there?" came the Secretary of Defense's voice over the phone.

"You saw the video we just transmitted?"

"Yes. Incredible. Horrible. That platform is obviously some sort of enemy device. Maybe it's even—and I can't believe I'm saying this, because it sounds like something out of a James Bond movie—some manner of weather control machine."

"I share both your opinion and your incredulity, Mr. Secretary. Furthermore, we've lost comm with everyone on the other side of the barrier. We can't get in or out. I've already lost one pilot; I'm not going to lose another, even if we could get someone through. We sent two surveillance sorties up to determine how far it extends."

"It. You mean this water barrier?"

"Yes, Mr. Secretary. We also have a submarine, the *Stingray,* doing soundings to see how deep it goes as well."

"Well . . . how large is it?"

"According to the *Stingray,* it goes all the way to the bottom. No way under it. Or through it. Or over it. Or into it."

For a long moment the Secretary of Defense was dead silent on the other end of the line, then he said, very softly, "Holy shit."

"Yes sir," said Shane, "I think that about sums it up."

USS *JOHN PAUL JONES*

On the bridge, Ord personally transmitted the message that Hopper had dictated, earphones pressed tightly to his head in order to hear the reply. After a few moments he said, "Uhm . . ."

"Don't give me 'uhm,' Ord. Did they respond?"

"Nagata did, yeah. He said there's not enough battle space, and wanted to know if you were out of your mind."

Figures. Useless dumbass.

"All ahead flank," he said as if no one had spoken. He turned to Ord. "Tell Nagata I'm going with him or without him. His call. Tell him . . ." He paused, smiling grimly. "Tell him with the fate of the world on the line, I'd have thought he'd behave in an honorable manner. And that I'm sorry I overestimated him."

There were soft murmurs of "Whoa" on the bridge. No one there was Japanese, but likewise none of them had any doubts as to the serious challenge Hopper was throwing down.

I'm taking on an alien fleet; I really don't give a damn about pissing off a single human officer.

Nevertheless, he was curious as to the response he'd get from Nagata.

"Sir," said Ord, sounding apprehensive, "you really want to attack this thing?"

"Yes. Yes, I do."

"Sir, they've killed everything that has fired on them!"

Hopper rounded on Ord. "If you're bucking to be relieved of duty, keep going. Just say anything to me other than 'Aye, sir.' You understand?"

Ord's jaw twitched and then he said, "Aye, sir."

The *John Paul Jones* slowly turned and prepared to take on the stinger. As it did so, Ord turned to Hopper. "Sir . . ." Hopper fired him a warning look but Ord simply indicated the communications board. Understanding, Hopper nodded and indicated Ord should speak. "Sir, Nagata says you obviously *are* out of your mind. But he also says that they're in, all ahead full on battle line 110. And that he'll see you in hell."

"Tell him I have dibs on the top bunk. On second thought," he said as Ord reached for the transmitter, "don't tell him that. Tell him to stay on 110 and attack its starboard side." He toggled the link to CIC. "Raikes, are you good to go?"

"Good to go, sir," her voice filtered back.

His eyes were locked on the stinger with murderous intent. "Can you see it, Raikes?"

Raikes didn't even have to ask what "it" he was referring to. "Five-inch gun locked on target. I can see it, sir."

"Kill it."

"Killing it, sir."

The moment they were within range, Raikes unloaded, firing directly at the stinger, giving it all she had with the pounding fury of the 5-inch gun. Coming in from the other direction, Nagata's vessel followed suit, spitting shells at the stinger that then exploded against the ship's force field. It flared to life, repulsing as many of the shells as it could.

It wasn't all of them, however. Hopper couldn't tell if it was one of his that had managed to punch through to the stinger's surface or if it was the *Myoko* that had the singular honor of landing the first major blow against the alien invaders on behalf of the human race. Either way, he was rewarded with the sight of the stinger rocking on its pontoons, and a blackened, scorched dent appeared on the stinger's hull, on the starboard flank.

"*Ha! Got you, you—*" Hopper's crowing died in his throat as the stinger, elevating on its "legs," let fly with those white, cylindrical missiles. Half a dozen of them hurtled toward the *John Paul Jones.*

"*Countermeasures!*" he shouted as the cylinders streaked toward the destroyer. Seconds later there were explosions all around. Most of the cylinders were intercepted and blew up prematurely, but one managed to get through and slammed into the side of the ship, detonating a moment later. The *John Paul Jones* rocked violently and Hopper shouted, "Damage report!"

"Weapons systems down!" Raikes's voice came over the radio.

Hopper muttered a curse and then watched in horror.

He had braced for another round, but as if his ship were old news, the stinger swiveled around to face the *Myoko*. The action seemed to catch Nagata's vessel flat-footed. "Move! Move your boat, you son of a bitch!" Hopper in futility shouted.

The stinger moved deftly out of range of the *John Paul Jones*'s guns as it angled straight toward the *Myoko*. The launch array atop the stinger swiveled to aim directly at the Japanese destroyer. Seconds later, the stinger had launched a brace of its cylinder weapons, streaking across the space between themselves and the Japanese ship in no time flat. The *Myoko* tried to counter, and was as successful in the endeavor as the American vessels had been. Many of the alien missiles were intercepted, but a few were not. And those few were enough to have devastating results. The white cylinders thudded into the ship, and even from this distance, Hopper could see them transform from white to red and then detonate. He realized they must have hit the weapon magazines or fuel reserves, as the ship went ablaze in a massive explosion.

"Get the guns online!" said Hopper. "We're going in full attack!"

"Sir," said Ord, getting the report from Raikes, "guns are three minutes away! We don't have any weapons, sir!"

"Then set course for 33 degrees at 30 knots."

Ord clearly had no desire to be relieved of duty, but nevertheless felt compelled to point out, "Sir, just so we're clear, that's a collision course."

Hopper nodded. His next words weren't an order—they were a threat. "Get the guns online, or I'm going to ram this thing."

Witnessing the destruction from her vantage point behind the guns, Raikes watched in horror as the *Myoko* fought for her life. Raikes also realized that the *John Paul Jones* was continuing on a collision course with the alien vessel, showing no sign of slowing down or attempting to provide aid to a crippled vessel that had just been attacked. Immediately she got on the horn with Beast, down in the engine room. *"You've got to pull him back. He's going to kill us all."*

"You do it," came back Beast's voice.

"I can't afford to leave my post! You can! And he'll listen to you before he'll listen to me!"

Hopper was listening to nothing, save the pounding of his pulse in his head and the way his heart was driving him to avenge himself on the stinger. Everyone on the bridge looked terrified, keeping themselves together purely because training had drilled into them a directive that superseded even the instinct for self-preservation: respect for the chain of command.

Even if the person in command was the weak link in the chain.

"Goddammit!" Hopper shouted down to Raikes, who had inexplicably stopped talking to him. "Target that thing before it jumps clear! Get me in there so I can hit it!"

Suddenly Beast was standing next to him, as if he had just appeared out of thin air. But Hopper didn't even acknowledge Beast's presence, so focused was he on the enemy before him. When Beast said, slow and serious, "There are sailors in the water," it didn't register on Hopper at any level.

"This thing can go faster!" Hopper bellowed. "What are you dragging your heels for, for the love of Christ! They killed my brother and every sailor on his ship! Are you on *their* side or—?"

A hand clamped on his shoulder like a vise of iron, sending pain jolting through him, commanding Hopper's attention by its presence. He turned and looked up at Beast, confused, having to remind himself that the huge engineer was standing there, focusing on the sentence that Beast slowly repeated, stopping every few words to drive home the emphasis. "There are *sailors*. In the *water*. *Sir*."

Finally the words sank into Hopper's mind like a bucket of ice thrown in his face. There was the smell of smoke wafting in the air, blowing through the shattered windows of the bridge, and he saw Nagata's ship, the once-proud *Myoko*, ablaze in the water. The explosions had turned the vessel into an inferno, and as the fire devoured it, men were indeed leaping into the ocean. Boats were being lowered where they could be, but it was all happening too quickly. Many of the men were simply jumping from the ship. They were wearing life jackets, but they wouldn't last long out there. A few had managed to get their hands on life rafts and they were quickly inflating them in the water. The men who had been severely injured were being given first priority, shoved into the boats, while those who were in better shape were clinging to the sides.

The stinger had them at their mercy and proceeded to . . .

. . . do nothing. Nothing save pull back and return to its first position, guarding the structure in the water.

What the hell are they waiting for?

And do I really want to find out?

He put aside his concerns and second-guessing as he said briskly, "Hard port. All engines. Get us over to what's left of the *Myoko*. We're going to save everyone we can."

The *John Paul Jones* quickly made her way toward the scene of the *Myoko*'s death throes. The Japanese sailors weren't even looking at the men coming to rescue them. Instead they were focused on the remains of their vessel as it slowly began to collapse in on itself.

Beast never took his eyes off the stinger. "Why do you think they aren't attacking?"

"Maybe they're scared," said Ord.

Hopper and Beast looked at him.

"They are not scared," said Hopper.

Then a sound like screeching metal suddenly ripped through the air.

Everyone on the bridge jumped slightly, bracing themselves, certain another attack was imminent. They looked toward the alien tower and realized that the noise was being produced by two massive doors opening on the far end of the structure.

"What are *those*?" said Hopper, looking to Beast, hoping that the engineer might be able to provide some sort of answer. Beast shook his head. He had nothing to offer.

What they were seeing were two metallic spheres rising into the air. They were identical, glinting in the sun, each about the size of a large beach ball. There seemed to be no visible means of propulsion. They just rose in the air and hovered for a moment, as if gravity was of no consequence to them. Then they angled around and Hopper braced himself for the things to come straight at them. Instead they soared away, moving—in Hopper's estimate—at a speed somewhere around 85 knots. And he realized what direction they were heading.

"Direct course for Pearl."

Beast's eyes widened and Hopper knew exactly why. The engineer's wife and children were there. It was one thing to have his own life at risk, but the notion of his family being threatened clearly shook the big man to his core. "We've got to radio for anti-aircraft," said Beast.

"The only radio we have available to us is ship to ship, and barely that," said Hopper. "We don't have ship to shore."

"Dammit," said Beast.

Minutes later, Hopper watched the survivors from *Myoko* disembark from the lifeboats that the *John Paul*

Jones had dispatched. Ord, standing near him, stared at the alien vessels. "Sir . . . what are they doing?"

His voice flat, his mind far away with his dead brother, Hopper said, "Whatever they damn well please."

"No, I mean . . . why didn't they finish us?"

Hopper had no clue. "Maybe they figured we weren't worth their time anymore. Or they wanted to rub our noses in our helplessness. Or . . ." Then, faced with a question that had no real satisfactory answer, he started to look for a more practical one. "When did the targeting alarms stop?"

"When our weapons went off-line. So . . . when we weren't able to attack . . . maybe they stopped looking at us as any kind of threat."

Slowly Hopper nodded.

Ord was clearly astonished at the concept. "God, that's incredibly binary thinking. Fire when fired upon. We hail them with our horn, they blow out our eardrums. We fire a warning shot, they sink our ship." He paused. "You think they're machines? You know: totally automated."

"I know they're not. Those ships have viewports." He glared toward the stinger sitting out there; if a ship could look smug, he was sure the stinger had that look. "Some *thing* is looking out at us right now."

"So if they don't care about us . . . what *do* they care about?"

"That's what we have to figure out." He gestured toward the alien ships. "As soon as the last of the men are out of the water, get us away from the stingers, Ord."

"The what, sir?"

"Those ships. I call them stingers."

"Aye aye, sir. Good name, sir. You should trademark that." When he saw the look Hopper gave him, Ord quickly headed off to the bridge.

The last one to climb over the *John Paul Jones*'s rail was Nagata. His face and uniform were blackened from smoke, and there was also blood on his jacket. It didn't appear to be his own, though. *He was trying to save someone. Someone bled to death in his arms. Oh God . . .*

Hopper went to Nagata and stopped short a couple of feet from him. Nagata stared at Hopper—stiff-backed, stiff-lipped, shoulders squared—waiting for him to say something.

"I'm . . . sorry about your men," said Hopper slowly. "And for the, you know . . . the thing about your honor."

Nagata did not deign to respond. Instead he turned his back pointedly and went to attend to his wounded men.

There was a swirl of activity around Hopper, and there wasn't a damned thing he could do to contribute. Medics and the quartermaster were attending to everything. All he was doing was taking up space, standing there and trying to stay out of the way.

He headed back to his quarters, and with every step he took, he felt rage building within him. He ran, faster and faster, unable to control it, sprinting in the same way that someone who feels his dinner coming up hustles to the nearest toilet so he'll have something to vomit into.

The second he reached his room, he slammed the door behind him, just as his rage boiled over. He yelled, and it was a deep and primal sound. When he turned and saw his own image in the mirror, he drew back a fist and punched it. The tempered glass held together and he hit it again and again, figuratively battering his own face, causing cracks to ripple through it, distorting his image.

He turned his fury on the rest of the room, knocking over anything he could get his hands on. Books flew, plaques, newspaper clippings, old photographs, reports that he was supposed to go through. Everything was tossed, pieces of his life tumbling around him with nothing to hold them together.

For long seconds this went on, this cyclone of devastation with Hopper in the middle of it. And finally, when he had expended the last of his energy, he dropped onto the edge of his bunk—the only stick of furniture that hadn't been thrown—and his head sank into his hands.

He still kept expecting Stone to walk through the door. To look around at the mess and say "What the hell—?" and scold Hopper for his lack of control. And then Stone would make it all better, because that's what Stone always did. He made things better, and he always came through.

Stay out of trouble while I'm gone.

Hopper sobbed in the privacy of his quarters, and hated his brother for abandoning him.

The humans seek to help the others, plucking the survivors out of the water. Let them gather themselves together so they are a single target. That will allow the most efficient means of utilizing resources. The object is not to overwhelm them. The object is to prolong this engagement in order to fully determine what they are capable of doing when presented with various opportunities. Dead, they are of no use. Alive, they make interesting . . . experiments.

The jamming array continues to function within acceptable parameters.

The spheres have been dispatched.

Soon the transport vessel will be launched. It will depart underwater and only surface once it is beyond range of the human vessels.

All is well.

OAHU

Vera Lynch exited Interstate H-1 and guided her minivan onto Route 92, also known as the Nimitz Highway.
She'd rather not have left her parents alone while they
were watching all the news reports about the worldwide
insanity, but she really didn't have a choice. She had a PTA
meeting that evening and, what with being the recording
secretary, there was simply no way she could not be there.

*The PTA. People around the globe are being ham-
mered by debris from some shattered space station or
whatever the hell they think it is, and we're busy getting
worked up about bake sales.*

Still, the simple fact was that life goes on in all its massive trivialities, even if people a continent away are dying.

Her twin boys were in the back, buckled into their
booster seats. Emmett, the older by ten minutes, was
pushing against the restraining straps. Walsh, the younger,
had fallen soundly asleep, which was something of a relief. It was always easier to handle the twins when one of
them was unconscious. She was grateful for the fact that
her father never tired of playing with the boys and he'd
managed to wear Walsh out completely. Emmett, by con-
trast, seemed to be an endless fount of energy. *I wish I
had that much.*

They drove past the Pearl Harbor shipyards. From
where she was, she could see that the harbor was empty
of vessels save for the docked *Missouri* and some utility
boats. It made her wonder briefly how Walter's ship was
doing during the war games. Putting some of her random
thoughts together, she suddenly worried that a piece of
space debris might have fallen on the *John Paul Jones*. As
quickly as she could, she dismissed the notion. If anyone
was in a position to elude damage as a result of debris, it
would be Walter. *(Why do they call him "Beast" anyway? Stupid nickname. The sweetest man in the world.)*

Certainly the *John Paul Jones*'s radar would detect any incoming objects long before they got there, and Walter's engines would immediately steer the vessel to safety. The most they'd have to deal with would be a big splash when it came down.

"I really have to go," Emmett piped up suddenly. He was holding a juice box and sucked on the straw, which produced a hollow sound to indicate that it was empty. "I mean, I might go in this juice box."

"That's nasty," said Vera in her brisk, "we are not amused" voice—even though secretly she kind of was. "You'll hold it."

He fidgeted in his seat. "I'm gonna need a second juice box once I get started."

She saw that traffic was slowing in front of her. Probably tourists clogging up the arteries because they were heading to the *Missouri* to check it out. Freaking tourists. She decided to exit off 92 and seek an alternate route through the surface streets.

That was when she perceived a distant, humming sound. She'd never heard anything quite like it before. It wasn't the whistling sound of a bomb being dropped, something she'd never actually experienced but had certainly heard enough times in movies. Instead it sounded more concentrated, like a swarm of angry bees. But not even quite that. It was different, and disturbing, and it was getting louder.

She glanced around to make sure the windows were rolled up. If it was some sort of insects, she sure didn't want the damned things in the van. As she guided the car under an overpass, Emmett suddenly shrieked, *"Mom!"* and pointed. Normally when Emmett felt the need to draw her attention to something, she never looked, because it meant taking her eyes off the highway and it was invariably something fairly inane, like a billboard announcing some new television program. But there was such confu-

sion and fear in his voice that her head snapped around to
see what he was indicating.

There were two bizarre metal spheres heading in their
direction.

They were tearing down 92 right above them, smashing
through the traffic as if it was nothing. They tore the tops
off vans, knocked cars aside, and the air was alive with a
combination of the humming of the spheres, the shrieking
and wrenching of metal and the screams of the people.

One of the spheres angled downward and smashed into
the overpass just as the minivan was about to drive under
it. Vera screamed and slammed her foot on the gas, correctly intuiting that if she hit the brakes, the van would
have skidded to a halt right under the overpass. The speed
limit sign indicated that maximum speed in exiting should
be twenty miles per hour. The minivan leaped to fifty,
springing forward like a vaulting puma, and tore along
the off-ramp just as the overpass blew apart from the impact of the sphere. Debris rained down—huge chunks of
concrete—and one of them ricocheted off the rear of the
van, surely creating a big dent but otherwise leaving them
unscathed. The overpass collapsed and, to Vera's horror,
a Ford 4 x 4 tumbled with it. The last thing she saw was
the terrified expression of the driver, an old man, visible
through the windshield of his vehicle before more debris
crashed down upon him and obliterated him from her
sight.

Emmett was howling in fear, great wracking sobs seizing him and tears rolling down his face. *"Ma! Ma! I
peed my pants! I'm sorry, I'm so sorry!"*

"It's all right, honey! It's all right!"

"Don't be mad!"

"I'm not mad, it's all right!"

She kept shouting it over and over, like a mantra, as
the van sped away from the site of the wreckage. For an
instant she thought about jumping out, about trying to

help, but all she cared about at that moment was getting her two sons away from the scene of devastation and death. *Maybe it makes me a bad person, but at least I'm a good mother.*

The van sped away in one direction while the metal spheres went in the other, obviously unconcerned with the damage they'd already done, and clearly prepared to do more. Emmett's mortified howling continued and Vera kept saying soothing words to make it clear to him that she really didn't give a damn that he'd lost bladder control. Truth to tell, she'd almost done so herself. But she didn't feel that this was the time to share that particular piece of information.

Meanwhile Walsh the imperturbable snored peacefully, dreaming about his recent visit with grandpa.

There was an old Hawaiian legend about an angry and frustrated woman who complained about the brutality of her husband, whose cruelty was—by her description—as sharp as the edge of cutting bamboo. The eventual fate of the husband and wife were unknown. Perhaps he had tossed her into a volcano; perhaps she had stabbed him to death in his sleep with a spear fashioned of bamboo. Either way, her unhappiness had achieved a sort of immortality in the naming of Kaneohe Bay, since Kaneohe (or Kane'ohe, as it was more properly spelled) meant "bamboo man."

One of the more notable residents of Kaneohe Bay was the Marine Corps Base (MCB) Hawaii. MCB Hawaii maintained key operations, training, and support facilities and provided services that were essential for the readiness and global projection of ground combat forces and aviation units, and the well-being, morale, and safety of military personnel, their families, and the civilian workforce. They managed installations and natural resources situated on a total of forty-five hundred acres throughout the island of Oahu, including Camp Smith, Marine Corps Training Area Bellows, Manana Family Housing Area, Pearl City Warehouse Annex, Puuoloa Range Complex, and of course Kaneohe Bay.

The MCB was under high alert because of what was transpiring globally, but no one could have been prepared for what was about to happen.

Sirens sounded throughout the MCB as unknown, incoming objects showed up on the tracking instruments. Marines immediately scrambled, charging out of hangars, off drill fields, everywhere and anywhere, to defend the base.

Within seconds the twin metal spheres tore through MCB Hawaii. Initially they zeroed in on the airfield, ripping through helicopters and airplanes as if they were wet tissue paper. Huge pieces of metal were sent hurtling in all directions and the first thing the Marines needed to do was fall back, take shelter, lest they wind up being gutted or beheaded by flying shards. As soon as they managed to find cover, they then opened fire with their rifles and guns upon the spheres.

It proved to be ineffectual. For the most part the spheres were simply too fast. It would have been impossible to get a bead on them with anything short of computer tracking, and even then it would have been challenging. A few shots did strike them, more by luck than anything else, but all that happened was the bullets pinged off them without inflicting the slightest bit of damage.

Once every vehicle that could potentially have gone airborne was reduced to nothing but scraps of twisted metal, the spheres headed for the weapons depot. Seconds later the base was wracked with explosions. The air became thick with vast plumes of black smoke, and fire crackled through the MCB. And as the Marines struggled to find ways of containing it, the spheres—as if their assault had barely been worthy of their time—hurtled away, heading for Camp Smith and anywhere else that seemed as if it could provide even the slightest airborne military threat.

From the deck of the *Missouri*, populated mostly by tourists, old salts, and a grizzled gunner, they could see smoke rising in the distance from the MCB.

There had been no Japanese aircraft, no howling of bombs or staccato assault of bullets from diving Zeroes. Nevertheless the parallels to times long past were unmistakable. Men who were in their eighties now remembered being brand-spanking-new recruits, thrilled to be assigned to Pearl Harbor, only to wind up witnessing firsthand the assault that wound up waking the sleeping giant and sending the United States howling for payback into World War II.

They were seeing history repeating itself, and within their hearts, sleeping giants roared to life once more.

The wind was blowing steadily east. Sam and her client, Mick, were climbing up the hill, going west, and as a consequence didn't see any of it. Sam did catch, briefly, the faint whiff of something burning. But she heard no trees crackling, no indication of anything on fire. And then, with a slight shift of the wind, the smell was gone, and she chalked it up to somebody barbequing around a campfire somewhere.

The shirt she was wearing under her light jacket was thick with sweat as she walked along a dirt road. It was an access road, probably to accommodate park rangers, and so wider and a bit easier to maneuver. She needed it since she was starting to have trouble keeping her footing on the uncertain side paths, plus she was still worried that Mick might stumble and fall. She was certain he could physically withstand any bumps and bruises he might incur, but she didn't want his ego to take a battering.

She needn't have worried, though. His confidence seemed

to be growing with every step. Plus, she realized, he might actually be having an easier time of it in some respects because her heart had to push blood throughout her entire body. Since his legs were truncated, there could well be less strain on his system than there was on hers. "You sure can climb the hell out of a mountain," she said.

"*This* is not a mountain," he said disdainfully.

"It's more of a mountain than that chair you had your ass parked in this morning when I found you."

He raised an eyebrow. "You got a little attitude on you there, Miss Admiral's Daughter."

"I don't have an attitude." She reached down, picked up a large rock that was in her path and tossed it to the side of the road. "I'm just not real big on strong, competent men not living up to their potential."

Mick snorted at that. "You talking about me or the part-time fiancé that's got that vein on the top of your forehead going like a freight train?"

His casual reply annoyed the hell out of her, mostly because she despised the notion that she was that easy to read. In point of fact she had indeed been concerned about, and fretting over, Hopper. She just hadn't thought that it was so obvious.

Sam was about to tell him that her personal life was none of his damned business. Her job was to make sure he pulled his head out of his ass and made proper use of those extremely expensive legs taxpayer dollars had bought for him. Considering he'd spent the past months alternating between feeling sorry for himself and taking out his anger on physical therapists who were just trying to help him, he hardly had license to be judgmental about Hopper. It was high time he started getting his act together. She was prepared to unload this and more on him, but all of that vanished from her mind when something hurtled past just overhead, with an ear-splitting howl that reminded her of the old stories about banshees her grandmother used to tell her. *When you hear the howl of the banshee, death is near.* It froze her for a moment, and then the ground beneath her feet vibrated violently in response to whatever the hell it was that had shot past right over their heads, flying so low that it created a massive suction in its wake. Branches, stones, and dirt were all yanked into the air after it, and Sam and Mick—taking refuge behind some large trees—barely managed to avoid being hauled up along with all the detritus.

Seconds later the noise and jet wash subsided. Sam's hair was completely askew and she made vague attempts to tamp it back into place, having little to no luck. "What the hell was *that*?" she said.

"No idea."

"A low-flying jet? Something from the MCB at K-Bay?" That made no sense to her, though. Why would a jet be flying that low? It was insanely unsafe for both the pilot and anyone who might be in the area.

She knew there was a ridge nearby that would provide them a view of the base. It wasn't terribly likely that they'd get any answers from this distance, but at least they'd be able to see if fighters were scrambling. Sam clambered toward the ridge, Mick right behind her. No words were exchanged between them as they made their way up to the vantage point: a few minutes later they were staring down in astonishment toward the distant base.

They couldn't make out a damned thing. The entire base was blocked by black smoke, blowing away from the ridge.

"What's going on down there?" she said.

"Don't know. Fire, maybe."

"Fire definitely. But what caused it? Maybe we should go down and—"

"And what? Put it out? I left my fire truck in my other pants."

She nodded, silently acknowledging the absurdity of

the notion. A couple of additional bodies weren't going to do any good down there. The base was filled with marines who were trained to handle any situation. They didn't need a civilian and a soldier with a couple of artificial legs inserting themselves into the middle of it.

So they returned to the road they'd been hiking and continued on their path. The conversation between them became somewhat muted as they speculated on the cause of the fire at the base, wondering if that was somehow connected with the unseen jet that had hurtled past them at a dangerously low altitude.

Then they heard the sound of tires coming up the dirt path and they moved to one side, giving way, assuming it was some sort of official vehicle heading toward them. They turned out to be correct, as a police Jeep Wrangler cruised up quickly behind them and then pulled over.

There was a cop at the wheel who looked like he'd grown up watching reruns of *Walker, Texas Ranger,* and had modeled himself on them accordingly. Armed to the teeth, he had a name tag that read "Blake." He looked at Sam and Mick as if they had no business being there.

"You're going to need to get off the mountain and find cover," he said brusquely. He acted as if he was irritated that he needed to take the time to tell them this. "The roads are cut off and we're evacuating the area."

"What's happening?" said Sam.

Mick pointed toward the sky. "Something just did a flyby. Does this have anything to do with—?"

The cop didn't even let him complete the sentence. "The island is under attack."

They were stunned into silence for a moment. "From who?" Mick finally managed to say.

"We don't know for sure. They've taken out the Marine base. Some people are . . ." He paused, looking for all the world as if he felt he was insane even for thinking the next words. ". . . using the word 'alien.'"

"Alien?" Mick didn't understand. "You mean, like . . . Mexicans?"

Sam didn't know if she should feel more sorry for Mick or for the cop. She couldn't keep the skepticism from her voice. "I think he means like little green men from outer space."

Mick snorted at that. "Oh, well, that's not so bad, then. I mean, when they start giving me rectal probes, maybe they can check my prostate while they're up there."

"I'm glad you think this is some sort of big joke," said Blake. "Meanwhile the Navy's engaging off the coast—"

"Wait . . . what?" *Oh my God . . . Hopper . . . Stone . . . Dad . . .*

As Sam tried to reorient herself around the bombshell that the cop had dropped on her, another Jeep came skidding to a hard stop behind Blake's. There were three cops in that one. Two cops, with name tags indicating they were Officers Burns and Strodel, were in the front. A third, Kline, was crunched in the back. He hopped out and came around to the Jeep that Blake was driving, hopping into the passenger's side. He was carrying a shotgun and chambered it meaningfully as he climbed in. It wasn't a gesture meant to be threatening to Sam or Mick; instead he was simply preparing for whatever it was that lay up the road.

Sam was still working on processing what Blake had told her. "The Navy? What do you mean 'the Navy'? Which ship?" She had her cell phone in her hand but wasn't getting any signal. The bars were flatlined. *Piece of crap phone.* "Please, can I use your phone? I need to make a call."

Blake shook his head. "No service. Phones, radios, everything is dead. Miss," and he was clearly at the last of his patience, "we need you both off the mountain. *Now.*"

"Okay, well," Mick said, "can you give us a ride down to—?"

The only response the cops provided was to shift the Jeeps into gear. Seconds later both of them raced up the road, leaving Sam and Mick in a cloud of dust.

"Well, I feel so much safer now," said Mick. Then, realizing where Sam's head must be at, he turned to her and said, "I'm sure semi-fiancé is just fine—"

She put up a hand, trying to keep her voice from trembling. "Mick, could you just . . . not. Right now. Just not."

"Right. Okay." He actually sounded borderline contrite.

She needed a few moments to compose herself. It was one thing if she'd known in advance that Hopper was being deployed to an active war zone. She would have had time to mentally prepare for that and hope for the best. But this had caught her flat-footed. It was just supposed to be war games. Now all of a sudden they were . . . What? Battling alien invaders? She was suddenly feeling nostalgic for when the biggest problem they had was that Hopper was looking at a court-martial. *My God, what's going to happen next?*

The thought barely had time to cross her mind when there was a hellacious noise from where the cops had gone. The screaming of human voices was combined with the screaming of metal, becoming one huge cacophony of destruction.

Every bit of common sense would have dictated that Sam run in the opposite direction. Instead she ran toward the source of the upheaval, Mick doing his damnedest to keep up with her. The road curved to the right and suddenly a hand clamped onto her shoulder. She was about to let out a yelp when another covered her mouth and turned her violently around.

It was Mick, and the perpetual look of annoyance was gone, replaced with total focus on Sam's safety, not to mention his own. It was easy for her to forget that this was a trained soldier, a man who had been dropped into the middle of life and death situations and come through them . . . well, alive, if not in one piece.

He dragged her to the side of the road and whispered fiercely in her ear, "Are you stupid or something? Little Miss Admiral's Daughter should know better than to go running into the middle of a fight without a clear idea of what she's getting into. Now stay behind me, got that?"

She nodded, her eyes wide. Slowly he removed his hand from her mouth. She looked up at him and said quietly, "You caught up with me. That's . . . wow."

"Yeah, well, stopping someone from doing something incredibly idiotic can be a huge incentive." Then he put a finger to his lips to indicate they should stop talking. He moved slowly down the road, Sam following behind him.

Unfortunately stealth was a slight problem because the servos in Mick's legs continued to whir softly. He winced visibly at the noise and endeavored to keep his legs as straight as possible. If he didn't move his knees, then the noise was minimal.

Having taken the lead, he made his way to the bend in the road, gesturing for her to stay back and keep her mouth shut. Whatever the hell had caused the ruckus was gone, but Mick was determined not to run headlong into an unknown situation. Mentally Sam scolded herself; she should have known better and, if he ever heard about it, her father would have something to say.

Assuming he's all right.

Mick peered around the corner, minimizing his own exposure, and then he turned to Sam, looking utterly shaken. He gestured for her to join him, and she did. When she saw what he was looking at, her jaw dropped in astonishment.

One of the Jeeps was lying on its side. The other had been ripped into a grotesque shape, little more than shredded pieces of metal that wouldn't have been recognizable as a vehicle if there weren't tires lying on the road. There were no signs of human bodies in either of the vehicles.

She saw a large branch of some sort lying on the road, and it was only when she spotted blood seeping from it that she realized it was a human arm. There was a leg nearby, and a piece of a torso—not even the whole thing—that had the name tag "Blake" still attached to it.

For a moment she forgot where she was, forgot everything except the horror of what she was seeing. Reflexively she opened her mouth to scream, but Mick heard the sharp intake of air and fortunately turned fast enough that he could once again clap a hand over her mouth. He pulled her to the ground behind a tree in order to get out of the sight line of whatever it was that had done this, especially if it was still around. Sam screamed nevertheless, but it was severely muffled by his hand. "Shut up!" he hissed into her ear.

She breathed heavily. Again. Her eyes were still wide with terror, but she managed enough of a nod that he slowly removed his hand from her mouth.

"What . . . what the hell did this?" she said. Speaking too loudly wasn't a problem; she could barely get any words out at all.

"I have no idea."

Then something stepped into view, something that—although Sam could not have known it—was of the same race as the creature that Hopper had seen standing atop a vessel three hundred miles away.

The alien being was studying the dead police officers—or the remains of them—with what seemed to be a clinical detachment, as if trying to figure out how they had fit together in the first place before they'd been butchered.

Then, slowly, its attention turned toward Sam and Mick's hiding place.

At which point, Sam completely lost it.

Her body began to convulse and Mick had no choice but to cover her mouth again. In fact, he had to do more, because her impulse was to scramble to her feet and run like hell. Such a move would have been suicide. She didn't dare draw that degree of attention to herself.

But it was as if Sam had completely lost control. She was trembling violently, her eyes were bugging out of her skull, and tears were pouring down her face. It wasn't just her own safety that was tilting her into the throes of hysteria. It was the realization that the absurd claims the cop had been making were true, and that Hopper was facing a completely unknown enemy that, for all she knew, had already killed him and everyone on his vessel.

She tried to tear away from Mick but he only held her closer. He said, "Shhhh," into her ear, and that noise was enough to cause the alien's head to whip around and look in their direction again.

Mick quickly wrapped an arm under her chin with the crook of his elbow over the midline of her neck. Then he pinched the arm together and Sam suddenly felt dizzy, as if something had shut off the flow of blood to her brain. And she blacked out.

She came to some time later, jolted awake by the deafening sound of something else flying low overhead. Sam looked up and saw a vessel that was unlike any air vehicle she'd ever seen. It was huge, and appeared to be composed of two sections. The upper one was long, wide, and flat, like the top of an aircraft carrier. There didn't appear to be anything atop it, although she couldn't be sure from this angle. But the front was open, as was the back, allowing for the possibility of smaller vessels flying into and out of it. The lower section, the underside, was two-thirds the length of the upper, deeper than it and with what appeared to be a series of oversized clamps running along either side.

She was still in the exact same place that she'd been in when she'd passed out.

The alien was gone. So was Mick.

She felt a resurgence of the panic that had seized her earlier. Convinced she was alone, Sam had never been more terrified in her life. Then she heard soft movement from up ahead, and for a moment she came close to freaking out again before she heard the telltale sounds of Mick's hydraulics. Sure enough, there he came around the bend. He looked stunned, as if he couldn't quite believe what he'd seen.

So distracted was he that he nearly stumbled over Sam, who was just now sitting up. He crouched in front of her, his eyes flickering with concern. "Are you all ri— *ow!*" The last was a result of the fact that she'd just punched him in the solar plexus. Not hard, but enough to get a startled exclamation out of him.

"You put a *sleeper hold* on me?" she demanded. "You *dick*!" With no sign of the alien and Mick now speaking in a normal tone, she wasn't attempting to keep her voice down. "You could've *killed* me if you hadn't done the hold correctly!"

"Yeah, I know." He didn't seem particularly concerned over her ire, although he was rubbing where she'd struck him. "Because I've used it to kill people. So I know how to do it right and I know how to do it dead. Which is what we would've been, thanks to the Predator over there, if I hadn't done something to shut you up. You okay now?"

She nodded, although doing so made her neck sore. "What happened after you—?"

"Dropped you like a bad habit? Well, he was looking right where we were hiding, and he took a couple of steps toward us, and then suddenly that ship showed up and he lost interest. I guess he had bigger fish to fry."

"Or bigger planets." The entire thing seemed demented;

she felt like she was running to catch up with events as they were unfolding, except she was on a treadmill, getting nowhere fast while the world sped along without her. "Where did you go?"

"I followed him. He seemed pretty distracted by the new arrival. I saw others like him, setting up some kind of . . . I don't know what it was."

"But . . . what are they?"

"You mean our new pals? I have no idea."

"What are they doing?"

"If I had to guess . . . considering that they seemed to be setting up shop with some kind of satellite dishes ahead a ways . . . they're building something."

"Where is everyone?"

"Everyone? You mean our armed forces? Our Navy, who's out fighting them in the ocean? Our marines, who just got the crap blown out of their nearby bases? Gee . . . I don't know."

"Where's my father? Where's Hopper?" Tears, uncontrolled, started running down her cheeks.

Mick was clearly running out of patience. "Stop," he said firmly, and there seemed a chance that he might wind up knocking her unconscious again if she didn't get ahold of herself. She gulped deeply and snuffled a few times, doing the best she could.

"Mick?"

"What?"

"Am I dreaming?"

His face softened, but only a little. "I don't think so. I know *I'm* not, because I know that when I'm dreaming about gorgeous women, there's no scary aliens around." Despite the seriousness of the situation, that last comment actually made her smile slightly. "Can you pull it together, Sam? Can you?"

"Yes." She nodded. "I'm okay."

She got to her feet, dusting herself off. Almost as an

afterthought, she said, "Thanks for saving my ass, by the way. I shouldn't have lost it like that."

"I've seen professional soldiers lose it over far less. And you're welcome." He glanced in the direction of the Jeep. "We're gonna get some guns."

Sam looked at Mick and realized what he was talking about. The prospect of going over to the scene of such carnage, getting within range of those severed body parts . . . It wasn't as if they could hurt her, but still . . .

She shook her head. "No. I can't."

"You can." He pushed her firmly toward the still drivable Jeep. "Move. You'll thank me if you're holding a weapon when something jumps out at us."

Steeling herself, she stayed beside him as they crept toward the site of the destruction. She tried to ignore the blood that was seeping everywhere and stepped carefully around a stream of it that was staining the dirt dark red.

Mick made it to the nearest Jeep. It had been torn to pieces, but Mick could still access the backseat, where a shotgun was sticking out. He gripped it by the barrel, standing clear of the business end just in case, and slowly extracted it from the vehicle. He looked it over carefully to make sure that nothing was bent, which Sam thought was a smart idea. The last thing they needed was to have the thing blowing up in their faces if they had to use—

Suddenly there was a crashing sound and a streak of movement in the brush nearby. Mick spun, training the shotgun, ready to open fire on what Sam was certain would be an oncoming alien. *We were idiots to come out into the open like this, oh my God, we're going to die . . .*

And then a dark-haired, bearded man staggered out of the thick brush, covered in dirt and sweat. He took one look at the gun, and the man who was holding it, and let out a terrified shriek. He put his hands up in the air.

"Don't shoot! Are you trying to get away? If you're leaving, take me with you!"

"Why should we?" Mick kept the gun level. "How do we know you're not one of them? This could be one of those *Body Snatchers* deals."

"I swear to you, I'm not!"

Mick paused and then said challengingly, "What's your favorite football team?"

"What?" The man blinked and then said, "I'm . . . I'm not into football, really."

Mick chambered a round.

His voice going up an octave, the man cried out, *"I like baseball, though!"*

"Which team?"

"The Cubs!"

Mick took this in and then lowered the rifle. "He's legit. An alien conqueror would have said the Yankees."

Sam wasn't entirely sure she understood the reasoning, but it seemed to satisfy Mick, and he was the one with the field experience. "Who are you?" she asked the stranger.

"I'm Calvin Zapata. Doctor Calvin Zapata. We . . ." He tried to wipe the dirt from his face and only succeeded in smearing it around some more. "We sent out a beacon. To contact intelligent life in deep space. We monitor it from an outpost on top of the mountain."

It took Sam a few moments to fully process what Zapata was saying to her, and when she did, her eyes widened in shock. "So you *invited* them here?"

He started to nod but then quickly shook his head. "Not me. Them. Others. I mean, yes, I work for the Project, but I tried to tell them this could happen. The program really just hoped that if we ever made contact, they were going to be . . ."

"Nice?" said Mick.

Zapata nodded.

"Yeah, well," and he nodded toward the remains of the police officers. "They're not."

Understatement of the year, thought Sam.

USS *JOHN PAUL JONES*

Hopper had managed to pick up some of the damage he'd inflicted on his quarters. Now he lay on his bunk, staring at a photograph of himself and his brother. The picture was intact, but there was a crack in the glass. The crack ran lengthwise and divided the two brothers from each other. *Not too damned symbolic.*

There was a knock at the door and it swung open before Hopper even had the chance to signal that whoever it was could enter. Beast loomed in the entranceway, and Hopper could tell from the all-business expression on his face that he wasn't there to inquire after Hopper's health.

"Sir, we need you."

Hopper didn't respond at first. Then, his voice low and heavy, he spoke—not to Beast, but to his brother's image in the picture. "I can't do this."

"We need you, sir," Beast repeated, as if Hopper hadn't spoken, or even heard him.

This time he looked straight at Beast. "I. Can't."

"If you can't, who can, sir?"

Hopper propped himself up on his elbows. "What the hell's so important? What do you need me for?"

"We've pulled one out of the water. During the *Myoko* rescue—"

"What are you talking about? I thought we pulled all of them out of—" He stopped as he realized what Beast was talking about. His hands started to tremble. Immediately he sat fully upright. "One of . . . *them*?" Beast nodded. "But . . . how—?"

"Judging by the bullet holes in its armor, I'm pretty sure it's the one that Raikes shot to hell."

"But if that's the case, why isn't it just lying at the bottom of the ocean?"

"Best guess: some sort of internal buoyancy device in the armor."

"And how would that work?"

"I don't know. But I thought you'd want to be there when we dissect the bastard and find out."

Damned right I want to be there. This is the one small triumph we have over those creatures, and I want to be there for every second of it.

"Where is it?"

"Helicopter bay."

Hopper gave one more determined look at the picture of Stone and him. "We killed one of them," he said grimly. "And if we did that, we can kill all of them. Let's go."

Minutes later Hopper entered the helicopter bay. Raikes, Ord, and various crewmen from both ships were gathered around a table upon which a dead alien warrior was lying. Nearest to it was Nagata, who was staring down at it with cold fury. He looked ready to rip the thing apart with his bare hands. All eyes went to Hopper as he entered.

They were waiting for me. Of course they waited for me. I'm the commanding officer. He was still having trouble thinking of himself in that capacity. "Let's have a look at it," he said briskly.

Ord said nervously, "You're gonna *touch* it? Maybe it's radioactive or something . . ."

"Running a Geiger counter over it was the first thing we did when we brought it on board," said Beast.

"Okay, but maybe it's got some kind of alien virus or something."

"No one's putting a gun to your head to make you be here," Raikes said to Ord with obvious annoyance.

"It's first contact, Raikes. It's freaking history. Where else *would* I be?"

"Hiding under your bunk, swabbing yourself down with Purell?"

"Stow it, both of you," said Hopper, having no patience for his crew's banter right then. He looked silently at Nagata, who simply nodded his head, and the two of them got down to business.

It took them several moments to work the helmet free. Finally they managed to turn it counterclockwise and there was a loud *click-clack*. Taking that as a good sign, they slowly pulled the helmet free. It produced a strange sucking sound and then the creature's face was exposed. It was even more hideous than when Hopper had seen it from a distance.

He and Nagata looked down at it in bewilderment. Then a burst of liquid from some sort of tube spurted out at the two commanders, hitting them in the face.

"*Acid!*" Ord cried out. "It's spitting acid at you!"

"No," said Hopper, blinking furiously. "Salt water." A handkerchief was being thrust toward him. He turned and saw that Nagata was holding it, offering it to him. Without a word he took it and wiped the salt water from his face. In retrospect, maybe wearing a pair of goggles might not have been a bad idea.

"Must be some kind of hydration system," said Beast.

His comment barely registered. They were all dealing with various degrees of shock, and it was easy to understand why. Mankind's first extended encounter, face-to-face, with an alien life form, and it was happening right on their ship. And it was happening under the most mundane conditions possible. Not with a flying saucer descending into Central Park or perhaps on the front lawn of the White House—with an alien being in a silver lamé space suit stepping out and announcing in a stentorian voice, "Take me to your leader." No, instead it was on a make-shift operating table, like something out of a damned police procedural. *CSI: ET.* Or maybe *SVU: UFO.*

Hopper tried to keep his hands from trembling as he turned the head of the alien left, then right. In addition to the blue-green of its face, it had strange markings that he couldn't even begin to translate, and what looked more than anything like a growth of stalactites coming from its chin. The alien equivalent of a beard? Bone structure extending from its skull? He had no clue.

"My dad used to say they'd come," said Raikes softly. "Said it his whole life. 'We ain't alone. There's no way.' He said one day we're gonna find them or they're gonna find us."

"Yeah," said Ord.

"Know what else he said?" said Raikes.

"What?" said Ord.

"He said, 'I hope I'm not around when that day comes,'" said Raikes.

"Uh—" Ord paused and then asked innocently, "Did he say anything about you being there and shooting the crap out of it?"

"I'd do it again in a heartbeat. You want a firsthand re-creation of how it went down?"

"Last warning, the both of you," said Hopper sharply. He turned to Beast. "Give me your flashlight," he said.

"Gloves," said Ord urgently. "At least glove up, sir."

Hopper stopped and turned to him. "Ord, I understand you're a little freaked out. So I'm going to say this once, nice and patient: Calm the hell down."

Ord forced a nod. "Roger wilco, Captain. I'm calm.

I'm, like, neurosurgeon calm. Buddha calm. Buddha Buddha Buddha."

"One more word and I'm going to let Raikes shoot you."

Raikes smiled in anticipation.

Ord promptly shut up.

Beast handed Hopper a Maglite. The reluctant captain leaned in close to the alien's face, studying it. He flicked the light on and shined it directly into the alien's eyes.

Saline systems have been interrupted, but the damage is minimal. Fluids are rerouted; life support systems functioning at acceptable levels.

The Regent's regeneration cycle is complete. Internal damage repaired. External damage repaired. Retrieval signal has been sent. Retrieval is imminent.

His eyes, fully healed, focus on a light source. The system's star? No. Far more concentrated. A portable light device of some manner.

His eyes snap open and he sees a human staring down into his face. There are other humans nearby.

He does not perceive any of them as being the humans who attacked him in a tiny vessel. He does not recognize the female as the one who incommoded him by shooting at him and disrupting his armor. All humans look alike to him. They are not worthy of individual attention.

All he knows is that the human with the light source is within unacceptably close proximity, and the light is painfully bright.

The alien's eyes snapped open and, before Hopper could react, it lunged at him.

Ord leaped back, warnings of remaining silent forgotten. *"Not dead! Not dead!"* he screamed.

The alien's hands clamped around Hopper's throat.

Hopper gurgled helplessly as he felt long nails digging into his neck. *It's going to rip the skin clean off me . . .*

He was face to face with the monster, its burning eyes glaring at him, as Nagata and Beast came in from either side and tried to pull it off him.

It reacted to the light. It nearly freaked out at the light. Hopper immediately shoved the Maglite into the alien's eyes. If the flashlight had been a Taser, it couldn't have elicited any more of a response, as the alien jumped back violently, releasing Hopper as it did so.

The human is resourceful. It is adept at utilizing objects at hand in an offensive capacity. This notation had been added to the mission log.
Retrieval is imminent.
Retrieval is now.

Before Hopper could react—before he could do anything—there was a deafening explosion, similar to a flashbang grenade, but louder and brighter and with far greater concussive force. All Hopper knew for sure was that one moment he was still on his feet, pulling away from the alien, and the next he was hurtling through the air and coming down hard on his back.

The world around him was one huge riot of noise and strobing lights. From his vantage point on the floor, Hopper tried to shield his eyes and make out what the hell had happened.

The blood practically froze in his veins as he saw more of the aliens pouring in. He had quick glimpses of his crew on the floor, being either stepped over or kicked aside by the invaders. Hopper began to struggle to his feet but he never came close to standing fully upright, as a thick fist slammed down on the back of his neck, sending him sprawling to the floor once more. *This is it. They're going to kill us all. They're taking the ship. They're taking . . .*

. . . their man?

The aliens had grabbed their fellow, who'd been upright on the table. It was staggering but capable of locomotion, and hung on the shoulders of one of its rescuers as they headed out of the helicopter bay. Hopper worked on getting to his feet and this time he made it, lurching after them. He had no idea what he would do if he overtook them; he wasn't wearing a sidearm—a mistake he'd be sure to rectify in the future, should there *be* a future—and he was also considerably outnumbered. But the bastards had overrun his ship and he'd make sure there would be hell to pay for it.

As it turned out, his pursuit quickly became a moot point. He made it up to the chopper deck, only to stagger as he saw what appeared to be some sort of alien flying vessel rising into the air. *It's not a* stinger? *They have other vehicles? What else do they have at their disposal that they haven't shown us yet?*

Hopper stood there, bathed in the white light that the alien vessel was generating from beneath. Someone was suddenly at his side and he jumped slightly into a defensive posture before he realized it was Nagata. He saw his own exhaustion, confusion, and overall dazed demeanor mirrored in Nagata's face. *Who knew that we'd finally have something in common: total bewilderment.*

Together they watched helplessly as the alien ship angled away, the engines insanely quiet for something that big.

"I got a really bad feeling," said Hopper.

Nagata looked at him curiously. "What kind of feeling?"

"A 'We're gonna need a new planet' kinda feeling."

Nagata didn't laugh, or even smile. Which was fine, because as far as Hopper was concerned, it wasn't a joke.

The noiselessness of the huge vessel helped Hopper

understand why the aliens had managed to get the drop on them. With the radar out and the ship's instruments unable to detect the presence of alien vehicles anyway, the thing had probably dropped in from the sky so quickly, so quietly, that no one had time to react to it. Or perhaps it had even snuck up on them underwater and then leaped from beneath to land on the chopper deck.

"No man left behind," said Hopper softly. When Nagata stared at him, not understanding, he continued. "Maybe they're not so alien after all. That's got to be their version of 'leave no man behind.' You get one alive . . . they come for it."

Nagata nodded. "It makes sense," he said.

Wow. He's agreed with me on something. What're the odds?

Suddenly Raikes came charging out of the bay from behind them, urgency on her face. Hopper put up his hands and said, "Slow down, Raikes. They're gone."

As if Hopper hadn't spoken, she said, "We just got a report. Medical casualty C-52. Two men down."

"In C-52? That's—"

"Engineering," said Raikes.

The full implications of that news struck home. "They're still on board," Hopper whispered. Then, speaking with authority, he said, "Lock down the ship. And tell Beast he's not to go anywhere near—"

Raikes's expression immediately informed him what the next words out of her mouth were going to be. "He already made a beeline down there. It's his house, Captain," she added, as if apologizing for Beast's precipitous actions.

"Goddammit!" said Hopper, snarling. He was already moving, and seconds later was joined by a small craft action team—SCAT—weapons at the ready. "We have a hostile on board! Lock and load, people!"

* * *

As Beast sprinted toward the engine room, he heard a hollow, repeated booming sound in the distance, echoing through the corridors. He made it into the main engine control center just in time to see several of his people backing up, their eyes wide with terror, their gazes fixed upon a sealed hatch down at the bottom of a flight of stairs that led to a companionway. The hatch, or rather what was on the other side of it, was the source of the noise. Something was pounding on the hatch cover. A human fist wouldn't have even been heard. This thing was making a noise like a sledgehammer.

But even a human armed with a sledgehammer wouldn't have made any progress on actually getting through the hatch. The cover was designed to hold back thousands of pounds of water, should the ship's hull be breached, giving the sailors time to reach higher ground and safety.

Now, instead, the hatch cover was showing signs of wear and tear. It was visibly dented, and its bolts had begun to bend, to buckle. As if sensing impending success, the pounding intensified.

"Get out of here," said Beast, just as the door gave way.

The Regents fighting unit smashes through the impediment in his path. He registers dispassionately how much force was required to pound through the obstruction and the information is then sent to the central repository for all information gathered regarding the humans.

It is his job to test as much as possible the "ground level" resources that the humans possess. Both the Land Commander and the Sea Commander are very interested in the results of his study. It is impossible to know for sure where and when particular information is going to be useful. Ultimately he doesn't truly care about any of that. His job is to gather intel. The uses to which it will subsequently be put are of no interest to him.

There are more humans in front of him. This is not unanticipated. The primitive ship is infested with them.

His on-board attack systems examine the threat ratio each human represents. Several are fleeing. Their readouts register green. They are thus of no interest to him.

The largest one, however, glows a bright and furious red. It is approaching, coming down the stairs toward him. If there is fear in this specimen, it is being overwhelmed by what appears to be (he surmises) indignation. All of the human's bodily readings are in the upper levels of what the alien has determined to be human norms. Heart rate, blood pressure, everything is spiking.

It is doubtless preparing to attack him.

This will be interesting.

The alien that was facing Beast looked different from the one he'd seen sprawled out on the examining table. It was shorter, squatter . . . but even that was simply relative, because it was nearly as big as Beast.

"You think you're bad? Coming in this place like you're gonna start trouble? Like you're some thug? That's it, isn't it? You're just a punk who doesn't get that this isn't a game." Beast looks at the alien. "Well, all right, 'thug,'" he sneered. "Let's go."

The alien started climbing the stairs, coming right at him. Beast grabbed the stair rails on either side, elevated his upper body and swung his legs into the alien. He felt a shudder of pain up and down as his feet impacted with the armor, but it was enough to send the creature tumbling backwards down the stairs. It lay in the hatchway, stunned for a moment.

Beast seized the opportunity to vault to the bottom of the stairs. He grabbed the hatchway door, which had been broken open by the alien but was still on its hinges. He swung it as hard and as fast as he could. The alien's helmeted head was in between the hatchway and the door, and Beast slammed it with all his strength. It jolted the alien, causing its body to spasm.

Beast's strategy was simple: crack the helmet, get it off, have access to the creature's head and then pummel it into a fine paste.

He pulled back the door and slammed it a second time, a third time, but by the fourth the alien had gained control of itself. It caught the door and shoved it back wide. Beast jumped away, narrowly avoiding being crushed between the door and the bulkhead.

Beast came around fast and lunged at the alien, but it was too quick for him. Having regained its feet, it picked Beast up and threw him forward. Beast banged hard against the stairs and lay there for a moment, dazed. Then, digging his feet into the stairs, he propelled himself back as the alien lunged for him.

He crab-walked up the stairs, hurrying as fast as he could. The alien came after him, its armored feet clanking heavily on every step like a hammer being struck against a gong.

Beast got to his feet just as the alien almost reached the upper deck. While having the high ground advantage, Beast drove his fists into the creature's armor as if he were working a body bag. All he managed to do, however, was break a couple of his knuckles. The alien simply stood there, gripping on to the railings for additional traction, taking all the punishment that Beast could dole out and providing no visible reaction at all.

Then, with an almost casual sweep of its backhand, the alien knocked Beast aside.

Beast slammed up against the bulkhead again. He almost sagged to the ground, the world whirling about him, but he managed to keep his feet.

"This isn't going as well as I'd hoped," he muttered.

The alien came up the stairs and slowly advanced on Beast. It was hard to be certain about its body language but it didn't appear at all concerned that Beast would pose a threat for much longer.

Beast backed up, his mind racing, trying to think of something that would hurt it, something that could crack open that damned helmet. Then his eyes fell upon a fire axe affixed to the wall. He yanked it off its brackets and charged the alien.

The human is wielding something. Since it has not yet been proven to be any sort of known threat, the object in its hands is glowing green. Best to test its efficacy in order to determine whether it can, in fact, be a danger to any member of the Regents.

The alien stood there, apparently paralyzed with fear as Beast attacked, swinging the axe with all his strength.

The blade struck the helmet and there was a loud crack of something shattering. Fissures appeared in the faceplate, along with a small hole at the blade's impact point.

The object in the human's hand switches from green to red in the alien's sensory array. It has been reclassified from harmless to a threat. As such, it must be disabled.

The alien reached out for the axe, moving with speed that belied its size. But Beast wasn't exactly slow afoot either. He twisted to the right, dodging the creature's lunge, and struck again. The cracks in the faceplate widened and now Beast could actually see a single, alien eye glaring out from within.

He brought the axe around again, but the alien intercepted it with its forearm. The blade glanced off it harmlessly, and with a quick movement the alien sent the axe tumbling. It clattered to the floor near an array of steam lines.

Beast tried to get to it but the alien was blocking his way. He lashed out with a foot, kicking the alien squarely in what Beast imagined was its chest. It rocked slightly back on its heels but otherwise appeared undamaged.

Beast quickly feinted left, then right, then left again. The alien went for the third feint, lunged at him, and Beast quickly cut right again with the sureness of foot that only someone who had played plenty of soccer could possess. The alien had left just enough space for Beast to dodge past it. It swung a fist around and slammed it into the wall, barely missing Beast's head as he passed. Had the blow landed, Beast would have wound up as nothing but a red mass against the bulkhead.

Quickly, the towering engineer grabbed the fallen axe and turned to face the alien, who was advancing on him yet again.

The human's physical capabilities and resourcefulness have been sufficiently tested. It is now time to terminate this exercise and move on.

The alien moved toward Beast with what seemed like new resolve. Beast realized that another shot or two at the faceplate wasn't going to get the job done.

So instead of attacking directly, he swung the axe and severed the nearest steam line. Hot vapor blasted straight into the face of the oncoming alien.

The eye that Beast could make out within the helmet widened in surprise as the boiling steam enveloped the creature's head within. There then came an outraged howl of pain as the steam practically cooked the alien's head inside its helmet. It staggered back, still making those strange noises that sounded like a combination of a whale song and a lion's roar.

The steam was now blasting everywhere, turning the entire area into a blinding sauna. Boiling vapor didn't distinguish between friend or foe, and Beast turned and ran like hell, axe still in his hand.

As he sprinted down the hallway, he saw—to his relief—Hopper, with a couple of SCAT guys following him. "It's right behind me!" he shouted, and suddenly something heavy struck him in the back of the head. Beast fell to the side, tumbling into a cross corridor, the world turning black around him, and he saw something bounce away from him. It was a valve from the steam lines. The alien must have ripped it off the wall and thrown it like a Frisbee. *Son of a—* was the last thing Beast thought before he passed out.

Hopper barely had time to cast a glance at Beast—just enough to affirm that he was out of the way—and then he and the SCAT team opened fire.

The alien moved forward quickly, its torso twisting and turning in response to the impact of the bullets assailing it. It kept one arm up as a shield lest any of the barrage get near its damaged faceplate. The armor withstood much of the assault, although one shot did tear off some of its knee. The alien did not, however, slow down.

"Fall back, sir!" shouted one of the sailors, and two men converged and formed a blockade between Hopper and the alien. This momentarily angered Hopper, because he wanted to be in the thick of the battle. It only belatedly occurred to him that they were doing exactly what they were supposed to: protecting the ship's CO. In point of fact, he had no business being where he was at all. He should be someplace safe, ordering others into dangerous situations while he oversaw everything from a distance. But he wasn't accustomed to thinking that way. Besides, he rationalized, the death of Stone and of the *John Paul Jones*'s captain and XO were proof enough that, in this situation, there was no safe place.

The alien continued to advance and, as if adapting its

armor to up its protection, the impact from the blasts weren't even slowing it anymore. It reached out and a low, angry roar came from within its helmet.

Beast's "thug" snatches the glowing red weapons out of the hands of its assailants. They are hopelessly primitive, and nowhere near on par with the weapon that was actually able to do damage to the Regent they had captured. The Regent, however, has long since departed the ship, and now the warrior is finding that he can quickly assess and dispose of the other types of weapons the humans wield. These devices, for instance. They are easily broken, and can also be used against those who attempt to destroy him.

He snatches the weapons from the two humans facing him. The triggering mechanism is too small for him to utilize. Instead he simply reverses the weapons and uses them as bludgeons, slamming them onto the heads of the two humans. Their heads explode in a shower of bone and brain. The danger readout on both of them goes from red back to green. The humans go down immediately, leading the warrior to conclude that the inefficiently created humans only have one brain apiece rather than a far more elegant three. Poorly designed race. Next thing you know, they'll turn out to only have one heart.

The two terminated humans had come together to prevent access to the third. This would indicate that the third is of some rank. This merits further investigation.

The remaining human fires its weapon at him—both the man and gun are glowing red. Its hands are shaking, its vital signs are at the high end of the scale and beyond. The human is terrified. That is good. At least it shows that the human appreciates the gravity of the situation.

He reaches the human and grabs the weapon from its hand. He snaps the weapon with no trouble as the human *backs up. It bumps up against a wall and the warrior studies it meticulously, recording everything he sees. Of particular interest is what appears to be an insignia on its armor—extremely pathetic armor, it should be noted, being nothing more than some manner of thin material unable to repel even the most minimal of assaults. The insignia obviously denotes rank. This will be useful when it comes to deciding which of the humans to capture and which to simply dispose of. Certainly the higher-ranked ones will have demonstrably different brains and will be more useful and informative about the race as a whole when it comes to dissection.*

Suddenly the human shoves him, which he had not been expecting. Does it not yet realize that he is superior in every way? That resistance is futile? Perhaps a more convincing demonstration is in order.

Hopper watched in shock as, with a whir and a click, something snapped into place on the alien's armor. He didn't have to be a scientific genius to realize it was some kind of blasting weapon, and it was targeted on him.

"Crap!" shouted Hopper as he yanked away from the creature's grip, which happened to be on his uniform sleeve at that moment. The sleeve tore away from his shirt and he sprinted down the hallway. As he ran, he yanked out his walkie-talkie and shouted into it, *"Raikes! Combat! Right now!"*

He hit the bow deck running, the alien right after him, making a continuing, thundering noise as if it were a T-Rex in pursuit of its next meal.

Hopper burst out of the passageway leading to the bow deck, the alien in pursuit. *Please be there, Raikes, please be there,* he thought desperately. He could sense that, impossibly, the creature was gaining on him. A shot exploded just to his right, and then to his left, each accompanied by a high-pitched whine. *It's shooting some kind of ray blaster at me. Unbelievable.*

He'd been able to avoid it because of the twists and turns of the corridor, but now he had the straightaway of the bow deck in front of him and the alien would have a clear shot. There was nowhere to hide, no way of avoiding it, and as he heard the shrill sound of the blaster powering up again, he braced his shoulder blades, certain he was going to be cut down any second.

That was when he heard a loud clang from behind him. He turned, his feet still moving, so he almost tripped himself.

Nagata had come out of absolutely nowhere; maybe from the shadows, it seemed, like a freaking ninja. Hopper wasn't sure if that was an apt comparison or borderline racist, but he didn't care at that moment. All he knew was that Nagata was holding a sledgehammer that he'd acquired from God-knew-where and had just knocked the blaster clear off the alien's shoulder. The alien spun to face him and Nagata, with a furious yell, swung the sledgehammer and brought it crashing up against the alien's faceplate. Half of it shattered and the alien let out an infuriated roar, grabbing at Nagata. The Japanese officer spun out of the way like a dancer and whipped the hammer around once more. This time it took the alien in the back of the helmet, staggering it. Nagata ducked, spun, ducked again, and swung low, striking the area of the knee where some of the armor had been shot off. This caused more consternation and fury for the alien, who seemed to be flummoxed over the fact that it couldn't get its hands on the swiftly moving officer.

The human is formidable for one of its species, but it repeats its moves in a pattern that can be analyzed. It should attack with its weapon from over there . . . now.

* * *

The alien's fist lashed out, seemingly in anticipation of where Nagata was going to move, and caught him squarely on the side of the head. Had it been a human fist that had made contact, Nagata might have been able to shake it off. As it was, it was like being struck by a boulder. Nagata went down wordlessly.

The alien took a step toward him, looking ready to crush Nagata's head beneath its foot.

"Hey! Big ugly!"

Whether the creature understood what he was saying was anyone's guess. Nevertheless, it slowly turned toward Hopper, who was standing at the far end of the bow deck with his hands cocked in boxing form.

"Come on!" he shouted. "You and me! Man to . . . whatever the hell you are!"

The visible half of the alien's face stared at Hopper impassively, although Hopper realized that it could have been smiling or frowning or laughing uproariously and he still wouldn't have been able to tell.

The ranking creature demands personal combat. Perhaps they actually have some manner of honor system. How very surprising. That being the case, the warrior has no choice but to respect that request, even though it will mean the certain death of the ranking human. Which may well be a waste since the human could have been of further use to scientists. He will endeavor to leave as much of the corpse as possible intact for subsequent examination.

The alien advanced on Hopper. It brought its hands up slowly, mimicking Hopper's defensive posture. Hopper circled it, feinting, punching, trying to get into or at least near the part of the faceplate that would give him access to the creature's face. The armor could certainly withstand anything that he landed, but if he could get at the exposed area, he had confidence that his right jab would be able to do some serious damage. Maybe even take the bastard down.

The alien watched him carefully and, whenever Hopper tried to land a blow, the alien brushed aside his attempts, as if Hopper were a first grader challenging a high school senior. But that didn't deter Hopper as he dodged and weaved, staying just out of reach of the alien's return punches. "Yeah! Yeah, not so easy? Not so easy one-on-one! Not like when you're using your pop-guns to kill my brother," Hopper's voice was going up in pitch, his building anger beginning to blind him, make him faster, make him sloppy. "All you had to do was talk to us, man! We would've welcomed you! We were thrilled to see you! But no, you had to be a bunch of murdering alien douche bags—!"

An armored fist suddenly struck him square in the chest, knocking the breath out of him. He swung wildly, missed, and before he could recover, the alien punched him in the face, knocking him backwards and nearly tearing his head off.

Nagata had apparently recovered enough to shout, "Get the hell out of there!"

Hopper, dazed, reached back for the deck rail, swung a leg over. The alien stopped where it was, cocking its head, clearly puzzled by the move. It probably thought that Hopper was willing to commit suicide rather than continue what was clearly a hopeless fight.

Slowly Hopper raised the walkie-talkie to his face. He could feel his lip starting to swell, which irritated the hell out of him since it had only just recovered from getting punched by Nagata. "I sure hope you're there, Raikes," he muttered.

Raikes's voice came over the speaker, "Always am, sir. Fast as she goes, on manual."

The alien slowly advanced on Hopper, who continued

to lean against the rail. Below him the ocean was surging against the ship. In the distance the sun was drifting down toward the horizon line. It was probably going to be the longest night that anyone on the *John Paul Jones* had suffered through. He wondered briefly if he would be alive to take part in it.

With a slow, steady tread, as if waiting for some last-second offensive move, the alien came toward him, ready for anything.

The human flips over the railing and is gone.

He is startled. It seems that the human has gone to a good deal of work, displayed a sizable amount of bravado, only to throw itself to certain doom.

Perhaps it is some sort of human ritual for a person of rank to commit suicide in front of its enemy, thus acknowledging that it is supremely overmatched. There is still much to be learned about human culture before it is wiped out. Every little bit helps.

Or . . . is it possible that humans are capable of surviving in water? Perhaps some of the higher-ranking ones are partly aquatic? It is certainly something that needs to be discerned.

He walks over to the rail to make sure. He bends over it and looks down.

There, in the murk, is the human. It is not in the water. Instead it is hanging about forty feet above the water, clutching on to some sort of metal projection from the ship's hull.

No point in leaving it dangling there.

He brings his second phase blaster online, but just as it snaps out into position and starts to power up, he hears something behind him clicking into place.

He turns.

Not fast enough.

* * *

Raikes, in the CIC, watched in satisfaction as she lined up the crosshairs of the bow deck's 5-inch gun squarely on the back of the alien's head. Since the dumb-ass monster had been generous enough to stand still so she could draw a bead on it, she felt that thanking it for doing so would be only polite, even though it couldn't hear her.

"*Mahalo*, motherfucker."

She fired.

The alien was just starting to turn in the direction of the gun when the projectile punched through its head, in through the already cracked faceplate and out through the back. The now headless alien actually continued to stand there for a moment, its arms out to either side. Then it slumped backward and tumbled over the railing.

"Just in the Nearly Headless Nick of time," said Raikes, whose deepest, darkest secret was that she was a fan of Harry Potter.

Nagata had lowered a rope down to Hopper and now he was climbing it hand by hand, back up to the bow deck. He made it all the way up to the railing, but then almost lost his hold on the rope. Nagata reached over and gripped him by the wrist, hauling him to the deck with an impressive display of strength. Hopper had a huge bruise on the side of his head where the alien had struck him. "You all right?" asked Nagata.

Hopper managed a nod and then looked at Nagata levelly. "Thank you," he said.

Nagata shrugged as if it were no big deal.

Suddenly bright light illuminated them both. *Oh God, what now?* Hopper looked up and saw that another of those weird alien airships had risen up and was now shining light upon him. Or maybe it was the same one as before; there was no way for him to genuinely be sure.

It's going to blow us to hell and gone. After all that.

The ship instead did nothing. It just hung there, seeming to . . .

"It's studying us," Nagata said softly. "And I don't think it's done yet."

As if it had heard him, the ship pivoted in midair, and then hurtled away through the skies, heading toward the setting sun.

Darkness fell upon the *John Paul Jones*.

SADDLE RIDGE

It had taken long minutes for the three of them to get the Jeep that was on its side down onto all four wheels. Sam, Mick, and Cal had to rock it back and forth repeatedly until they finally succeeded in tipping it over. Unfortunately it had fallen straight toward Sam, and she had nearly wound up getting herself pinned under it. Luckily she had thrown herself backwards and the Jeep thudded to the ground, bouncing a few times before settling down. Sam had then clambered into the driver's seat, Mick riding shotgun—literally—and Cal crouched in the backseat, looking around nervously as if sure that something was going to leap out at him any minute.

Sam was driving as carefully as possible, given that it was night, the road was uncertain, and she was worried that attackers might be hiding anywhere in the darkness around them. And the nature of the potential attackers? Unwilling to accept what her common sense was telling her—because it just seemed too nonsensical to be "common" sense—or what Cal had just "explained," Sam asked softly, "Are they Chinese? Hopper always said if we go to war, it's going to be with the Chinese."

Cal Zapata stared at her as if she had lost her mind. "They're not Chinese."

"*What are they?*" she screamed. When both Cal and Mick lunged toward her frantically, desperate to get her to shut up, not to mention that in her franticness she could crash the Jeep, she put up one hand to indicate that she had regained her composure. Very quietly, she repeated, "What are they?"

Sounding both portentous and pretentious, Cal said, "I think it's safe to say we have successfully made contact with a life form from another world."

"Yeah. Some success." Mick looked at him with disdain. "I hope you guys threw yourselves a big end-of-the-world party."

The Jeep jostled Sam as she fought to compose herself. *Dad would have no patience with me freaking out. He'd be disappointed in me. He'd tell me to assess the situation, keep a cool head, try to understand the enemy . . .*

"What are they doing?" said Sam over her shoulder to Cal.

"I don't know for sure . . ."

"Best guess."

"Well," he said thoughtfully, "they've sampled soil, vegetation—and I'm guessing they like what they see."

"That would be just our luck," said Mick. "That being the case: what are we looking at?"

"Well, we're talking colonization," said Cal. He sounded astoundingly matter-of-fact about it, as if he were discussing someone else's problem. There was apparently a lot to be said for scientific detachment. "Look at history: explorers become invaders and if any indigenous people live, they'll be servants, slaves, or museum pieces."

"Thanks, Mick," said Sam, making no effort to hide her annoyance.

"Me? What did I do?"

"You asked him. I actually would have been perfectly happy not knowing." She sighed. "Why the hell couldn't it have been the Chinese?"

"Yeah," Mick said. "You get invaded by the Chinese and a half hour later, it's like you didn't get invaded at all."

Sam stared at him. Then, shaking her head, she turned back to Cal. "So . . . what, exactly, are they doing up there?"

"Everyone in my field knows that spectrum isn't the problem with inter-stellar messaging," said Cal.

"Was that *remotely* an answer to my question?"

"All I'm saying is that we all have a shot at open sky. Frequency boost power is what dictates how fast and how far your message travels."

To Sam's surprise, she actually understood the implications of what he was saying. "So those things they were flying in . . . I mean, bringing in up there . . ."

He nodded, actually looking proud that she was picking up on it so fast. "Power cells."

"Like giant batteries?"

He nodded again.

Mick turned in his seat, looking at Cal suspiciously. "And what is it *you* do up on this mountain?"

"Send and monitor deep space for messages. Why?"

"Well," said Mick, and his voice slowly became filled with a vague dread, as he understood what was happening and clearly wished he didn't. "When I was on Ops behind lines, first thing I did was try to make comms. Could they be . . . ?"

"Using our gear to communicate with wherever they came from? Seems likely to me. I'm guessing reinforcements. Occupational forces." Cal was way ahead of him. It made Sam wonder if the scientist had actually figured out everything the invaders were up to and was simply letting the two of them catch up at their own speed so they'd have an easier time both understanding and accepting it.

"Oh, so ET wants to phone home," said Sam. "Except they need something a little more sophisticated than a Speak & Spell." She looked at the bewilderment on Cal's face. "What?" she said impatiently.

"I have no clue what you're talking about. Is that a cultural reference? Because I don't really do well with—"

Her mouth moved but words failed to materialize. "Forget it," she said finally.

"We can't let that happen," said Mick firmly. "Stop the car." When she failed to do so, he raised his voice and repeated with fierce determination, "Stop the damned car."

The Jeep skidded to a halt, the tires churning up dirt under them.

"No! Are you crazy? We shouldn't stop," said Cal. He pointed toward the darkness ahead of them. "Drive straight for the Marine base, maybe they can—"

"There's no more Marine base," said Mick. He started checking the rounds in not only the rifle, which he was cradling, but the other weapons he'd managed to extract from the crumbled Jeep.

Cal slowly began to understand what Mick was saying. "We're not going down the mountain, are we?"

"Mick, that's . . . that's insane. That's Looney Tunes." Sam was shaking her head so vigorously it seemed as if it might tumble off her neck. "Doctor, doesn't that sound Looney Tunes to you?"

"I'm not sure. What is—?"

"Never mind. Mick . . . we can't do this on our own. We have to wait for someone who can handle—"

"You know what waiting around gets you?" he said coldly as he continued to check his ammo. "It gives the enemy time to find you, and target you," he looked bleakly at her, "and blow your goddamn legs off."

A deathly silence fell upon them, broken only by the soft *click-clack* of Mick chambering rounds in every gun to make certain he was ready to shoot anything that moved and wasn't born on Earth.

"Okay, so . . . what do we do first?" said Sam.

Minutes later they had driven the Jeep as near to the site of the initial attack as they dared. Then Sam pulled it over toward a small cluster of trees. They climbed out and proceeded to cover the Jeep with whatever branches and brush they could locate.

Sam was breathing heavily, scratching at bug bites and scrapes she'd gotten from the branches. The branches also kept snagging her hair, and finally she pulled it back into a tight ponytail and wrapped a rubber band around it that she'd had in her pocket. She stepped back and studied the camouflage. It looked to be a pretty good job.

"I need to call Hopper," said Sam abruptly.

Cal appeared confused, as if he was being presented information he should have but didn't. "Who's Hopper?"

"My fiancé."

"Semi-fiancé," Mick volunteered, laying some more branches over the Jeep for good measure.

She fired him an annoyed look. "He's my fiancé," she said firmly.

"Oh good. You need to call your semi-fiancé," said Cal, sounding decidedly snide. "*I* want to call my *mother*."

Sam was starting to feel as if Zapata was more in need of a good slap in the face than anyone she'd met in a long time. Mick, however, put a calming hand on her arm as he said to Cal, "He's also a weapons officer on a guided missile destroyer that has the resources to take a whole installation out."

"Oh." Cal suddenly seemed to realize how he had come

across when he'd spoken so disdainfully. Sounding vaguely apologetic, he said, "That makes sense."

Sam decided it would do little good to berate Cal for the way he'd replied to her. Yes, it was dumb, but she hadn't exactly covered herself with glory every minute of the last hour or so. Better to just let it go and move on. "You work with all that high-tech gear. Can you get us in touch with the ship?"

Cal gave it some thought. "They're using an electromagnetic field to block our signals. An alien version of a Faraday shield."

"A what?" said Mick.

"A Faraday shield. Invented by Michael Faraday back in the early part of the 19th century. You use a conducting material to form an enclosure to block out static and non-static electrical fields. Think of it as a sort of ideal hollow conductor."

"Okay, I'll do that." Mick glanced at Sam. She shrugged.

"But in any electrical field," Cal went on, oblivious to their confusion, "no matter how powerful, there's no such thing as a solid or an absolute. And perhaps they're using some momentarily unencrypted frequency among themselves, unless, of course, they use ESP or some other advanced, non-oral form of communica—"

Sam's head was starting to spin. "*What* is he *saying*? He's speaking English, right?"

"Could be," said Mick. "I'm a little rusty on my science."

"Sorry," said Cal, looking embarrassed that he had left them behind. He thought a moment, trying to come up with a simpler way to pose it. "What they're blocking frequencies with is like . . . a pulse. Not a brick wall. This means there are gaps. So if I can get to my spectrum analyzer, I can, theoretically, discover a frequency we can broadcast on for—I don't know—thirty, forty-five seconds, before it rotates and gets jammed again."

"You didn't answer the question," said Sam. "Can you get us in touch with the ship?"

"Your semi-fia—I mean, your fiancé's ship?" he said, quickly correcting himself when he saw Sam's expression. "If they flicker . . ." He nodded and then added, "I need to get to my lab."

"Then that's where we'll get you," said Sam. "If they're left unchecked, how long before they can make their call?"

Cal glanced at his watch. "Five hours and fifteen minutes. That's when our deepest satellite orbits into range. It only does it once a day. They'll use it to slingshot the transmission to wherever it is they're from . . ."

"Then we've gotta hurry," said Mick.

Rifles slung over their shoulders, they set out to save the world.

THE HIMALAYAS

Doctor Nogrady had fantasized about moments like this. The notion of being face-to-face with high-ranking officials, and their hanging on his every word. Being accorded the importance that he felt a scientist of his status and achievement was due.

Never had he dreamed, even in his wildest imaginings, the circumstances that would lead him to this "achievement." His mind flew back to the conversation he'd had with Cal Zapata about being wary over what you wish for, since you might well get it.

Zapata. Zapata, with whom they'd lost contact, along with the entire Honolulu base. *Have they taken it over already? Have they destroyed it? And are we next?*

He returned his attention to the image of the Secretary of Defense on the viewscreen in front of him. "And what," the Secretary was saying, "is the update of the fragment that crashed in China?"

"Scientists have been scouring the debris field," Nogrady said, consulting the latest updates. "And the pieces they're recovering suggest they were designed for multispectrum data transmission across every electromagnetic wavelength from visible to x-ray."

The Secretary nodded. Apparently he understood. Nogrady was impressed.

"What does that mean?" asked the Secretary.

Nogrady was less impressed.

Normally Chinese scientists weren't quite so forthcoming with information they gathered, particularly with findings on their own shores. The Chinese government was relentlessly territorial with such things. But the Beacon Project was an international endeavor and all the scientists involved were sharing up everything they learned, whether the governments liked it or not. "It is the strong belief of the Chinese," Nogrady said, "that what crashed down in Hong Kong was some sort of communications ship."

"You're saying a flying telephone cratered and took out two hundred and fifty people?"

"Like most death tolls, I'm sure that number will increase exponentially as they find bodies. My point is, what I'm saying is that our visitors appear extraordinarily concerned with establishing a line of communication home."

"But if they lost their ship, how can they do that?"

"The same way we did. Our communication station on Hawaii has the ability to send a message to deep space through our LANDSAT 7 satellite. I believe it's for that asset that they've domed the islands."

"So if we can't get into Hawaii, why don't we just take out the satellite?" The question wasn't being directed to Nogrady. There was doubtless some general or other army officer sitting just out of sight in whatever secured bunker they were communicating from. Maybe the Situation Room, maybe the Pentagon. It wasn't Nogrady's business to know; just provide information.

From nearby the Secretary, a gruff voice said, "Well, sir, that's orbiting seventy-eight thousand miles out. We don't have a weapon in our arsenal we can launch that distance at a moving target and be assured of hitting it. In fact, I can almost guarantee we won't. It could take weeks of trial and error for our weapon to reach it."

"Do we have a . . . I don't know . . . some sort of self-destruct button we can push and just blow up the satellite from here?"

Nogrady didn't quite trust himself to answer that question. Fortunately enough the unseen general did it for him. "Mr. Secretary," and he was clearly trying to keep the incredulity out of his voice, "we're not talking about a spy plane. We don't build self-destruct mechanisms into everything."

"Well, assuming we survive, we should look into that."

"I'll get right on it, Mr. Secretary."

The Secretary shifted his attention back to Nogrady. "Speaking of survival . . . what happens if they establish communications?"

"Based upon the destruction we've seen them uncaringly rain down upon us . . ." He paused and then said, "In scientific terms: we're looking at an ELE, an extinction level event."

"Less scientific terms?"

"We're history," said Nogrady.

If Calvin is alive, thought Nogrady as he watched the

Secretary of Defense contemplate the end of mankind's time on this planet, *then he's doubtlessly coming to these same conclusions. At least he's in a position to do something about it.*

Although I wouldn't hold my breath.

USS *JOHN PAUL JONES*

Hopper looked across the faces of the assembled officers and crewmen as they sat in the CIC. Nagata, Raikes, Ord, Beast, and the rest of the CIC crew. They were waiting for him to say something, to tell them what to do.

He had no blessed clue.

But he had no time to wait until he did.

Hopper drew in a breath and let it out slowly. "Okay. What do we know? And what does it mean?"

"We know they're not here on some goodwill mission to feed the children," said Ord.

It was his typical lame attempt at humor. Surprisingly, of all people, Nagata picked up on it and went with it. "Not *our* children."

There was a faint chuckle, shared by people who didn't actually think anything about the situation was remotely funny. The laughter of people sitting on death row, trading morbid jokes while hoping that a pardon from the governor would be forthcoming.

Hopper ran his fingers through his hair. "Those throat tubes were full of salt water. Maybe . . . maybe that's what they're here for. Maybe salt water is something they need for survival, just like we need desalinated water to survive. And maybe their supply on their homeworld is running low, or there was climate change, or it was polluted. So they sent—"

"Three ships," Ord interrupted him. "They sent three freaking ships. How much could they possibly transport?" Then he added quickly, when he saw the annoyed look from Hopper, "*Sir.*"

"Not just three," Raikes reminded them. "Those three mobile combat ships, plus that transport thing, plus who knows what else."

Nagata leaned forward, his eyes thoughtful. "Three, four ships, only the beginning. Water is only the beginning."

"You think this is an advance party that they're setting up for a land invasion?" said Hopper. He could scarcely conceive of it, the magnitude of the undertaking. "But there are seven billion people on this world. Millions of miles of territory, hundreds of different governments. And you're trying to tell me—?"

"They want the whole damned place," said Beast.

"More coming for certain," said Nagata, nodding.

They exchanged looks. Hopper realized the enormity of what they were discussing. More than that, he considered the distinct possibility that they might be alone in this realization. They had no idea what was happening elsewhere or what others might have figured out. If the aliens were raining down destruction worldwide, launching ships and attack vehicles, then the secret was pretty much out.

But that didn't seem to match with their method of operation. They were coming across to Hopper as being extremely methodical. Testing, probing, seeing what the humans were capable of doing, while preserving their own resources. It seemed far more likely that they would be concentrating minimal forces here, trying to determine what it was that humans were capable of mounting offensively, so they would know how much of their ships and personnel they'd need to commit. Only then would they send for reinforcements, enough to take whatever they needed and lay waste to whatever they didn't.

"Not if we can help it," said Hopper, as much to his inner concerns as to anyone there. He turned to Beast and said briskly, "Damage report."

"Starboard engine is down. Whatever that thing was, it tore through the drive shaft."

"Fixable?" said Hopper.

Beast shook his head. "Negative."

"Port engine?" Hopper was nervous to hear the response. "We're sitting ducks without it."

"It tore into the turbines pretty good, but we can fix it."

Hopper sighed in relief upon hearing that. At least he had some small fragment of good news to which he could cling.

Abruptly Nagata called out something in Japanese. It certainly sounded like an order. In response to it, a short Japanese man with a round face and glasses entered and looked to his commanding officer expectantly. Nagata gestured toward the new arrival and told Hopper, "Lieutenant Commander Hiroki is my chief engineer. He is quite excellent and can help you."

"Thanks, but I don't need any help," said Beast. Clearly as far as he was concerned, that was the end of the discussion. He stood up, stooping in order to keep his head clear of the low ceiling, and started for the door, barely giving Hiroki a glance.

He was brought up short, however, when Hopper said sharply, "Beast." He turned questioningly toward Hopper, who continued in a tone that was gentle but also firm, with a hint of warning that there were bigger things than Beast's ego at stake. "We are under attack from what appears to be a force from another world."

"Yes, sir."

"We have lost two destroyers."

"Yes, sir."

"We are effectively dead in the water. Sitting ducks, until you get our engines back online."

"Yes, sir," said Beast. He obviously knew where the conversation was going, but was content to let Hopper take it all the way there.

"We'd be appreciative of Captain Nagata's offer to assist us and would welcome Lieutenant Commander Hiroki's assistance in our engine room."

Beast and Hiroki exchanged looks, this towering American and a diminutive Japanese officer. They looked like a comedy duo.

"Sir," Beast rumbled, "if the lieutenant commander would follow me, I'm sure we have plenty of work for him."

Nagata nodded to Hiroki, who saluted his captain. Then he stared up at Beast, looking as if he didn't care in the least that the American had been resistant to working with him. A silent understanding seemed to occur between the two of them and they actually nodded in unison. Beast walked out first and Hiroki followed him from the CIC.

Hopper looked with certainty at Nagata and forced a smile. "They're gonna get on great."

Nagata harrumphed.

"So . . ." Hopper settled into the captain's chair, feeling awkward in doing so, but knowing it was expected. He stared up at the big screens on the wall that displayed the Hawaiian theater. Using the controls in front of him, Hopper moved an icon to articulate his point. "So, we're here," he said, sliding a small boat-shaped image onto the screen. Then he tapped a spot on the map and an arrow appeared. "Pearl Harbor is here. They—whatever 'they' are—are here in the middle," and he created a circle in the general area of the aliens. "We have plenty of conjecture, but ultimately we don't know for sure their true objective. And at night, without radar, we can't see them."

"Correct, but I don't think they can see us either," said Nagata.

That possibility had not occurred to Hopper. "Why's that?"

"Because we're still floating," said Nagata.

"Good point. So the radar jamming works both ways," said Hopper. Then he added reluctantly, "Of course, they could have blown us to hell before the sun set. Why didn't they?"

"Conserving resources. Maybe they used up their fire-power. Maybe they have to recharge or reload their missiles."

"Which they've probably had enough time to do by now. And that brings us back to the theory about their being as blind as us."

He stared up at his screen, an empty battlefield. Nagata stared at it as well. But where there was just a sense of hopelessness on Hopper's face, a frustration over the challenge he was facing with no real answer presenting itself, the wheels that were turning in Nagata's head were practically visible. "There is a way," he said after a time.

"A way?" said Hopper.

"A way of seeing them, without seeing them."

Hopper had had a brief surge of hope, but when Nagata said that, it was like the air going out of a balloon. "Is this going to be some kind of *Art of War* reference? Fight the enemy where they aren't? 'Move like the water' . . . ? 'Cause I have to be honest, I've read that book and it didn't make a whole lot of sense to me."

"The book is Chinese." There was mild annoyance in Nagata's voice.

Hopper couldn't have given a·damn at that moment.

"Yeah, well, I don't understand the damned thing. Not a word of it."

"My way is much more simple," said Nagata.

"And what would that be?"

"We've been doing it to America for twenty years."

Now Hopper's attention was firmly engaged. He leaned forward in his chair, his eyes narrowing. "How?" he said so slowly it became a three-syllable word.

"Water," said Nagata. He said it with a touch of pride, as if quite pleased with himself that he was having the opportunity to inform some dumb-ass American about something the Japanese had pulled over on them.

"Water?" said Hopper slowly. It didn't make any sense to him.

"Water displacement. We can tell where your ships are by the amount of water displacement."

Hopper felt as if he were being left further and further behind. "How do you trace water displacement?"

"Tsunami buoys."

"Tsunami buoys?" That actually sounded vaguely familiar to Hopper, but he couldn't quite place where he'd heard it.

"You have them surrounding your islands," said Nagata. "Transmitting displacement data. We hack into their transmission. Form a grid and identify military ships based on displacement signature."

Hopper stared at him. He felt a degree of grudging admiration. "You sneaky bastards."

"We would practice it as a contingency plan should we lose fire control radar."

Hopper waggled a scolding finger at him, as if chastising a child. "Sneaky, tricky, dirty playing."

Nagata didn't seem the least bit chagrined. "Rough world," he said indifferently.

"I like it. Can you do that? Here? Now?"

"Possibly."

Without any hesitation, Hopper got up and gestured sweepingly toward the captain's chair. "Captain Nagata, my CIC is your CIC."

The rest of the crew could not have been more stunned if Hopper had peeled off his face to reveal he was one of the aliens. The words "Who are you and what did you do with Alex Hopper?" certainly occurred to more than a few of them. Here he was turning his baby over to a stranger—no, not even a stranger, a guy he'd had a major punch-out with that might well have wound up scuttling his career.

Right now, though, his long-term career plans could not have been further from Hopper's mind. All he cared about was finding the best man for whatever tasks were necessary to get his people out of this situation alive. As far as he was concerned, if that meant Nagata in the captain's chair while they took on the aliens, so be it. He had neither the time for, nor the luxury of, pampering his ego.

Even Nagata was astounded, although his was not the reaction of wide eyes and gaping jaws as was seen from the rest of the sailors in the CIC. He merely arched a single eyebrow as he stared at Hopper. The unspoken question was easily discerned: *Are you sure about this?*

Hopper replied even though the question hadn't been voiced. "It's what my brother would have done," he said with a small shrug, as if it was so obvious, it didn't need to be spelled out.

Nagata's arms were stiff at his sides as he bowed crisply from the hip, and he kept his eyes fixed on Hopper's. Hopper bowed in response.

The Japanese officer wasted no more time as he sat down in the captain's chair and began working on the *John Paul Jones* computer system. As he did so, he said softly, "Your brother was a good man."

"Yes."

"I heard his younger brother was an idiot."

Hopper froze, scowling. Was this all some sort of joke to Nagata? Was he going to take the grand gesture that Hopper had just made, trusting his ship to him, simply so he could make a few more snide remarks at Hopper's expense?

Then Nagata looked up. "But it appears I was misinformed. I will be sure to remember that in the future." With that pronouncement, he went back to work.

Hopper smiled for the first time since the death of his brother.

He hoped he would have further opportunities.

It took Nagata about half an hour to thoroughly master the differences between the *John Paul Jones*'s computer system and that of his late, lamented vessel. There was tense silence during that time, only broken when Nagata had a question, which would quickly be answered by Hopper or one of his crew. While Nagata worked, everyone was braced for the possibility that maybe the aliens could, in fact, perceive them, and that any moment they might be fired upon.

Nothing happened, though, lending further credence to the notion that they were as invisible to the aliens as the aliens were to them. But after thirty minutes of working on the problem, Nagata had gone a long way to remove that differential.

The main computer screen was now alight with a massive grid that presented the locations of all the buoys floating in the ocean within miles of the area. It was more than they required, but there was no point in doing this in half measures. Besides, if more ships landed anywhere nearby, or even not that nearby, they wanted to be able to know immediately.

Hopper leaned in near Nagata, staring at the complex

grid system of hundreds of buoys, all of them transmitting water displacement. "Now what?" he asked.

"We're looking for patterns of water displacement," said Nagata.

Hopper studied the grid for another few seconds. A buoy had been activated. He pointed and said with satisfaction, "There."

"Maybe," said Nagata noncommittally.

Another buoy grid two hundred yards south was activated. "It's moving," said Hopper.

"Maybe."

A third buoy was activated. "That's a ship," Hopper said with growing excitement. A trajectory line was being established. That meant if they could determine a heading, then they could line up a shot and be one step ahead of the enemy.

"Looks that way." Nagata didn't sound especially enthusiastic, but he was obviously one to play things close to the vest. Plus he'd gotten his ship shot out from under him, so it was understandable he wouldn't be too quick to celebrate.

"Good job."

"Bad news is that it's heading toward us," said Nagata.

Hopper did a double take and he was pretty sure the blood was draining from his face. "Fantastic," he muttered.

Beast and Hiroki, with the aid of some additional men, were busy tearing apart the starboard engine when the call came down from CIC.

The chief engineer knew Hopper as well as anybody and probably better than most. So he was able to tell from Hopper's tone of voice that they were in deep trouble. Not that Hopper would be sharing that information over the radio. It wasn't his style. He would focus on the problem at hand and leave everyone else to deal with their specific tasks.

"Beast," Hopper's voice filtered through the radio, "we need some power." He said it casually, as if he'd suddenly realized they'd run out of booze and was asking Beast to make a beer run down to the local 7-Eleven.

Beast didn't bother to ask why there was a sudden need for propulsion. He suspected that the answer wouldn't be anything good. "Working on it," he said into the radio.

"Work faster," the admonition came back.

"Roger, working faster." He clicked off the radio, returned to work, and looked at Hiroki. "Your boss like that? Always want it faster, quicker? Done yesterday?"

Hiroki stared at him, peering owlishly over the tops of his round glasses. It was fairly clear that he had no clue what Beast was talking about. Beast actually knew he was wasting his time. Thus far he'd communicated with the Japanese engineer entirely through emphatic pointing and gestures; clearly the smaller man spoke no English. Beast was talking to himself as much as he was talking to Hiroki. Instead, as he did his best to stitch his beleaguered engine back together, Beast kept a running commentary going. "It's never fast enough. No matter how quick you turn it around, it's always 'Fix it faster. Faster faster faster.'" He snorted. "Like to see *them* fix up their gear after a two-fifty-pound Hippo Robot goes full berserk in *their* department."

Beast looked up in surprise as, out of nowhere, Hiroki asked, "Your mother named you 'Beast'?"

Everything stopped, the other sailors pausing in their endeavors and looking with barely restrained amusement at the way Beast was staring at the smaller man.

"Don't worry about my mother," Beast said curtly, and got back to work.

* * *

Nagata had been absolutely correct. There was a clear track on the monitor of one of the alien vessels—a stinger, most likely—heading straight at them.

Raikes, observing their approach from her station, said, "So they can outgun us, outmaneuver us, and more or less fly . . . and the one thing we have in our favor is that they don't know we know they're coming." Hopper nodded. Raikes forced a smile and said heartily, "I love this plan. I'm thrilled to be a part of it."

"That means a lot, Raikes." He spoke into his walkie-talkie. "Spotters on deck?"

"Spotters ready, sir," Ord's voice crackled over the walkie-talkie. Ord would be at the port observation deck, since the other one had been blown to hell by the aliens. Other young men were scattered around the deck, armed with binoculars.

Are they terrified? A bunch of kids, many fresh out of the Academy, keeping a lookout for alien vessels that can come out of nowhere and annihilate us with weapons the like of which we've never seen before? Yeah, well . . . it's not as if I'm not outside my own comfort zone right now . . .

Nagata was completely focused on the monitors in front of him, calibrating the speed and course of the stinger. "I thought they couldn't see us," Raikes said.

"It's entirely possible they can't," said Hopper, hoping he was right. "They could just be heading in this direction by coincidence, and they'd stumble over us purely by accident."

"Would that be any better than if they were heading toward us by design?"

"Not really, no."

Raikes stared at him. "Great."

Hopper couldn't bring himself to come down on Raikes. He knew that she was wound up. Her trigger finger was visibly twitching, indicative of the mounting tension she was feeling from having a potential target and not being allowed to shoot at it yet. That tension was reflected in the faces of everyone else in the CIC.

"Hold it together, Raikes," Hopper said sharply. "All of you."

Raikes nodded in acknowledgment, but she was clearly not winding down anytime soon. The bottom line was that Hopper had every confidence that—when the moment arrived—Raikes would be all business and hyperefficient. It was the waiting that could get to her. That could get to all of them.

"Can we hit this thing, please?" Raikes said to Nagata.

Nagata was the only one on the CIC who seemed immune to any sort of pressure. *The man must have ice water in his veins.* "We need to be sure of its speed," said Nagata calmly. "Are we ready to fire missiles?"

"Raikes, do we have some Harpoons for the captain?" said Hopper.

Raikes smiled. Discussion of an impending opportunity to shoot at something always brightened her day. "Yes, sir, I've got some beauties."

"Very well. Prepare to target; everyone in position." Nagata checked the screen, although Hopper suspected it was purely *pro forma*. He probably had the image and position embedded in his mind. The stinger was definitely getting closer. Whether that meant that their own danger level was being ratcheted upward or that the aliens were presenting themselves as a better target pretty much stemmed from one's worldview.

"Target ECHO 11," said Nagata.

Raikes immediately threw herself into her work, entering the coordinates into the computer that controlled the ship's store of RGM-84 Harpoon anti-ship missiles. It took her only seconds and then she announced, "Coordinates loaded, target impact twenty-one seconds. On your clock, Captain." She paused and then added in a tone of forced casualness, "By the way, you know it's not going to matter if they're heading in this direction by accident or not. When we fire, they'll know where we're at."

Hopper had known that. Still, Raikes saying it aloud brought it to stark reality. All eyes were upon him, including Nagata's. It was his call. There was always the option that they could just sit tight, hope that the stinger cruised past them without being aware of their presence . . .

Then, in his mind's eye, he saw the look on Stone's face right before he was blown to hell. It was impossible to know which ship was the one coming near them, but it could well be that the same bastards that had murdered his brother were now within striking distance.

"Hit that son of a bitch," said Hopper.

Raikes grinned wolfishly, although her voice was all business. "Roger that."

From the foredeck missile battery, a huge plume of flame erupted from the missile tube. Raikes's perfectly targeted Harpoon launched from the ship, arcing into the darkness in a blaze of light. A second followed a heartbeat later. Everyone in the CIC looked at the grid on the board, waiting to see the likelihood of their surviving the night.

On the port observation deck, Ord watched through binoculars with mounting concern as the *John Paul Jones*'s two missiles tore across the sky. He hadn't had to hear Raikes's comment down in the CIC; he knew perfectly well they were going all-in based upon readings from a series of buoys. "Like this will ever work," he said under his breath. "Why don't we just close our eyes and throw the missiles at them?"

He kept his eyes open, though, and watched carefully, counting down, listening to the roar of the missiles as they hurtled into the distance, a tiny light receding further and further.

Then he heard it.

A distant, hollow splash, followed by a second.

Oh, crap.

Hopper's voice crackled over the walkie-talkie. "Ord, anything?"

Keep it together. Keep it together. Be all business.

"Negative. It's a miss."

Then he saw the last thing he wanted to see under the circumstances: lights, glaring pale green in the distance, coming toward them. "Contact bearing 340. They're following us . . ." Suddenly plumes of flame erupted in the night. "I think we've got a launch. Yeah . . . we've got incoming."

We're dead. We are so dead. D-E-A-D. God, Raikes is so hot. Dead dead dead.

"Twenty degrees hard starboard! All hands, brace for impact!" said Hopper.

As if they weren't under attack, Nagata was focused on the board, studying the buoy transmissions. But none of that would matter if the enemy missiles struck home. Their only prayer now was that it really had all been happenstance that the stinger was heading in their direction. That the aliens didn't really have any clue as to the location of the *John Paul Jones*. That they were likewise firing blind, and that their luck would be as poor as Nagata's.

Might be seeing you again sooner than either of us would've liked, Stone . . .

They heard the whistle of the incoming missiles. Hopper closed his eyes, braced himself. Everyone else in the CIC did the same, save for Nagata, whose calm gaze never left the monitor.

Then the ship rocked violently, but there hadn't been any impact. It was being caused by geysers of water blasting upward from the starboard side. Hopper's eyes snapped open wide, astonished. Crackling over the walkie-talkie came Ord's ecstatic voice: "That's a miss! I love when they miss!" Then his tone changed back to its typical sense of impending doom. "Sir, they're, uh . . . they're getting closer. Close enough that we should, uh . . . are we planning on firing something, sir?"

Nagata studied the grid, thinking, seemingly impervious to the prospect of impending doom. "FOXTROT 24," he said at last.

Raikes dialed up the coordinates. "FOXTROT 24," she confirmed.

"Fire," said Nagata.

Two more Harpoons exploded from their tubes. Raikes quickly loaded two more in anticipation of having to use them.

Seconds passed, and Hopper was certain that during that time not a single person exhaled.

Suddenly there was the distant sound of explosion, and if they had been up on deck, they would have seen an abrupt and brilliant burst of light upon the horizon. Ord's voice came screaming over the walkie-talkie, *"Holy shit! Hit! Big hit!"* But the celebration was short-lived as, seconds later, Ord shouted, "Sir, they're coming from both directions!!"

"All engines, full stop! Countermeasures!" Hopper immediately ordered.

Instantly the CWIS was employed, and again it was a waiting game to see if the anti-missile system did what it was supposed to do.

It did, but, again, only partly.

The ship rocked, and this time there was no mistaking it was as a result of impact. But Hopper knew immediately that they had averted catastrophe. The CWIS had managed to intercept at least some of the missiles, but apparently not all. They had sustained some damage;

now it was a matter of determining just how much. He grabbed the 1MC—the shipboard public address system—and called out, *"Damage report!"*

It was Beast who responded first. "Sealing the aft magazine. We'll stay afloat." Seconds later other sections of the ship were reporting in, stating that there was no damage.

Okay. That's a relief.

"Captain Nagata, we seem to have multiple targets. Care to do something about that?"

"Hai."

"I take that as a 'yes.'"

Nagata nodded. A moment of mutual respect passed between them. Then it was back to business. Nagata carefully tracked the second stinger. "Target . . . INDIA 37," said Nagata.

"INDIA 37," Raikes repeated. "One more time."

Ord watched with growing enthusiasm and blossoming hope as another Harpoon missile leaped into the night sky, an avenging angel carrying considerable firepower. It streaked through the air, zeroing in on the alien.

The stinger tried to leap out of the way, but the missile caught the port pontoon, ripping through it and sending the ship tumbling back onto the water. It landed with a hellacious splash. The stinger listed in the water, and Ord could hear the engines misfiring, sputtering. It attempted to bound to the right but landed heavily, like a crippled bird.

"That's a hit," he said. "She's dead in the water, about fifty yards to the right of where you hit her."

Seconds later another missile launched from the deck of the *John Paul Jones*. The stinger apparently saw it coming, because it tried to launch one of its own missiles directly at it, hoping to counter it. It failed to do so. The white cylinder tumbled out of the launcher rather than being propelled, and slid into the water. The firing mechanism had obviously been damaged and the stinger was a dead duck.

Except it wasn't. There was a surge of the waves, as if the ocean itself had a bet on the aliens and was trying to prolong the action, that pushed the stinger to one side. An instant later the Harpoon hit the water and sank uselessly beneath the waves.

"Miss. That's a miss. You're 10 degrees right," said Ord.

In the CIC, Hopper nodded at the new information, making his own adjustments to the trajectory. "Second coordinates, ROMEO 36." He nodded toward Raikes and said, "Have a nice day."

Raikes, with a missile ready to go, fired.

Ord watched the third missile track launch. He followed its trajectory, murmuring, "Please, please, come on, please," the entire time as the missile streaked through the air.

This time when it hit the stinger, there was no doubt. The alien vessel erupted in flame, blown apart by the power of the Harpoon. Even more, the second vessel got caught up in the backlash of the inferno and went up as well. Flames blasted upward like a volcano eruption, and cheers rang from all over the deck. *Hit! Sink! Big hit! Big sink!*" Ord shouted into the walkie-talkie, doing an exuberant dance that would have gotten him roundly lampooned by anyone else in the crew under ordinary circumstances. But these were far from ordinary, and all that resulted was several others joined him in his terpsichorean celebration. Through the still-open walkie-talkie, he could hear the sounds of jubilation coming from the CIC as well.

Then he glanced at his watch and he was filled with considerably less joy. The night had fled and the sun would soon be rising. Once there was full visibility, the playing field would be level once more.

And he wasn't convinced, when that happened, they'd be around to see another sunset.

SADDLE RIDGE

"What the hell are they doing?"

Sam had spoken so softly that Cal, who was right next to her, could barely hear her. But her exact wording wasn't necessary; he was able to infer it from context.

The three humans were concealed in the tall, overgrown grass high on a hill that surrounded the Beacon International Project building. They'd gotten there by slithering along on their bellies, moving a foot at a time, stopping, waiting to make sure there was no reaction and then moving again.

Sam supposed it was entirely possible they could have made the approach in the accompaniment of a brass band and it wouldn't have garnered any attention. The aliens seemed far too involved in their work: walking around, engaged in various tasks, none of which Sam understood. She saw, though, that there appeared to be two different types of them, perhaps arranged along some manner of caste system. There was one who appeared to be in charge: the commander. He was taller, his armor a different color from others, who were broader and mostly in-volved in doing the serious grunt work.

Watching their movements, Cal whispered, "They're connecting what I think are the power cells that are going to be required to boost the transmission. They're wiring everything to the satellite dishes."

"Then that," Mick said, "is where we're going to shut this whole thing down."

He crawled forward toward the edge of the hill where the drop-off would take them down toward the building. He brought his shotgun up to bear, aiming it squarely at one of the shorter aliens. Sam was right beside him, and then they were brought up short when they heard loud breathing behind them.

They turned and saw that Cal Zapata hadn't budged. Instead he was busy hyperventilating—or at least very close to doing so.

Mick looked scornfully at him, clearly in no mood to deal with a faint-of-heart scientist. He met Sam's gaze, and she quickly shook her head, silently imploring him to hold up. She didn't see any choice; they needed to peel Cal off the metaphorical ceiling before they could proceed any further, as he was crucial to their overall plans of contacting Hopper's ship. Mick looked like he desperately wanted to ignore her, but then—with clear reluctance and a poisonous glare at Cal—he lowered the shotgun.

They remained where they were as another transport passed overhead, lights glaring. It didn't illuminate their hiding place, fortunately, thanks to an overhanging tree that obscured their presence from overhead. *Must be bringing another power cell,* she thought grimly.

The workroom that was the destination of the three humans was visible from their vantage point, so that was something, at least. But it might as well have been on Mars—or even whatever planet these creatures hailed from—for all that they were going to be able to get near it . . . at least for as long as Cal was proving himself to be completely useless.

The scientist clutched at his chest, trying to steady himself. She prayed he didn't have a heart attack. That was the last thing they needed. They wouldn't be able to seek help for him and would probably have to leave him to his fate. Except she wasn't at all convinced they could possibly do what needed to be done without his scientific acumen. Some part of her was appalled she was measuring the worth of a man's life purely in terms of how it was useful to her, but ultimately she knew she didn't have a choice. At this point all that mattered was the mission.

"I'm sorry, but there is *no way* I'm going down there," Cal finally managed to say. "I do not possess that particular courage."

Sam was determined to talk him into it. There was an entire litany of things she could say. She could tell him that the world was literally counting on them, even though no one knew their names. She could tell him that she was positive he had vast stores of inner determination that could be tapped, enabling him to rise to the occasion. She could remind him that, since it was his project that had brought these creatures here, it was his responsibility to jump into the middle of this thing with both feet. To clean up the mess he and his scientist friends had made. She could even remind him that if he showed timidity now, then in the long term his life wasn't going to matter, since—if they failed to interrupt or, better yet, terminate the aliens' message home—the planet would be overrun and he likely wouldn't *have* a long term *or* a life. So if he wanted a chance of survival, he needed to pull it together right now.

Before she could articulate any of that, however, Mick said between gritted teeth, "You're going to acquire that

particular courage right now, or I'm going to break my
steel leg off in your ass."

Cal absorbed this new information. "Acquiring courage," he said briskly, as if he were downloading it off the
Internet.

Sam realized that out-and-out threatening the guy
hadn't occurred to her. *I've just got to broaden my rep-
ertoire of techniques for dealing with stubborn people.*

They started moving down toward the workstation.

Their stealth served them well. They covered the distance to the simple, square building in a fairly short
amount of time, or at least in as short a time as possible
when one was crawling on one's stomach, propelling
oneself via elbows. Sam had to think she would never
freak out about snakes again, considering they had to
live like this all the time.

They froze at one point, when one of the bulky aliens
walked by. It stopped and stood there for a moment,
seemingly inspecting the air. Sam wondered if it had
somehow caught wind of them, and perhaps was even
about to open fire. But then, seemingly satisfied that it
was alone, it went on about its business. It was all she
could do not to breathe a sigh of relief, which would
most certainly have been audible. Once the alien was
gone, Cal and Sam got to their feet, remaining hunched
over as if that would do them the slightest bit of good,
and ran quickly to the side door of the darkened structure. Mick remained where he was, keeping his weapon
at the ready. If this thing turned into a firefight, he was
definitely prepared for it. Sam even wondered briefly if
he was hoping it would turn out that way, because these
monsters had destroyed a military base and she was sure
that Mick was itching for some payback.

Once inside, Sam continued to stay crouched, keeping
an eye on things. She saw Mick propped on his elbows,
shotgun at the ready. Cal was rooting around in the

work area, which more or less took up the entirety of the building. They didn't dare turn on any lights since that would unquestionably catch the attention of the aliens. Instead Cal was employing a flashlight that they'd taken from the Jeep, but was doing so as judiciously as possible. He kept low to the floor, making sure not to get anywhere near a window that would allow the light to be seen from outside.

And then, as she peered around the corner, she saw the taller alien, the one she took to be the commander, slowly striding their way.

Reflexively she sucked in air sharply between her teeth. The alien didn't hear her, but Cal did, and he froze where he was, near stacks of equipment. Even in the darkness she could see the panic in his eyes. She frantically gestured for him to keep his mouth shut.

The alien stopped a few feet away and slowly removed its helmet, accompanied by a hissing of air. She saw the creature's hideous, inhuman face and bit down on her lower lip not to let out a loud screech. There was no reason for her to be startled at this point. She knew what she was dealing with. Freaking out upon seeing it so close up wasn't going to help matters in the slightest.

It brought some manner of narrow tube to its mouth, closed its eyes and then lit the tube with a blue flame.

Oh, you've gotta be kidding me. Of all the things that these creatures and humanity could have in common, that's where we overlap? On cancer sticks? Really?

Cal had stopped what he was doing so that he could peer out the nearest window as carefully as possible. When he saw what was happening, he scuttled over to Sam and said, practically in her ear, "I do *not* wanna die from secondhand alien smoke."

"One thing at a time," Sam shot back under her breath. "How long is this going to take?"

"I'm on it." Moments later he had gathered coiled

cord and batteries and brought them over to Sam. "I tuck it away for safekeeping."

"You mean, like, in case of an alien invasion?"

"Actually, most of this stuff's for gaming." Leaving it with her, he crawled under a desk that was piled high with hard drives and CD-ROMs, reaching for what looked to Sam like a pretty high-tech-looking box in a corner. He managed to get a grip on it with the fingers of one hand. "Got it."

"Great," said Sam. "Just don't make any noise extracting it."

He endeavored to do as she instructed as he began to pull. This nudged the box forward toward him, close enough that he was able to get a second hand on it. Then, slowly, he began to back out from under the desk, hauling the box a few inches at a time and then moving with greater confidence.

That confidence cost him when his back leg bumped into another desk nearby. It had a towering pile of stuff on it, and the impact from Cal's leg jolted it. Sam tried to lunge toward it, to catch the pile before it fell, but she wasn't even close to getting there in time. The pile tilted, slid and crashed to the floor. Cal whipped around, a look of wide-eyed fear on his face.

The Land Commander finds that he cannot take even the slightest break without being disturbed.

He hears the crash within the nearby human structure. It is as frail and poorly put together as any human shelters are ... indeed, as much as actual humans are. It could easily be falling apart all by itself. Nevertheless, attention must be paid, in the unlikely event that any of the creatures are lurking inside.

He summons two of his subordinates and they approach hastily even as he tosses away his salt stick. They await his orders. He gestures for them to head into the structure, to determine just exactly who or what it was that caused the things inside to fall over.

Each of the soldiers is carrying a cleeb, a bladed instrument that could slice any human in half with the slightest contact. They head toward the structure, their cleebs at the ready. When they approach the structure, the door is shut. Without hesitation the foremost grunt kicks it open and enters with full confidence that nothing inside can possibly pose a serious threat. They are warriors in the service of the Land Commander, and there is nothing they cannot accomplish. Nothing they cannot defeat. Nothing—

—in the room.

The first soldier steps in, the second right behind. They clear the corners, making sure that no one is hiding there.

The rear window. It is hanging open. They move to it and look out.

No sign of anyone.

They report their findings—or lack thereof—to the Land Commander. He considers the information carefully. Which seems the most likely? That some random stack of human leavings tumbled over because of a possible gust of wind, or maybe it had never been properly aligned in the first place and had eventually given way to gravity? Or that some human or humans had braved all manner of threat just to search around in an empty building and had barely managed to escape out the back window before they could be seen?

The answer is self-evident.

He orders the two back to work and resolves to give it no further thought.

Sam had come to think of the area where the first contact had been made—the spot that was now occupied by the overturned Jeeps—as her own personal Ground Zero.

The place where her view of the universe, her understanding of reality itself, had been upended.

Now she and her companions had taken refuge on a hill overlooking it and were doing everything they could to take down the creatures that had performed the actions of total destruction. *God, I show up at someone's place, I come with a bottle of wine, maybe some dessert, and if it's a party, I offer to stay after and help with the cleanup. These guys come a bazillion light-years to our place and the first thing they do is blow shit up. I swear, some people . . .*

Calvin Zapata had worked with surprising speed and confidence—surprising, Sam reasoned, because thus far she had only seen him out of his element. Now that he was operating within his area of expertise, he was all efficiency. He had effortlessly set up the spectrum analyzer and rigged it to batteries. Then he had put on the headphones as if he were crowning himself and, with complete certainty, snapped on the analyzer.

That was where his confidence came to an abrupt end. Needles, dials, readouts—all of it just lay there, unmoving. Dead.

"You doing this right?" said Mick.

Cal shot him an annoyed look and started double-checking the connections.

Speaking as much to herself as anyone else, Sam said softly, "Yesterday my biggest fear was that my dad wouldn't accept my boyfriend. Now . . ." Her voice trailed off and then she looked back at Mick. "You?"

"I thought I couldn't climb a little mountain. Good one?"

Suddenly they both jumped at a nearby surge of sound. Sam automatically thought it was some sort of weapons blaster aimed at them, about to blow her head off. Judging by Mick's expression, he'd probably thought it was the same thing. She relaxed when she realized it was just the analyzer humming to life. Cal looked at them with an expression of smug triumph and then began adjusting the dials. "Oh, I should have mentioned this before," he said in an offhand manner, "but if this works, and we get a good frequency—"

"We'll only have a few seconds to communicate. You already told us," said Sam.

"Yeah, that. But . . ." He was trying to sound casual about it and wasn't being terribly successful. "Also those monsters are pretty much guaranteed to get a lock on our position, too. So we'll only have a few seconds to get out of here."

Sam took in this new information. "I almost wish you hadn't mentioned it."

He shrugged and returned to the spectrum analyzer, fine-tuning the dials so delicately that he seemed like a safecracker trying to discern the combination through subtle clicks of tumblers. Sam mused that, in a way, that's exactly what he was doing: he was trying to crack into a wave band in order to gain access to it.

"Anything?" said Mick.

Cal shook his head and continued to adjust and refine it. The needles and dials were now flitting about, bouncing from one side to the other. And then, all at once, they stopped their twitching and became rock steady, pointing straight up with only the most minute of quivering. As they remained steady, Cal whispered in amazement, "I hear them. I'm listening to aliens communicate."

"What's it sound like?" said Sam.

He pulled a headphone free so they could hear it, too. To Sam, it sounded like a steam wand on a giant cappuccino machine. Apparently it came across that way to Cal as well. "Starbucks," he said.

Great. Thanks to him, now I'm craving a latte.

Mick nudged Cal, who made a final adjustment, getting the patched-together device online with where they needed it to be. Then he took the police radio they'd salvaged from the Jeep, plugged it into the spectrum analyzer and handed the microphone to Sam.

Sam worked to keep herself calm. She needed to be all business. There wasn't time for histrionics or sounding like the frantic girlfriend in one of those horror films.

"*John Paul Jones,* this is an urgent message for the USS *John Paul Jones,* do you read?"

No response was forthcoming. She repeated it again and again, and with utter despair crushing in on her, she heard a familiar voice come with an excited, "*Sam? Sam, is that you?*"

It was Hopper. His voice was static-filled and phasing in and out, but it was most definitely him. "*Sam, what the hell are you doing on the naval emergency channel?*"

She didn't have time for a back and forth. For all she knew the aliens were detecting the transmission. Plus the horizon was beginning to redden—the sun would be coming up soon, making her feel even more exposed. Without even acknowledging him by name, she got right down to business. "Three items. One: these things are here and their immediate goal is the satellite array on Makapu'u Head above the watershed, near Saddle Ridge. Two: at 10:30 a deep-space satellite will orbit by, which they'll use to slingshot a message home. And you can guess what that means."

His voice was still laced with static, but at least she understood him. "*Millions of 'em. Everywhere. What's the third?*"

She paused, and for the first time, she allowed emotion to fill her voice. "You better stop 'em, because we're getting married and they're not invited."

"*Sam! Sam, get out of there! You've got to get out of there! I love—!*"

The static overwhelmed the clarity of the transmission, and Sam winced from the feedback as she removed the headset. "He's gone."

"I know," said Mick, "we could pretty much hear his side of it leaking out of the headset. We better get gone, too."

They rose to their feet. The spectrum analyzer having served its purpose, they left it behind. As they moved quickly away from it, Mick said, "By the way, I'm pretty sure that the last word he was going to say was 'you.'"

"Pretty sure?"

"Well, it might've been 'pizza.' Or 'baseball.' Or maybe 'being a semi-fiancé and we shouldn't make it any more serious than th—'"

"Shut up," she said as they disappeared into the rain forest.

USS REAGAN

Seated behind his desk with a phone to his ear—which was where he felt like it'd been forever—Admiral Shane was starting to have trouble recalling a time when he didn't think he was losing his mind.

I've had meals with this man. Hell, I've golfed with this man. He seemed sane and reasonable all those times. When did he turn into such a flaming asshole? Guess it takes an alien invasion to bring out one's true character.

As Shane's aide, Ensign Chavez, came in with a cup of coffee, Shane tried a different approach. "I'm asking you to reconsider, Mr. Secretary . . ."

"And I'm asking you," came back the Secretary of Defense's voice over the phone, "to keep following orders, something I'd think I shouldn't have to ask. Your orders were to continue trying to find a way through that water obstruction they've tossed up."

"We've *already* lost two planes and a fully manned attack sub trying to do just that—"

"And we're willing to lose more if we must."

Shane's voice was low and flat, an unmistakable tone of *screw you* in his response that not only could he not hide, but he wasn't even trying to. "*Are* we."

There was a pause on the other end. Message sent. Message received. Message rejected. "Just scramble the jets, *Admiral,*" said the Secretary in a way that drew the divide between them in stark relief. "Circle that barrier. Find a hole in it. We need to get in there—"

"*We* need to get in there?" *Calm. Stay calm. He's not one of us, he can't understand, he answers to the President, don't say what you're thinking.* His mind split down the middle, one side listening to the very solid advice being presented by the other side. After listening, the other half of his mind completely ignored the first, and Shane said what he was thinking. "While you sit six thousand miles away, I'm on the enemy front line, with four hundred of my men *and my only daughter* trapped inside that dome! I am far more aware than you of the need to get inside there, but wasting lives *will not help.*" He paused, and heard the Secretary inhaling on the other end, about to speak, but the admiral steamrolled right over him. "You want me to send up another plane? I'll do it the second you come up here and *sit your ass in the copilot seat!*"

He slammed down the phone, killing the uplink. Waves of anger radiated from him, and it was that moment he realized that Chavez was still standing there, waiting to hand him the coffee. In a fit of uncontrolled rage, he snatched the mug from Chavez's hand and threw it with all his strength. It shattered against the wall.

Chavez stared at the mess in shock. Shane looked directly at him, his eyes like twin thunderstorms. Chavez gulped, his Adam's apple bobbing up and down. "I . . . I'll get you another cup."

He got out of there as quickly as he could.

USS *JOHN PAUL JONES*

"Dammit," muttered Hopper as he watched the seemingly random, unpredictable movements of the remaining target.

He was still having trouble processing that somehow Sam had managed to get in touch with him. He'd always known she was resourceful, but this was beyond anything he would have thought she could have cooked up. There had to be someone there with her, out on Saddle Ridge. Maybe someone military. He hoped so. It made him feel a little better knowing that perhaps there was an experienced soldier or Navy man by her side, working to get her the hell out of there . . .

I wonder who it is? Should I be jealous?

Then he pushed such dead-end thoughts out of his mind. This sure as hell wasn't the time for them.

Nagata was right next to him, seeing the same thing that Hopper was when it came to the alien vessel. "They're learning from their mistakes."

Hopper nodded. "We can't hit him. Can't lock a missile on his movement."

"They're smart."

"Yeah, well we're not exactly a bunch of dummies ourselves. If nothing else, we bloodied them up pretty good, so that bought us some time. They're not going to come right after us."

"Too bad," said Nagata. "Recklessness on their part could have worked in our favor."

Hopper hated to admit it, but Nagata was right. *Can't be helped now, though. No sense dwelling on it. We need to focus on what's next, not what was.* "We know a few things," said Hopper. He ticked them off on his fingers. "If you hit them, they come after you. They value their own. So if you kill them, they seem to resent that. Agree?"

"Agree," said Nagata.

"We also know they don't handle light very well, and their ships are not bulletproof. They are hittable."

"Yes, agree."

Hopper considered all of it a moment and then picked up the radio. "CIC to engineering. Beast, give me good news."

"We've shored up the port engine," Beast's voice came back. That alone was enough to prompt a sigh of relief from Hopper. Beast continued, "I can give you 10 knots now and 20 in ten minutes." Then Beast's voice suddenly became fainter and Hopper realized Beast was facing away from the radio on his end, speaking to someone else softly, thinking his voice wasn't being heard. He was saying, "Hiroki, can you give me twenty in ten?" A second later he came back on and said, "Yeah. Definitely twenty in ten."

Hopper smiled at that, but he didn't let his amusement sound in his voice as he said, "I'm holding you to that."

He clicked off the radio and glanced at the monitor. The stinger was showing no sign of slowing its movements. "I don't think this one is going to make the same mistakes."

"No," said Nagata.

His gaze drifted to the island of Oahu. His mind racing, he said, "Let's see if we can take him somewhere he doesn't want to go, and hit him somewhere he doesn't want to be hit." He looked to Nagata for approval, but Nagata just appeared puzzled. This actually pleased Hopper—he was one step ahead of Nagata. This was shaping up to be a good day after all. "Miss Raikes."

"Sir?"

"What time is sunrise?" He exchanged looks with Nagata, and this time it was clear that he was now on Hopper's wavelength. Nagata didn't smile—that would have been too much—but the edges of his mouth actually seemed to twitch ever so slightly.

Raikes, not sure why it was of that much relevance, checked her chronometer. "At 0553," she said briskly.

"Okay." He clicked back on the radio. "CIC to engineering. Beast, you said twenty minutes?"

"Yeah."

"Fine. Meet me on the bridge in twenty-one minutes."

"Aye, sir," came Beast's voice, but he sounded as confused as Raikes.

Moments later Hopper and Nagata were heading up to the bridge at a brisk pace. As they did so, Nagata startled Hopper by saying, "Why?"

"Why what?"

"You are all that your brother was and more. So why do you act as if you were so much less? Why such self-destructive behavior?"

He glanced at Nagata as they walked and then laughed softly. "Do you have any idea how many people have asked me that?"

"Not really, no."

"It was rhetorical." He paused and then said, as they

continued to move, "When Stone and I were kids, I was better than he was at . . . well, lots of things. School. Athletics. Strategic thinking. Everything. And I loved rubbing it in his face, because I was a typically obnoxious kid brother. And one day we were in the woods near our house, playing some game . . . I don't even remember what it was . . . and he just got fed up. He stalked off and I ran after him, shouting and being snide. Suddenly the ground went right out from under me and I fell straight down a hill, which sent me tumbling into a river. Got knocked cold by a branch and the water just started carrying me downstream. I'd've drowned, no question. Next thing I knew, I was waking up in a hospital. Stone had jumped in and swam after me and pulled me out. And what woke me up was my father shouting at Stone. Telling him it was all his fault. That it was his job to watch out for me. And I thought, *Son of a bitch, he saved my stupid life and he's the one getting his ass chewed.* And that was it."

Nagata looked at him, confused. "What was it? That was what?"

"I swore I would never do anything to make Stone look bad again. That he'd be the hero of the family. Because I might have been better at all this stuff that, in the end, doesn't matter . . . but he was the better person. And he deserved to have the world recognize that."

"That is . . . very noble of you."

"Thanks."

"But I would point out that it doesn't explain your obvious rage issues. Your tendency to solve problems with your fists. Your knack for self-destructive behavior."

"What are you getting at?" said Hopper suspiciously.

"Simply that, at some level, you hated the decision you made. That you likely resented your brother for that decision, even though you're the one who made it. You're suffering from misplaced aggression. You really wanted to lash out at your brother or your father, but since you didn't dare, you lashed out at others . . . including me."

"Yeah, well . . . you had it coming."

"Fortunately, you hit like a girl."

Hopper stopped in his tracks and stared at Nagata, who simply stood there with one eyebrow raised.

Then Hopper laughed. Nagata's face never moved a muscle.

Hopper started walking again, Nagata falling in step behind him. "Whatever, man. Hell, the only reason I told you any of this was because we'll probably both be dead by noon anyway."

"That's very comforting."

"'Rage issues.' 'Misplaced aggression.' Jeez. What were you, a psychiatrist before you joined the Navy?"

"No. But my mother's one."

"She is?"

"Don't get me started on my mother," said Nagata. Hopper didn't.

Once on the bridge, Hopper spread out navigation charts on the wide table and started tracing a line from their present location toward the island that was the target of his developing strategy. Nagata stood to one side of the table, Beast on the other.

"When we round this point can you hold her here tight? Just off Diamond Head?" Hopper said to Beast.

Beast studied it and was obviously running calculations through his head. "It ain't gonna be easy. There's an ass crack of a current in there. We get on its bad side, we're gonna need a proctologist to pull us out."

"Then it's elbows and assholes all around." Hopper tapped the link and called up the CIC. "How close is the stinger to us?" he said as soon as he raised Raikes.

"Seven miles and closing fast," her voice came back. She was trying to sound unconcerned, as if an oncoming, swiftly approaching and seriously pissed-off alien vessel was just another day at the office.

Hopper shifted his attention back to Beast. "No kidding around. Can you do it?" asked Hopper.

"I can try," said Beast. "Sir, I don't get it . . ."

I can try wasn't good enough. "*Can* you *do* it?"

Beast wasn't going to promise something he couldn't deliver. He stared at the map, at the area of the current, and he started to mutter a string of numbers. Hopper realized Beast was running engine revolutions through his head, making calculations. Finally he nodded. "I can do it."

Hopper wanted to sigh in relief, but he kept it to himself. Instead, he turned to Nagata. "Captain Nagata, how's your aim?"

Nagata nodded slowly. "Excellent."

Hopper looked back at Beast, who appeared somewhat dubious for some reason. "Problem, Beast?"

"Permission not to be the one who has to tell Raikes that Captain Nagata will be handling guns . . . no offense," he added quickly to Nagata.

"We're going to need her behind the 5-inch," Hopper said. "I have something else planned for Captain Nagata. Now get down to CIC and get us heading in the right direction. Leave the rest to me."

"Yes sir," said Beast.

Nagata watched as Beast headed off. "He is not sure what you have in mind. But he does not question."

"Of course not. That's not his job."

"Yes. His job is to obey you. And your job is to issue those orders."

"Are you telling me my job, Captain Nagata?"

"No," said Nagata mildly. "It is simply a pity that your brother is not able to see you do it."

"Yeah," said Hopper. "Just think. If I hadn't made the

decision I did, it might well have been me on the *Sampson*. And Stone would still be alive."

Nagata studied him and then said, "You are blaming yourself for your brother's death." When Hopper didn't respond, Nagata continued, "That is foolishness. You did not kill your brother." His voice hardened. "*They* killed him. And yes, I will tell you your job now. Your job is to make them all pay. Do not lose sight of that."

"I won't."

"Good. As for your survival . . . I suspect, Alex Hopper, that you would have managed to survive the Great Flood."

"We may yet have the chance to find out."

The human vessel is fleeing.

They are under the impression that they can forestall the inevitable.

They believe that succor is possible elsewhere. They think that the Regents will allow them to flee the field of combat. They are under the impression that they have a say in when, and how, the testing will be ended.

Foolish humans. Only the decisions of the Regents commanders—the Land Commander and the Sea Commander—matter. The test is not over until the Regents say it is over.

How wrong they are. How greatly they will pay for their underestimation of the Regents' resolve.

How utterly they will be destroyed.

The Regent ship is in pursuit. The end for them will come soon.

Diamond Head was a volcanic tuff cone, known to the natives as Le'Ahi, since the shape of its ridgeline was similar to the dorsal fin of an ahi tuna. British sailors had come upon it in the 19th century and, mistaking the calcite in its rocks for diamond, had dubbed it with the name it retained to this day.

The *John Paul Jones* was now making for it with such speed that one might think actual diamonds were waiting for those who could get to it the fastest.

The stinger was in pursuit and closing in as Hopper and Nagata hurriedly assembled a .50 caliber sniper rifle on the ship's bow. Nagata glanced over his shoulder at the alien vessel as it drew nearer. "It's not attempting to close the distance by jumping," he observed.

"Don't you get it?" Hopper said. "They're testing us. Pushing our limits, seeing what we can do. They figure they have us cold, so why not see how fast we can go and how long we can sustain it?"

"Testing us because . . . ?"

"Because they're sending more, like Sam said. That's got to be it. They want to see how much of a challenge we present so that they can be sure to be prepared for it."

"And if we blow them all to hell?"

"Then maybe they'll figure they're overmatched and look for easier pickings, like . . . I don't know, whatever planet the tribbles come from."

Nagata's eyebrows furrowed. "Trib . . . bulls?"

"Never mind. Not important." He adjusted the sights of the sniper scope. "If I'm right, their bridge window is three feet wide. It's inlayed a couple of feet. A 5-inch can't take it out. Still, that doesn't mean Raikes isn't ready to rock."

Nagata nodded and then glanced up at the bridge. Beast was behind the wheel, handling the *John Paul Jones,* as the point of the island loomed closer. "And your engineer is steering . . . why?"

"Because the best man for the job got blown to hell, and Beast's stepping in."

"Ah. Of course. I am . . . sorry."

Hopper's eyes glazed over for a moment. The faces of

all the men who had been killed by these creatures so far floated in front of him. The creatures would pay. They'd pay for all of it. He forcibly shook himself back to the here and now. "Beast and I go back a ways. He always gets me. It's like we share a mind. When you're in this kind of pinpoint situation, that's who you need. Someone with whom you're on the same wavelength."

Beast was grateful that the sea was relatively calm at the moment, considering the slightest surge of the ocean might be something that he couldn't adjust for quickly enough. Tucking the *John Paul Jones* close to the shore behind Diamond Head, he glanced down at Hopper on the foredeck, setting up a second sniper gun.

He looked toward Hiroki, who was standing nearby and watching events unfold with clear apprehension. Hiroki was accustomed to rooting around in the depths of the ship; being up top didn't seem to be wearing well on him.

Beast nodded toward Hopper and said, "Usually I get him. This time . . . not a clue. Is it the same way with you and your CO?"

Hiroki stared at him and shrugged. Not a word.

"Glad we could have this talk," said Beast. "I feel like we've really bonded over it." He glanced toward the horizon and frowned. Light was filtering over the ocean.

The sun had risen.

Beast noticed that the *John Paul Jones* was beginning to drift uncomfortably close to the rocks. If they were lying in wait here for the stinger to show, they couldn't wind up losing their maneuverability—what little they had—by running aground.

Judging by Hiroki's reaction, he was seeing it as well.

"Let's do this," said Beast briskly, and he handled the wheel with the finesse of a concert pianist.

* * *

On the foredeck, Hopper and Nagata were side by side, eyes on scopes, waiting for the stinger to show its ugly face. Without taking his eye off the impending target, Hopper said out the side of his mouth, "How good of a shot?"

"Pardon?"

"Back in CIC. You said your aim was excellent. How good of a shot are you?"

"Ah." Nagata allowed a touch of pride in his normally dispassionate voice. "Champion rifle competition, Natsu Campu."

"Natsu Campu?"

"Correct."

"Natsu Campu?"

"*Correct.*" Clearly Nagata wasn't accustomed to having to repeat himself.

"What is . . . ?" Hopper tried to say it but was having trouble with the enunciation.

"I'm not sure how you say it in English."

"Nutso . . . campus—?"

"Nat . . . su . . . Cam . . . pu."

"You are the champion of . . ." He paused, working on getting it right so that he wouldn't piss off Nagata. ". . . Natsu Campu?"

"Yes." Nagata seemed relieved not to have to say it again. "In Hakone."

He waited for Nagata to further clarify, but the officer said nothing. Finally he couldn't stand it anymore and, taking his eye off the scope, said in irritation, "*What the hell is Natsu Campu?*"

"Natsu Campu! Natsu . . ." He struggled to remember the English equivalent and then his face cleared as it partly came to him. "*Summer* campu!"

"Summer campu?"

"*Hai.* Yes. Correct," said Nagata.

"Summer camp?"

"Yes. The 1991 Champion Summer Camp. Long Rifle." He said it with such pride that it was as if he were telling Hopper about the Olympic gold medal he'd picked up during the biathalon in 2004.

Hopper became aware that he was staring openmouthed at Nagata, and then suddenly he realized from Nagata's reaction that their target had just come into sight. "Remember," he said quickly, the words all in a rush, "we'll have to be both accurate and quick. The first shots will be for punching through the shields. Once that's done, we'll carve them to pieces." He took aim, and his finger tightened on the trigger. "Let's get her done," he said, and he opened fire.

His .50 caliber gun cut loose, as did Nagata's. The rounds ripped into the shields on the stinger's command deck. As expected, he saw the shields flare up, and at first they were able to hold back the weapons fire. But then they began to crack and, within seconds, blew out.

He had a clear view of several of the aliens in the bridge, none of whom were wearing helmets. They threw their arms in front of their faces, their mouths open in what he was sure were screams of pain. They tried to escape the glare of the newly rising sun, like vampires seeking shadow, but there was none to be had. It was flooding every inch of their bridge, blinding them, sending them scrambling for helmets.

Along Waikiki Beach, Hopper noticed that tourists and locals, up and around to watch the sun rise and maybe even catch some waves, were getting way more than they bargained for as they watched a once-in-a-lifetime battle unfolding in front of them, courtesy of the U.S. Navy. *Your tax dollars at work,* he thought with grim amusement as he flashed a quick thumbs-up to Beast.

It wasn't merely a congratulatory gesture. Instead it was the signal Beast had been waiting for. Immediately he radioed down to CIC. "Raikes! Cover target point, alpha with guns and birds."

"Hello, there," Raikes's voice came over the radio, and Beast knew what that meant: She had the stinger in her crosshairs.

Hiroki, with a pair of binoculars, watched one of the aliens fumbling blindly for its helmet. "Hit him!" said Hiroki.

Raikes's gun started firing. So did the guns of the other officers. Every available weapon on the ship was hammering away at the stinger.

The alien vessel tried to come about, but was hit by a broadside of 5-inch shells. It was clear that systems were failing all over the ship. Shields flared once again, trying to keep the ship impervious to attack, but after numerous shots the ordnance was getting through, punching into the ship's shell, ripping the stinger apart. A blast tore apart the supports of one of the stinger's starboard pontoons, ripping out the entire leg. The mortally wounded ship toppled sideways into the water. It started to slide beneath the surface.

"Oh no you don't, you bastard," said Raikes, moving to the missile station. "No quarter asked or given. You don't get away that easy." She targeted the sinking vessel faster than she'd ever targeted anything in her life. "Been saving one for ya," said Raikes, and she fired.

The missile flew straight and true and struck the stinger just before it could disappear beneath the water. It was possible that the ship offered no further threat. It was also possible that it was trying to get away so it could regroup, quickly repair itself somehow and come at them again. Either way it didn't matter, as the missile struck home, blowing the stinger to pieces. The explosion was massive, a gigantic spout of water leaping skyward.

Some of the spray fell upon the bridge, where Beast endeavored to fist bump Hiroki. But the diminutive Japanese officer was so convulsed with joy and excitement that he returned the bump with force that seemed insanely out of proportion to his size. So much so, in fact, that he wound up slamming Beast's fist back into his face, causing the much larger man to stagger and almost fall over.

The civilians on the beach screamed in joy as the ocean water rained down on them, dancing around, shouting, "U.S.A! U.S.A!" It was likely they didn't fully understand everything that was happening. But as far as they were concerned, if a Navy destroyer was blowing some other ship to smithereens, then the other guys were up to no good and were enemies of the United States.

Hopper watched from the foredeck as the stinger burned furiously. Then he turned to Nagata. "What was it again? Mitsubishi?"

"Natsu . . . cam—"

"Right, right. Natsu campu. Are you *kidding* me?" He stuck out a hand. "That's some damn fine shooting, my friend. I give it up to you, Nagata, I really do. I—"

Nagata didn't take his hand. Stirrings of the old animosity began to awaken in Hopper. *Are we back to this? Are we back to dissing each other and—?* Then he realized that Nagata wasn't even looking at him, but instead past him. "Captain," Nagata said slowly, "we have a problem. Something's coming our way."

The time of testing is over, and the Sea Commander is deeply furious. The pilot of the guardian vessel is his hatchling mate . . . was his hatchling mate. He is the best of the best, and now he is gone, thanks to the test subjects.

The Sea Commander will not tolerate this insult. Nor does he see any reason to prolong the encounter. He orders the top bay doors opened and the spheres launched.

That should attend to them.

* * *

Hopper stared at four whirring globes hovering in the distance nearby that strange alien structure, as if determining where to go. "Those things again?"

Ord's eyes widened. "Oh shit."

The globes were heading their way. Whirling blades had extended all over them, spinning away, and they were heading straight toward the *John Paul Jones.*

"Can . . . can the hull withstand those?" Hopper asked Beast.

"Captain, I don't know what those things are, or what the blades are composed of, but if I had to guess, I'd say they're going to shred us."

"Not to mention," Nagata added with his customary sangfroid, "even if the hulls were capable of withstanding the assault—which I suspect they aren't—the crewmen . . ."

Oh my God. "Beast! Get below on damage control! Keep us afloat for as long as you can! Ord . . . just get the hell out of here!" As the two men scrambled to obey, Hopper hit the shipwide PA system and shouted, "Brace! Brace for . . ." He groped for a word and, remembering what Beast had said, shouted, ". . . for shredders!"

Using the defense systems was simply not an option. The shredders were too fast and too small.

The shredders fanned out, two of them coming in from the port side, the other looping around to the starboard. Fore and aft, a coordinated attack, leaving the ship nowhere to move and with no means of defending itself. They tore into the *John Paul Jones,* sliding down the length of her, tearing deep furrows in the metal.

Within the ship, crewmen who had moments earlier heard the captain's warning and said to one another, "What the hell is a shredder?" cried out and jumped back as glistening blades tore through the bulkheads, slicing through the ship like a laser beam. The shredders dug into the *John Paul Jones,* jackals ripping into a crippled lion, tearing up everything they could get near.

On Waikiki Beach, the jubilation from mere moments earlier now seemed nothing but a distant memory. Tourists and natives alike stood there in horror, many of them screaming, but their screams were drowned out by the shrieking of the metal as the shredders tore through it.

The shredders crisscrossed the ship with such elegance that it almost seemed choreographed. Once each of them reached the far end of the vessel, they simply doubled back, creating more gigantic gashes in the hull. The *John Paul Jones* trembled and shuddered under the assault, helpless to return or slow the attack, helpless to do anything except take it for as long as it could. And that wasn't going to be much longer at all.

The Sea Commander watches with silent approval, but also belatedly with just the faintest tinge of regret.

The spheres are not his preferred weapons. Missiles at least provide the prey a sporting chance. An opportunity to use their resourcefulness, to display signs of personal mettle.

Not that they do not deserve death for what they did to the Sea Commander's hatchling mate. No, they most certainly do. But the Sea Commander would far prefer to attend to it himself. To pound the vessel into submission, then have a shuttle bring him over to the boat, have the ship's commander brought before him, whereupon the Sea Commander would crush the life out of the creature himself. He would enjoy looking into its eyes as darkness claimed it.

However, that is an indulgence, and the Sea Commander—much like his other surviving hatchling mate, the Land Commander—does not believe in indulgences. Tests are for results, and wars are to be won. There is no room in that narrow formulation for personal ven-

*dettas, no matter how much satisfaction they may bring
with them.*

Let the spheres take them, then.

It's a more merciful end than they deserve.

Two X-shaped gashes now festooned both sides of the
ship. Explosions rocked her, making it look as if the *John
Paul Jones* was trembling with fear over her impending
demise. She began to list, water pouring in through the
tears in the hull the shredders had ripped into it. The
shredders promptly came back together in midair as if
having a quick conference—baseball players converging
on an invisible mound to decide how to handle the next
batter—and then they descended upon the ship in four
different directions, seeking to wreak havoc upon the
crew itself.

One of the shredders came straight for the bridge. Nagata and Hopper were the only ones remaining upon it,
and they hit the deck as the shredder tore through. The
glass may have been gone from the windows, but the
supports were all there, and the shredder ripped them
apart, sending the upper part of the bridge crashing
down upon the lower. Debris landed all around Hopper.
He twisted and turned, trying to avoid it, and a jagged
piece hit the ground not more than an inch away from
his head. Had he been a half second slower or a fraction
less lucky, the thing would have bisected his skull. Then
again, with debris raining down upon him, it was hard
for him to think of himself as lucky.

Nagata was as buried under debris as Hopper was. He
was struggling to push it off himself, and then Hopper
said in a low, taut voice, barely above a whisper, *"Don't
move! Don't even breathe!"*

Having torn the bridge apart, the shredder was now
hovering above it, slowly drifting right and left. Hopper
was certain it was looking for signs of life and if it found

him and Nagata, it would tear through them with as much ease as it was destroying the ship.

The shredder descended slowly toward him, blades whirring, coming closer and closer. Sweat beaded his forehead and his eyes were fixed on the edges of the blades approaching him. *It doesn't know I'm here . . . it's not sure,* he thought furiously. *If it knew, it would come right at me, finish me off. As long as I don't make any move against it, maybe it can't distinguish me from the rest of the crap around me. Playing dead is the only chance we have, because we're sitting ducks right now. This thing has us cold. So the only shot we've got is to hope it doesn't know we're alive.*

Inch by inch it drew nearer, the steady breeze from the blades wafting in Hopper's face. It came to within less than three inches of him, and he felt sheer, stark terror building inside, seeking release. He kept his teeth clenched against it, suppressing it, and closed his eyes so he wouldn't see the blades descend.

And then, just like that, the shredder was gone.

For a moment he thought it might be some sort of trick. That perhaps it was pulling back to see if anything moved, and once found, it would then attack again. But no. Through the demolished remains of the bridge, he could see it angling down toward his ship. It struck the foredeck and sliced right through it, sounding like a buzz saw, penetrating with ease and heading belowdecks.

Desperately he started trying to work the debris off him. He was at a bad angle, though, with no leverage, and couldn't shove it away. Then he heard a sudden crash to his immediate right and inwardly jumped, afraid the shredders had returned.

Instead he saw Nagata, rising up from the dust and debris, taking only a second to brush at his uniform. Then he moved quickly to Hopper and yanked upward.

With Hopper pushing from underneath, the last of the wreckage was shoved aside.

Quickly Hopper flexed his arms and legs to make sure everything was still functioning properly. Nagata put out a hand and Hopper took it, and Nagata yanked him to his feet. Hopper staggered, coughing, over to the 1MC and punched the button, activating it. It was just about the only thing in the bridge that was still functional.

His heart died within his chest as his voice rang out through the ship: "This is the captain. All hands, abandon ship. Repeat, all hands abandon ship."

Hopper's voice sounded in the bowels of the ship, but it was making little difference to Ord at that moment. He was busy running for his life.

He sprinted down a hallway and the high-pitched whine of the shredder pursuing him was drawing closer and closer. Every second that passed he was sure he could feel the blades about to slice through his spine. He screamed at the top of his lungs as the shredder closed in on him.

And suddenly, as he passed an open hatch, a hand reached out and yanked him through it. It was Raikes. There was desperation etched on her face, but also determination. She was a survivor, and she clearly had no intention of letting the flying puree machines put paid to her or anyone near her.

The shredder reached the end of the corridor, whipped around, and was about to head right back after Ord. Suddenly a massive cascade of water crashed in through the hold. It immediately enveloped the shredder, which was helpless in the grip of the water's crushing force.

Side by side, Raikes and Ord pushed the hatch door forward. Water came roaring up, pounding against it, nearly knocking the two sailors off their feet. But they maintained their footing, shoving with all their strength against the hundreds upon hundreds of pounds of water that were trying to shove the hatch door open. On the verge of being overwhelmed, they pulled desperate strength from somewhere at the last second and managed to slam home the door. Raikes spun the locking mechanism for good measure.

"It's gonna flood all the holds!" shouted Ord.

"Yeah, no shit, Sherlock! What do you think 'abandon ship' means? Come on!"

They ran as fast as they could, trying to find corridors that hadn't been rendered impassable by water or that didn't have shredders maneuvering through them looking for new victims.

Their actions were being mirrored throughout the ship. Sailors were desperately struggling to close hatches against the increasing flooding, yanking their fellows out of danger whenever and wherever they could.

But there were the screams as well. The screams of men and women who were lost to the shredders, or their bodies broken by sheets of water hitting them with the force of jackhammers. The survivors knew that the howls of their lost shipmates would stay with them for the rest of their lives . . . assuming they managed to survive.

Hopper and Nagata were moving through the corridors and passageways, helping the evacuation wherever they could. Everywhere they turned they saw the devastation the shredders had inflicted upon the vessel. The air was slowly becoming thick with smoke from distant fires as explosions rocked the ship. *You'd think the water would put out the damned fires,* Hopper thought grimly.

The worst were the bodies they discovered. Men, women—shipmates—who were destined for a watery grave because there were too many to do anything about.

Hopper's face and uniform were smeared with ashes and blood. Nagata was much the same.

Soon they were up to their ankles in water, and then their shins, and it was rising steadily. They sprinted up the gangways, having done everything they could, seeking higher ground, which wasn't going to remain high for much longer.

More explosions rocked the vessel, and Hopper was thrown against Nagata, who caught and steadied him. The destroyer was shifting under their feet, angling sharply. It was easy to tell which direction by the tilt of the water that was rising below them. "Head to the stern! The stern!" shouted Hopper as the ship began to tip on its bow.

They raced toward the non-existent safety of the upper levels, hauling with them anyone they found.

And suddenly a blast of water roared in from a cross corridor. It knocked Hopper completely off his feet, sweeping him away from Nagata. He had a brief glimpse of Nagata's eyes widening in dismay, his hand reaching for Hopper—not coming close—and then Nagata rapidly receding as the water bore him quickly and furiously down the passageway. Hopper tried to get his feet under him but the swirl of the water knocked him right off them again. He went under, splashing his arms wildly, and suddenly something hauled him upward. His head broke the surface and he looked around wildly.

It was Beast. He'd come in directly behind him, and although the water came up to Hopper's chest, that was less of an issue for Beast, for whom it was barely waist high. *"To hell with this whole 'captain goes down with his ship' thing,"* Beast bellowed over the thunder of the water. *"Come on!"*

Propelled forward by Beast, Hopper was quickly able to get his feet under him. Seconds later they were clambering to the deck. Crewmen were diving off the rails, plummeting to the water. And it wasn't all that far below, because the ship was going down fast. There was an ear-splitting roar of metal that evoked the noises that dinosaurs must have made when sinking into tarpits. Seconds later the super-structure of the ship collapsed.

"Go! Go!" Hopper shouted, and Beast leaped clear. Hopper had lost track of Nagata, and hoped the Japanese officer was already out of harm's away, or as much out of it as he could be under the circumstances. Hopper was about to jump clear as well, but he couldn't bring himself to do it, despite Beast's admonition. Instead he stared up, and he saw, in the distance, the alien tower sitting far off in the water. The thing that must have launched the shredders and was now watching Hopper's first command disappear beneath the waves.

And as the *John Paul Jones* fell out from under his feet, he screamed up at the structure, shaking his fists in impotent fury. *"You . . . you son of a bitch! You sunk my—!"*

He didn't have time to complete the sentence as Nagata came to him out of nowhere and shoved him clear of the ship. Hopper's arms pinwheeled as he fell and then he hit the water. He went under, then kicked his feet, fighting his way to the surface. Seconds later Nagata was by his side, and he was shouting, *"We need to get clear of the propellers or—"*

"I know! I know!" If they weren't clear of the ship when it went down, either the vortex created by its sinking could pull them down, or the massive wave caused by the water displacement could swamp them.

They swam as hard as they could, cutting through the water furiously. The *John Paul Jones* bobbed a few more seconds, as if trying to buy them time with its last moments and then slowly—as was inevitable—the destroyer descended beneath the surface of the water.

Alex Hopper's first command ended the way it had started: with death, tragedy and violence. And there was no guarantee any of that was going to abate anytime soon.

The Sea Commander monitors the transmissions that are coming in from all over the globe. The humans, of course, do not have the instrumentation to penetrate the watery dome that seals them in, but that does not present a problem for the Regents. What does present a problem, however, is the human's language. It is painful for the commander to have to listen to. So, as he scans the transmissions, he kills the volume and listens solely to the translation provided by his instruments.

There is someone whose primary job seems to be imparting information: "Scientists have confirmed that there was a UFO landing in the Pacific Ocean off the coast of Hawaii. We still have no communication with anyone in Hawaii. The aliens have set up a barrier around the islands, which is preventing anyone or anything from getting in or out."

There is someone who purports to be a man of science, or at least as close to science as these primitive creatures can command: "For years we have been sending out radio signals in the hopes of making contact with intelligent life."

There is someone who appears to be some manner of leader. "Today I want to update the American people on what we know about the situation in Hawaii. First, we are bringing all available resources to bear to closely monitor the situation, and to protect American citizens who may be in harm's way . . ."

There are more and more of the talking heads, an endless array of them, it seems. Why there cannot simply be one talking head, the Sea Commander cannot begin to understand.

"International efforts continue as the crisis in Hawaii grips the world."

"*Governments search for solutions as time appears to be running out.*"

"*Scientists now believe that invading forces are attempting to use the satellite transmission capabilities on Oahu, and with less than one hour before transmission becomes possible, all hope remains with the three Navy warships on the inside.*"

The Sea Commander finds this quite entertaining since he is aware that the three Navy warships are, in fact, now zero Navy warships.

SADDLE RIDGE

This wasn't supposed to happen. This isn't how it all turns out.

Sam had conjured the final scenario in her head, the way the world was going to be saved. In the movie that was unspooling in her mind, of which she was now a part, she was convinced that she and her valiant companions were going to find themselves in a position to put an end to the alien invaders' plan . . . and they'd do so with the help of—and in a perfectly coordinated attack with—Hopper and the intrepid crew of the *John Paul Jones*.

Now, as she, Mick and Cal stood on a ridge with a clear view down to Waikiki, she watched in mute horror as—far in the distance—the last remains of the destroyer sank beneath the waves. She saw men, small as dots from her vantage point, bobbing in the water, trying to get to shore. She was suddenly aware that Mick was pressing up against her, and for a moment thought it was presumptuous of him to try to take advantage of the situation—right up until she realized that in fact her legs had given way and Mick had stepped in to keep her upright. Cal was coming in on the other side, also lending support.

"Hopper," she managed to say.

Cal patted her arm. "I'm sorry."

Seized with rage, none of which was directed at the men who were supporting her, Sam pulled away from both of them and stood there, on her own, staring at the place where a ship of the line had once been and now wasn't.

Mick had pulled out a pair of binoculars and was studying the scene more closely. "Don't give up hope. There are lifeboats deployed."

She knew there had been, and nodded. She knew there was still hope; it just seemed to be growing fainter by the moment. "The *John Paul Jones* can't stop those things from sending their message now," she said. She and Mick traded looks.

"You know what that means," said Mick.

She nodded.

Cal stared at the two of them as they started moving back to the Jeep. They paused when they realized he wasn't following them, and Mick gestured impatiently for him to climb on board.

"You're getting that weird violent look again," said Cal. "I don't like that look."

Sam could not have given a damn at that moment about what looks Cal liked or didn't like. Obviously Mick was of the same mind, as he said to Cal, "You said that satellite only orbits by once every twenty-four hours."

"Right."

"So if they miss it, they have to wait," said Mick.

Cal frowned, thought about it, then shrugged. "I suppose."

"Then we're gonna go try and buy the world another day," said Mick. Sam nodded in agreement.

They got into the Jeep, and then Cal stopped where he was. "You're planning to attack them directly, aren't you."

"That's the plan, Einstein. Now come on . . ."

And slowly Cal shook his head. "I can't," he whispered, and he was trembling. "I'm not like you. I'm not heroic. I'm . . . I'm sorry."

"Get in the damned Jeep, Doc. I'm not kidding around."

"Neither am I."

Sam just looked at him with a combination of anger and disappointment, and said, "We don't have time for this." Before Mick could get out of the Jeep and go after Cal, Sam had gunned the engine and taken off.

Calvin Zapata stood there and watched them drive away, left alone with his cowardice.

PEARL HARBOR

The small fleet of RHIBs, carting the last remaining survivors of the doomed *John Paul Jones,* glided across the water, a deathly silence having descended upon them like a blanket. In every direction Hopper looked as he sat in the prow of an RHIB, he saw on the faces of his men a sense of crushing defeat. Every crewman was suffering in his own personal hell, knowing they had failed, that the world was lost . . . because of them.

There was every temptation for Hopper to join them.

No one would blame him. He'd gotten some licks in, he'd taken out those stinger vessels. He'd simply been overwhelmed by a weapon he could not possibly have defeated.

He'd done his best, but it wasn't enough.

Except he refused to accept that.

He stared resolutely at the horizon, eyes flinty, his mind racing. "No," he said firmly. "It doesn't end like this."

Nagata was in the small ship with him. There was skepticism in his eyes, the same look of defeat that was reflected in the faces of everyone else in view. "What do you want us to do, Hopper? Ram them with the inflatables? We have no ships left!"

Slowly Hopper shook his head. "We have one."

"One what?"

As the RHIBs came into the harbor, Hopper pointed straight ahead. "We have a battleship."

Nagata still looked confused. "What? You mean behind the *Missouri?*" It took him a few more moments to realize what Hopper meant, and when he did, all of his usual reserve dissipated. "Are you *crazy?* That's . . ." He gestured toward the ancient vessel that was permanently moored in Pearl Harbor. "That's a museum!"

"Not today," said Hopper.

Minutes later Hopper and his command crew were striding across the deck of the antiquated battleship. The rest of the survivors from the *John Paul Jones*—the ones who weren't in immediate need of medical attention—were spreading out, looking around the vessel with the same sense of wonder that one might have seen from wide-eyed tour groups. They'd seen it all before, of course, but never with the notion of it being sent into combat.

"This ship is seventy years old," Beast was saying. "It's completely outdated." He started ticking off the problems on his fingers. "The firing systems are all analog.

The engines probably haven't been started in a decade, which would be fine, but they're *steam,* which I have no idea how to fire up. And even if you did have a user's manual and gave me six weeks to go through it all, we still don't have enough crew to physically run the damn thing!"

"I already thought of that," said Hopper. "Stone brought me here to visit once, back when I first enlisted. I've stopped by every so often, talked with them. Great guys. There're experienced hands ready to serve; more than enough to fill our needs."

"What are you talking ab—?"

But Hopper had stopped walking, and was now pointing ahead of them. Beast, Raikes, Ord and several others stared where he was indicating, and it was all they could do not to laugh. Then, faced with the seriousness of their situation, not laughing suddenly became quite easy.

An assortment of old salts—Navy men who were actually more ancient than the ship whose deck they were striding across—were approaching them. They were grizzled, and they weren't moving particularly quickly. But they walked with their heads held high, distinct pride and—of all things—an attitude of certainty that, now that they'd been called in, everything was going to work out just fine.

There was one who seemed to be the natural leader. Tall, angular, with a square jaw and quiet blue eyes, he strode up to Hopper and straightened his back. "Captain," he said, and saluted. "Saw you fight those bastards. Hell of a thing. Sorry about your boat."

Hopper nodded. "Schmidt, isn't it?"

The old salt nodded. "Lieutenant J. G. Schmidt, yes sir. That was a long time ago, though. 'Andy' will do for an old man."

"Well, Andy, everything old is new again." His gaze

took in all the elderly sailors who were waiting to hear what he had to say. "You men have given so much for your country over the years. No one has the right to ask any more of you. But I *am* asking."

"When we saw what was happening," Andy said slowly, in a rough voice, "we said 'not again.' Not in our lifetimes." His eyes were haunted; he seemed to be looking inward to images that he had witnessed decades earlier, on that terrible day in 1941, images seared into his mind that could never be erased. Then his eyes hardened to steel. "What do you need, sir?"

"I need to make this ship ready for war."

Andy grinned. "War we can do."

Hopper's crew moved with renewed energy, prepping the *Missouri* for action. Some of them were muttering about how ridiculous this whole venture was, but invariably they'd wind up saying it within range of one of the old salts, whose collective hearing was apparently still pretty sharp. As a consequence the reluctant sailors would be on the receiving end of a sound *thwap* to the head and a growled, "Show some respect, sonny," from whichever of the elderly sailors happened to be within earshot.

Everything that smacked of either tourism or the ship being a museum piece was quickly scuttled or tossed overboard. Down came the large banner that read, *"USS Mighty Mo Museum,"* accompanied by a loud ripping noise that garnered some cheering from the old sailors. Hopper spotted, with amusement, one old sailor sweeping his arm across a shelf full of merchandise, knocking it all to the deck and then kicking it off the edge of the ship. A particularly joyous moment was when Beast, Ord and several of the old salts combined their efforts to heft a six-hundred-pound "Mold-a-Rama" wax machine, a particularly cheesy device that—for a buck—would produce a small wax replica of the *Missouri* while you waited. Kids loved it, and the old salts hated it particularly with a passion. For some reason it struck them as the ultimate trivialization of a once proud fighting vessel. Andy seemed especially enthusiastic about lending a shoulder to the endeavor. Slowly they hoisted it up over the deck. They grunted and shoved and for a few moments it seemed as if the machine was going to win the battle and thud back onto the ship. But then the momentum shifted to them and seconds later the wax machine tumbled down, crashed into the dock and shattered.

"Wax on, wax off!" shouted Beast as the old salts and he high-fived one another.

Andy started chanting, "Way to go, Mighty Mo! Way to go, Mighty Mo!" The rhythmic cheer caught on and soon all the elderly sailors were saying it, too.

Beast turned to Ord, chucked a thumb at Andy, and said, "Check it out. The rhyme of the Ancient Mariners!"

Ord stared at him. "The what now?"

Beast closed his eyes in annoyance. "Just get your ass up to the control room, okay?"

"Fine. Uh . . ." He glanced around. "Never actually been on a battleship, much less one this old. Where—?"

Overhearing the exchange, Andy called, "Segar! Bring the young man up to the control center!"

"Right this way, young feller."

Ord turned and saw what appeared to him to be the oldest man on the planet. Segar's eyes were set in what seemed a permanent squint, and his face was all jowl and bristle, with his head thrust forward defiantly on a thin neck. He was wearing white ducks and a short-sleeved blue shirt that had the *Missouri*'s name emblazoned above the right breast. His forearms were incredibly well muscled, given his age.

"You're a sailor?" said an astounded Ord.

"D'ja think I'm a cowboy?" said Segar. He gestured for Ord to follow him and then moved with surprising speed. He didn't walk so much as he waddled with long strides. Ord hustled after him.

Segar brought him straightaway to the control room, which was blocked off by cordons meant to keep tourists out. Without hesitation Ord picked up the wooden barriers and chucked them aside. Then he entered the room, Segar right behind him, and stopped dead in his tracks.

Where there ordinarily would have been a computer array, Ord was faced with what seemed to be ten thousand analog dials.

He stared at them, not knowing where to begin. Then he said hopefully, "Is there, like, a mouse or something?"

"Nope," said Segar, shaking his head. "Used to be, but we got cats on board, so that ain't a problem. Which is good 'cause sometimes the little buggers could get up inside there and start buildin' nests. Screws up all the readings."

Ord stared at him. "Riiiiight."

Meanwhile another old salt, named Grumby—rotund and with a hearty laugh—had accompanied Beast down to the engine room. Beast stopped in awe, having much the same reaction as Ord had up in command. Massive boilers loomed over him like iron sentinels. He didn't even know where to start, and looked to Grumby in bewilderment.

The old man laughed. "Step aside, son." He reached into his pocket and pulled out a book of matches. He lit one and then held it up in Beast's face as if he were about to perform a magic trick. Then he tossed it to one side. It sailed through the air like a tiny shooting star and landed inside one of the boiler's pilot burners. "Here there be dragons," he said solemnly.

An instant later Beast understood what he meant as, with a massive roar of flame—as if indeed belched up from the mouth of one of those mythic reptiles—the oil that was deep within the bowels of the boiler ignited. "Best hold your ears," Grumby advised him. Beast clapped his hands over his ears, although he noticed that Grumby was not doing likewise. Instead the old man was manipulating a complex array of dials, firing up the engine, which gave off a hellacious roar that was quite simply the loudest thing Beast had ever heard. Yet Grumby wasn't flinching from the racket, which led Beast to conclude that years spent down in this cacophony had probably made the old man partly, if not mostly, deaf.

Grumby shouted over the noise, *"Like a kitten!"*

And Beast thought, *Right, purring like a kitten. A thousand-pound kitten.*

Hopper arrived at the helm, Nagata right behind him. A sailor named Driscoll was there waiting for them. Driscoll had narrow, canny eyes beneath bushy white eyebrows, and carried with him an air of adventure, as if he were a sailor on a quest to hunt down some great, legendary monster.

There was a sense of majesty in the room. Heroes in a great war had tread here, and—in a sense of ironic turnaround—had done so in battling the very people from whom the man at Hopper's side had descended. *Funny how enemies can become friends,* Hopper thought, and wondered briefly if that meant someday the aliens now trying to annihilate them would eventually be allies.

Then he remembered the explosive death of his brother and hoped he wouldn't be alive to see it. He didn't want to live in a world where he had to be best pals with the monsters that had killed Stone. If that made him some sort of racist, if that was shortsighted of him . . . fine. He was really okay with that.

"How we looking on fuel?" he asked Driscoll.

"Six hundred tons, sir. Just enough for maintenance runs."

"Ordnance?"

"Scraped what we could from storage. It ain't much."

He nodded and then said, "Cast us off, sailor. Set course for Saddle Ridge."

Driscoll ran off to carry out the orders. As the combined crew of young men and old salts made final preparations for the ship to depart, Hopper—as he walked around the helm, running his fingertips along it with reverence—said, "You got kids, Nagata?"

"Children, yes. Three. I have three girls."

"Three girls." Hopper whistled softly.

"I am hoping to try for a boy, but my wife . . . she only makes girls." There was something in his voice that sounded like a trace of humor, although with him, it wasn't easy to be sure.

"Girls aren't so bad."

"They are my angels," he said softly. "Do you have children, Mr. Hopper?"

It seemed to Hopper that the time for formality was long gone. "Alex. Please . . . call me Alex."

"Children?"

"Not yet. But I'm going to. And I'll tell you something, Captain Nagata."

"Tell me what?"

"I can't wait to put my arms around that little guy and give him the biggest hug that he's ever gonna have in his life. Don't think I'll ever let go." He sighed, his expression changing, and then patted the bulkhead. "Let's just see how mighty she is."

Minutes later, everyone on the ship was at their stations aboard the vessel that had the unenviable task of being the last, best hope of the human race. Hopper, standing up on the flying bridge, picked up the PA and clicked it on.

"I'm not good with words," he said, his voice echoing

throughout the entirety of the ship. "So let me just give you a fact. World War II ended on this ship. The Japanese Instrument of Surrender was signed on the very deck you stand on." He paused, glancing at Nagata, who was standing next to him. *No offense*, he mouthed to Nagata. *None taken*, Nagata mouthed back.

Hopper continued: "I don't think that's a coincidence. This old girl ended one war. We do our jobs today, and she'll see to it we end another . . . and just maybe save the world in the bargain. My . . ." He hesitated, trying not to choke up. "My brother always said the same words to his men before a mission. Since he's not here, I'm saying them to you: Be safe out there. Look out for one another. *And let's keep chargin'*.

"Mr. Ord . . . take us out."

"Aye, Captain."

There was a slight lurch, and a groan, and for a second Hopper was worried that someone had forgotten to clear the last of the moorings and the ship was going to rip out the dock in its departure. But then the Mighty Mo eased from its resting place like a coma patient waking after a decades-long slumber. She slid into the water, the propellers picking up power and speed, and a raucous series of cheers went up from all over the deck. Hopper even fancied that he could hear the cheering from deep within the bowels of the ship.

Nagata cleared his throat to get Hopper's attention. Hopper turned to him, his face a question. With his customary calm, Nagata reached toward a switch, the purpose of which Hopper didn't know, and flipped it once.

The song "Anchors Aweigh" blared through the speakers, not only setting off a rousing cheer, but also prompting many of the men to start singing along.

"Nice touch," said Hopper. Nagata bowed slightly. Then Hopper noticed that a number of Nagata's men were also singing the song, but in their native tongue.

"Man, you have *got to* teach me how to sing it in Japanese."

"I'd rather not."

"Why?"

"Because at some point in the future, you'll attempt to sing it in front of one of my superiors. He will demand to know who is responsible for your butchering our language, and I will be obliged to commit ritual suicide."

Hopper stared at him. "You're kidding."

"Do you want to take that chance?" he said solemnly. After considering it, Hopper shook his head. "Wouldn't be fair to your unborn son."

"Hai," said Nagata gravely.

Driscoll was on the flying bridge with them, and he said, "If you don't mind my asking, Skipper . . . what's the plan?"

"Here's the deal, Driscoll: the enemy doesn't seem to register us as a threat so long as we don't do anything threatening. With me so far?"

"Yessir."

"Okay. So for all any of them knows, we're just going on a nice little pleasure cruise to Saddle Ridge, which my . . ."

Girlfriend? That's gonna sound good.

". . . my away team has informed me is Ground Zero for the aliens' transmission tower. We blow it to hell and that way they won't be able to get word to what we believe is the rest of their invasion party, waiting for the 'go' order."

"I see. Got it." Driscoll moved his chin around as if he were chewing on something, and then said, "And just out of curiosity, once we show we're not just a heavily armed cruise ship out for a jaunt, what happens then?"

"Very likely all hell breaks loose. But we'll have bought our planet valuable time. These creatures aren't invulnerable, Driscoll. They can be hurt, they can be killed and they can be blown the shit out of. I'm not sure what the hell is keeping the rest of our fleet at bay, but once the aliens are facing the combined armed might of Earth, nothing," and Hopper, repeating it with pride, "*nothing can stand in our way.*"

"Captain, there's something standing in our way."

At first Hopper thought Ord was just trying to be funny, but then he saw where the sailor was pointing.

The alien structure that the stingers had been guarding was now blocking their path, as if it had anticipated what direction they were going. It looked the same as it did before: a strange, central body, jagged angles and industrial panels, weird shapes of unknown composition.

Hopper fought to keep his voice casual, as if he were observing some minor weather event that hadn't been in the morning report. "I didn't know that one moved."

Ord said apprehensively, "I got a super-duper bad feeling about this."

So did Hopper.

The Sea Commander activates the morphing circuits through the command ship. It begins to charge with energy, its surface pulsing, its five segments extending to reveal their full fierceness.

Now the humans will experience the consequences of their actions. Now they will see the full power and potency of the Regents.

And it will be the last thing they ever see.

Everyone watched in shock as what was now clearly a vessel—probably the flagship of the alien fleet—began to rise upward, water cascading off ragged metal, splashing white as it poured out of armored sheathing, revealing itself in sections: teethed and buck-knifed with jagged segments that slowly unfolded into five identical pieces of malevolent construction: twelve hundred feet of gritty, industrial danger.

There was deathly silence throughout the *Missouri.*

It was Ord who broke it as, in a very soft voice filled with barely controlled panic, he said, "We're gonna need a bigger boat."

SADDLE RIDGE

The Land Commander is satisfied with the way in which matters are proceeding, even as he fights his frustration over the manner in which he must work.

He surveys the readiness of the power cells, all of which appear to be running at full capacity. He nods in approval as he appraises the various displays and vertical satellites, the human technology that they have cannibalized for their own purposes. He supposes that there is a certain irony to utilizing the very equipment that summoned them in their campaign against the current residents of this ball of dirt and water.

Yet it appalls him that it should be necessary.

He cannot help but dwell on his meeting with the World Commander. That smug bastard, looking down at him with such arrogance, making decisions about how they were to proceed based upon his understanding of how such matters were supposed *to proceed. All of it theoretical, none of it taken from actual firsthand experience. The World Commander, sitting there safe and sound in his so-called "strategic center" back home, sent in troops as if*

Regents' lives mean nothing to him. Let's see him at the helm of a combat vessel being dispatched into a war zone and see how he likes it.

And crippling their resources while he was at it? The unadulterated nerve of him. If the landing teams had had the redundancy equipment that they'd asked for, it wouldn't have mattered that one of their arrays had been destroyed during the unfortunate mishap upon landing—there would have been backup resources. Instead the World Commander dares to talk of how the Regents are spread thin throughout the galaxy. He talks of how—rather than providing the landing troops with all that they could possibly require so as to enable the invasion to run smoothly and flawlessly—they are to take only what they need and make use of found materials upon the target world should there be problems. What sort of nonsense is that? How are they supposed to eradicate the humans with minimal difficulties if the World Commander hampers them? Who sends troops into a war situation without properly outfitting them? Even the humans likely wouldn't do something so stupid, and they're primitives.

It prompts the Land Commander to wonder if politics are not being played here. If the World Commander doesn't have priorities and agendas of his own that are being pursued. Once this operation is completed, it might well be worth the Land Commander's time to join forces with his hatchling mate, the Sea Commander, and see about having done with the World Commander once and for all. A seemingly unthinkable notion, but still . . . worth considering.

That is when the Land Commander hears an unexpected noise. It is a loud roaring; not living, but mechanical. His best guess is that it sounds like the sort of noise made by an engine propelling a primitive human vehicle, similar to those vehicles that they destroyed upon first making landfall. So it couldn't be one of those . . .

Wait . . .

The Land Commander suddenly tries to recall. Did he wind up actually destroying all of those vehicles? Or did he leave one in working order because he got distracted with dismembering the humans, the first of the species he'd had a chance to inspect close up?

His answer arrives seconds later as one of the vehicles tears into view. The humans—two of them, sitting in the front—are shouting loudly, their words incoherent but their intentions clear.

The vehicle's wheels churn up dirt beneath them as it heads full bore straight at them. Its speed and solid construction are proving to be a formidable combination as the Land Commander's troops are knocked aside by the vehicle's velocity. Before the Land Commander can intercede, before he can even target them, the creatures hurtle directly between two power cells, ripping cables loose. The power cells go dark. The vehicle continues on its path of destruction, heading directly for the main dish array.

If it had been constructed solely of solid Regents materials, it would be impervious. But thanks to the damned World Commander, it is a hodgepodge of Regents technology combined with more breakable Earth tech. That proves the sort of devastating problem that the Land Commander had anticipated, but had been unable to convince the World Commander to take precautions for.

One of his warriors comes running out of nowhere, his helmet off, clearly having been in the midst of a salt stick break and not having had time to reattach it. He attempts to get in between, and then the vehicle crashes directly into him, pinning the soldier to the base of the makeshift tower. The impact crumbles the front end of the vehicle, beams and debris tumbling down upon it.

The Regents-provided components of the antennae,

deprived of power from the cells, begin to wilt. They slump forward and are now angled toward the ground, rather than the sky for which they are designed.

The Land Commander cries out a trill of alarm. He ignores the humans in the vehicle—they will be dealt with soon enough. Instead he struggles to repair the ripped cables. If he does not . . .

. . . the alternative is simply too horrible to contemplate.

U.S.S. MISSOURI

"Permission to panic, sir," said Ord as the gigantic flagship loomed before them. Under the circumstances, for Ord, that was a fairly restrained response. It was likely that he was trying to do the same thing Hopper was at that moment: fight down an overwhelming sense of despair.

"Denied."

"Permission to ignore denial, sir."

"Shut up, Ord. Stay focused."

"With all respect, sir, I am focused, because there's really nothing else to look at. Sir, we've got to turn around!"

"No time," said Hopper curtly. "We have to get to the Ridge."

Technically Nagata was the senior officer. He would have been within his rights to assume command of the situation, although considering it was a U.S. ship, it might have been debatable. As it was, the subject didn't even present itself. Nagata simply turned to Hopper and said, "What are we going to do?"

"Their launchers are going hot!" Raikes informed him from the firing controls.

Sure enough, two massive launchers had clicked into position upon the alien flagship. Hopper could discern from the shape of them that they were packed to the gills with those same white cylinders that had both sank Nagata's ship and utterly destroyed Stone's.

The voices of his people were coming at Hopper fast and furious over the 1MC, so quickly that who was actually speaking seemed to blur together. "How do we respond, sir?" "We're a sitting duck here, sir!" "We're gonna be swimming in a minute!" "Sir!" "Hopper!"

Hopper felt as if he were outside his own body, watching the rest of the world telescope away until he was alone, isolated, focused. Time slowed down and the entirety of all his experiences—everything he'd learned, everything he'd read—was laid out right there in front of him like a pure white corridor of understanding, waiting for him to pluck out some strategy that would save them all, something that the aliens couldn't possibly see coming, because they were rigid and binary in their way of thinking, while the human understanding of war was . . .

"Holy shit," he whispered, and then practically shouted, *"The Art of freakin' War!"*

"What?" Nagata was clearly bewildered. "What are you talking about?"

Hopper ignored the question. *"Battle stations, people!"*

As the klaxon sounded throughout the battleship, Ord turned to Nagata. "Did he say, *'The Art of War'*?"

"*Hai.* That scares me."

"Why?"

"Because he doesn't understand a word of it."

* * *

Hopper, his eyes wild with the fire of inner vision, continued on his seemingly hopeless quest to get to Saddle Ridge, shouting orders as quickly as he could. "Beast, all engines ahead full! Ord, come to course one-two-zero."

"That's right at it, sir!" said Ord, suddenly recalling the berserk Hopper sending the *John Paul Jones* on a collision course with the stinger. "We're engaging head-on?"

"We ain't buying it flowers, Ord. Fire control, weapons status?"

Raikes's voice filtered through. "All turrets up and ready to send some hell downrange, sir."

"Hold your fire. We don't have enough ammo. We can't afford to waste a single shot." Hopper paused a moment, considering, and then said, "Bring all three turrets to two-three-zero degrees."

Raikes sounded puzzled. "The target's at *one-two*-zero."

"I know."

"But sir," she pressed, "that's the wrong direction . . ."

"That's an order, Raikes."

On the deck below, the crewmen watched in complete shock as the primary offensive weapons of the ships— the three turret towers with the 16-inch guns—rotated to face away from the enemy. The flagship was looming like a vengeful steel god, and the *Missouri* was speeding toward it with its three 16-inch turrets pointed 180 degrees in the wrong direction. It was as if they were inviting the enemy to take a free shot. There were confused cries from the old salts:

"He's gonna get us killed!"

"Has he lost his mind!"

Only Andy appeared sanguine. "Shut up, the lot of ya. We lived this long and every damned day's a gift. Men like us ain't born to die in our beds. 'Sides, I like the cut of that young man's jib," and he indicated Hopper, visible through the windows of the flight bridge. "He's got a trick or two up his sleeve."

"Hope you're right," said Grumby.

"'Course I'm right. My lips are movin', ain't they?"

On the bridge, Nagata grabbed Hopper by the shoulders and turned him so their eyes were locked. "Hopper . . . do you know what you're doing?"

"God, I hope so," said Hopper. Then he pulled away from Nagata and continued rattling off orders. "Hard left rudder! Port engine back full! Beast, squeeze those engines! I need everything you've got!"

"Hopper, what the hell—?" said Nagata.

"Watch," said Hopper, and he pointed at the array of cylinders on the flagship that were bristling and ready to cut loose. "The aliens are all about predictability. About what's known. They haven't been fighting us. They've been putting us through our paces. Studying what we do now so they know what we'll do next."

"I still don't see . . ."

"We're cutting hard to port. Right now, whatever targeting systems they have, I'm betting they're calculating the physics and predicting where we're heading. I'm betting they're about to turn clockwise in order to intercept where they think we're about to be . . ."

"You keep saying you're 'betting.' You realize our lives are the chips on—"

"*There! There it goes!*" Hopper pointed in excitement.

Sure enough, the flagship was turning, its missile launchers swiveling and adjusting not to where the *Missouri* was, but to where it anticipated the battleship's current trajectory would take it.

And then, just when it seemed to his officers that Hopper knew what he was doing, he issued an order that convinced them he'd lost his mind all over again.

"Drop port anchor!"

"What?" said Nagata.

"Do it! Now!"

The old salts on the decks turned in astonishment at a loud splash, followed by a clanking sound that was wholly unanticipated. They ran to the port side to verify with their eyes what their ears were telling them was happening.

Sure enough, the ten-ton port anchor had dropped into the water and was now dragging the gargantuan chain behind it, each link weighing over two hundred pounds, like a gargantuan fishing line being dragged out. The sound of the anchor chain playing out over the gunwale was deafening, and confused and panicked looks went between almost all the old salts.

All but Andy. He calmly lit up a pipe and chuckled softly to himself, a high-pitched, nasal laugh.

Then he noticed that the sky was suddenly filled with white cylinders hurtling toward them gracefully. They were actually kind of pretty if you didn't think of them as harbingers of doom.

Which Andy didn't.

Instead he said under his breath, "Idjits. Wait and see." And he gripped the rail tightly with both hands.

Ord watched with horror as the fusillade of white death angled toward them. "Oh my God . . . oh my God . . . we're gonna die."

"You're right, Ord," said Hopper. "You *are* gonna die."

Ord's head whipped around as he stared with a look of pure betrayal at Hopper. "What?"

Hopper turned to Driscoll as the cylinders drew closer, closer. "You're gonna die, too." He pointed to Nagata. "And you. And even I'm gonna die. You hear me? We're all going to die!" And then, with a fiery end almost upon them, he shouted, *"But not today! Now hold on to something!"*

And at that exact moment, the *Missouri* was suddenly yanked hard to port.

Andy watched with tremendous amusement as everyone on the deck but him was sent staggering, tumbling, falling all over one another. With his firm grip on the railing, he was secure, and he bellowed over the crew's shouts and the roaring of the water, *"He's club-hauling! Old Barbary trick! It's the Blackbeard slide, mateys, and a pirate's life for me!"*

Hopper knew that it was a maneuver not without risk. The ship could be swamped, even capsized. Worse, the ship's very super-structure could be ruptured. The *Missouri* could wind up tearing herself apart and save the aliens the trouble. In short, club-hauling was a dangerous tactic that should only be used in cases of extreme emergency.

On the other hand, Hopper really couldn't think of a situation that qualified as more of an emergency than this one.

The *Missouri* creaked and groaned but held together as she tossed up a massive tidal wave, whipping around in a jaw-dropping, ninety-degree turn. As it did so, the crew watched in astonishment as the death-laden cylinders sailed clear past them, missing them by almost literally a mile as they splashed down harmlessly into the water.

The unexpected turn brought the ship's gun turrets perfectly into flanking position against the flagship, and the aliens in the flagship—having discharged their weapons and thus not having a second flight prepped—were caught flat-footed.

"Raikes, fire! Fire! Fire!" shouted Hopper.

The turrets erupted, blasting rounds the size of Volkswagens at what was essentially point-blank range. Huge chunks of the flagship were obliterated and the ship, for all its vastness, shuddered under the unexpected assault.

I was right! Hopper thought triumphantly. *They didn't have their shields up! They weren't taking any defensive action because they thought we weren't attacking them!*

"Fire everything we've got! Don't stop!"

The *Missouri* continued blasting away, firing freely, pounding relentlessly at the flagship as it endeavored to reacquire them in its sights.

"Incoming!" shouted Ord, and he was right. The alien flagship had managed to lock and load even under the *Missouri*'s assault, and now a new barrage of the white cylinders were heading their way. And this time Hopper didn't have a stunt maneuver to pull out of nowhere.

Nevertheless he said defiantly, "This girl's lined with two feet of hardened steel. She can take it."

"Brace! Brace!" shouted Ord.

Seconds later the cylinders impacted against the hull, sticking, turning red and exploding. The mighty vessel was rocked in the water by the explosions, pieces flying off the ship and tumbling into the water. On the deck, everyone scrambled, trying to get out of the way. All save old Andy, who stood there with a fist clenched while defiantly shouting, *"Is that it, you bastards? Is that the best you can do? Bring it on!"* Meanwhile her assault on the far larger vessel continued unabated.

Alex Hopper had been given a front-row seat at the Apocalypse. The Mighty Mo's big guns, all twenty-nine of them, were now unloading, spitting flame and hurling massive metal shells into the belly of the flagship. It was fury incarnate as the flagship was struck, ripped, speared, torn apart by the violent onslaught. It was King Kong versus Godzilla in a final fight to the death.

"Forward guns beginning to run low, sir!" came Raikes's

voice, which was not what Hopper wanted to hear at that moment.

In quick succession the *Missouri*'s guns took out one of the flagship's missile turrets and then the other, but not before two final white cylinders had been fired and arced down—toward the *Missouri*—sticking to one of the ship's 16-inch guns. The cylinder switched from white to red and a second later the turret blew up. Shards of metal fell everywhere on the foredeck. Huge chunks fell toward Andy and thudded into the deck to his immediate right and left. Nothing hit him. Slowly he raised a defiant middle finger to the alien flagship.

"Turret three's been hit!" said Ord, rather unnecessarily since Hopper had a clear view of it.

Hopper wasn't deterred. "We've neutralized their launchers! All weapons, target those upper panels!" To him they looked like some manner of broadcasting devices, and he had a hunch that they were responsible for whatever the hell was keeping the rest of the fleet at bay. There was nothing to be lost by annihilating them and seeing what happened.

Working together, the crew of the *Missouri* converged all fire on where Hopper had instructed. The flagship shuddered under the attack, began to crack, and Hopper howled defiantly, *"You ain't sinking this battleship!"* as the targeted area erupted in a blast of light and fire.

And seconds later, the flagship erupted in a massive explosion. The heat from it was so intense that Hopper could feel his eyebrows and nostril hair crisping as it spread across the water, and he automatically shielded his eyes from it. Pieces of the flagship rained down around the crew, yet cheers rang out from all over the ship.

"I can't believe that worked!" Nagata said. He wasn't joining in the raucous celebration. Instead he said it almost analytically, as if with curious scientific detachment.

"Yeah, well, it did, Mr. Spock," said Hopper. "*Art of War*. 'Fight the enemy where they aren't.' After all these years, it just finally clicked."

"But that's . . ." Nagata paused. "That's not what it means."

Hopper blinked. "Really?"

"No. Not at all."

"Oh." Hopper thought about it, wondered where he'd "remembered" that conclusion from, and then just shrugged and shook his head. "Whatever, man."

"But you misinterpreted . . . we could have been . . ."

Nagata was having trouble finding the words, and Hopper didn't really see the point of letting him find them. "Target destroyed. That's all that matters. Let's get her back on course to Saddle Ridge."

USS REAGAN

Chavez practically exploded into Shane's office as the admiral sat there trying to determine whether sending a letter of resignation to the Secretary of Defense was going to mean anything while the world was ending. "Admiral! You're needed topside, right now!"

Shane didn't even bother to ask what could have prompted Chavez to come flying in there in that manner. He got up from behind his desk so fast that he banged his knees on the underside. Swallowing the automatic moan of pain, he ran after Chavez, limping slightly, and minutes later was standing on the flying deck, looking at nothing.

Actual nothing.

Where the dome of water had been erected that had cut them off from their other three ships, there was now nothing.

"It's like it just collapsed, sir!" Chavez said. "Like whatever was creating it was shut off—"

"Or destroyed," said Shane, as hope swelled within him. Even as he ordered the communications officer to raise the Pentagon, he thought that maybe, just maybe, a Navy vessel had managed to rally and get the job done. And he was reasonably sure he knew who was responsible for it. "Good going, Stone," he said under his breath, not realizing that he was addressing the wrong Hopper.

"Pentagon, sir!" called the communications officer. "Got Fitzroy on the horn."

The vice admiral. Good. Shane was in no mood to talk to the Secretary of Defense. Shane grabbed the phone and said, "Sir, the jamming array has been terminated. I repeat—terminated." When the communications officer gave him a quick thumbs-up, he added, "Comms are up, the signal is down. I'm getting our birds in the air and radioing the other carriers. With any luck, we're turning this thing around."

They were bold words, he knew, but there was just one problem: the *Reagan* was a super-carrier, not exactly built for speed. The ship topped out at about 30 knots, which meant it would still take them a while to get to the scene of the action. And if there was one thing Shane had learned in his time, it was that in combat situations, things could turn around very, very quickly.

The air was thick with the smell of smoke, which was in turn fighting for dominance with the aroma of ionization rising from the disrupted power cells.

In the Jeep, the airbags had deployed at the moment that Sam, at the wheel, had driven it headlong into the antennae array. Both driver and passenger sides, fortunately, were equipped, but nevertheless Sam and Mick were somewhat dazed from the impact. Sam looked up and made a face when she saw that there was a dead alien a few feet in front of her, pinned against the upright remains of the array by the front of the car.

Suddenly Sam picked up movement out the corner of her eye and saw that another of the wide-shouldered warrior aliens was coming toward her fast. She tried to climb free of the Jeep and get the hell out of its way, but the wreckage of the tower had fallen across her. None of its weight was upon her—the structure of the Jeep, including the front windshield, was supporting it—but it was blocking her ability to clamber free. "I'd really like to get out now," she said with growing urgency as the alien drew nearer.

Suddenly she shrieked as something grabbed at her from the other direction. She turned and saw, to her relief, it was Mick. He'd obviously regained consciousness, and was lucky enough to be unencumbered by any manner of obstruction. An army-issue fighting knife in his hand, Mick quickly cut apart the seat belt around her waist. He then tried to lift away the crossbar, but it wouldn't budge.

The alien warrior was practically on top of them, and that was when Mick distracted it while calling out, "Hang tough, Sam. This one is mine."

He rocketed out of his door and stepped between the alien and Sam just before it reached her, chambering a round into his shotgun.

The warrior stopped, looking momentarily confused, as if it wasn't sure what Mick's intentions were. Mick made it abundantly clear as he fired a round from the shotgun at point-blank range.

The assault rocked the creature back on its heels, but otherwise it was unhurt. Its hand speared forward before Mick could make a countermove and it knocked the shotgun effortlessly out of his hands. Automatically Mick tried to go in the direction of the fallen shotgun, but the warrior didn't allow it. Instead, with a casual sweep of its right hand, it knocked Mick to the ground, his steel legs going out from under him.

Grabbing the edge of the Jeep, Mick immediately hauled himself back to his feet. "Come and get it," Mick said defiantly, saying and doing anything to distract the thing from Sam.

The alien was all too happy to oblige him. It came in fast and proceeded to dismantle Mick with an array of blows to the head and chest. Sam watched, helpless and frustrated, as Mick waged a war of futility against his far stronger opponent. Whenever Mick did manage to land a blow, it was against the creature's armor, which barely seemed to register any of the impact. Indeed, the warrior appeared to be enjoying Mick's ineffectiveness.

Once more it knocked Mick to the ground. Lying there, the world swimming around him, Mick's hand fell upon a sizable rock with a pointed end. Even as he wrapped his fingers around it, he tried to wave the creature off, going so far as to plead in what sounded like a whining voice, "Please, no . . . don't hurt me anymore! Don't—!"

Apparently the alien enjoyed brutalizing helpless foes. It reached down toward Mick, yanking him to his artificial feet, and that was the moment that Mick swung the rock around, aiming for the junction point of where the creature's helmet was joined with its armor.

It staggered from the impact and Mick pounded away furiously. The noise was echoing within its helmet, and apparently the loud ringing it must have been causing wasn't something that the alien could easily endure. It had lost its hold on Mick when he first struck it, and now it flailed at him, trying to get its hands back on him. Mick sidestepped the alien and jammed the rock forward as hard as he could.

He heard a crunch and the sound of something breaking within the armor. The helmet came flying off its head, revealing a butt-ugly face, which Mick promptly made even uglier as he slammed the rock into it. There appeared to be some manner of tubes visible in the top of the armor, and Mick's assault broke some of them, causing what appeared to be salt water to pour all over the place.

"Kill it!" shouted Sam, even as she continued to try to push against the girder and free herself. "Hurry—!"

Her phone rang.

It was on the seat next to her, but she couldn't see it. She shoved her hand down to her side blindly and was relieved when her hand found it. She managed to extract her arm and shoved the phone against her ear. "Not the best time!" she said.

"Sam!" Hopper's voice crackled over the connection. "The comm's working! Can you hear me!"

"Hopper, is that you? You're alive!" Suddenly she felt a jolt in the Jeep and she turned to see that the pinned alien against the array wasn't as dead as it could have been. "Hopper, we took out the array—!"

"No you didn't! I see it!"

She looked up and her heart sank. He was right. Like a flower being restored to life, it—like the alien that was still trapped against the Jeep—was throbbing with renewed energy. The power had been at least partly restored and now the array was tilting upward, aiming itself at the satellite that would serve as the summoning beacon to the rest of the invading race.

"We're ready to fire on this end!" he said. "Where are you in relation to the dish! Did you get clear of it after you tried to take it down?"

Sam's eyes were on the power cells, fully glowing again, and the dishes, which were ninety percent fully restored and growing stronger with every passing moment. *These things aren't mechanical. They're bio-organic somehow. And if Hopper doesn't blast them to hell and gone . . .*

She checked her watch, saw that the deadline was drawing near, and forced a smile into her voice. "I'm on the other side of the island. I'm clear. Do it."

The pinned warrior was starting to shake the car violently in its endeavors to free itself. From behind her she heard grunts of struggling, Mick against his own opponent, but she didn't have time to do anything about it even if she could. There was a gun in the well of the passenger seat and she tried to reach for it with what limited mobility she had. The tips of her desperate fingers came three inches short.

"*Where* are you?" Hopper didn't sound convinced.

The trapped alien was pushing against the Jeep. She realized the ignition was still on, the car still running. She shoved the accelerator to the floor, trying to push the car forward. The creature grunted under the additional pressure and pushed the Jeep back, trying to free itself. She put it in drive and kept the alien pinned. Hopper was calling her name over the phone and then she saw what looked like some sort of ray blaster snap into existence on the creature's shoulder. *Oh, shit,* she thought, but then instead of anything lethal coming out of the business end, some energy crackled around it harmlessly before dissipating. She breathed a sigh of relief. She must have damaged the armor's offensive capabilities when she'd hit it with the car.

But then the warrior managed to free a hand and thrust it forward. A vicious curved blade extended from it and drove through the windshield. She yanked her head to one side and the blade sliced into the headrest.

"Sam!" Hopper was still working on getting her attention.

"I'm safe," she said, fighting to keep her voice calm. "No problems here."

"Sam, you sound terrified!"

So much for trying to keep her cool. "Yeah, I am. Terrified you're going to miss your chance. Listen to me, Hopper. The satellite will be in range in minutes. You *can't* let them get their message out. Hit it with everything you've got. I love you."

She clicked off the phone just as the alien—having retracted the blade—lifted the Jeep with its powerful arms. It raised it high and then dropped it, breaking the axle. That killed all forward thrust on the Jeep, and it was enough for the warrior to shove it clear and start heading around toward the driver's side.

Sam banged on the door. It didn't give way, compressed as it was by the initial impact and the further damage it had sustained from the creature just now. The warrior came at her with the blade on its arm and Sam threw herself back, prone on the seat. The girder that had kept her pinned was now her only salvation as it prevented the alien from getting a clear angle at her. The closest it managed to get was the upper part of the seat, which it shredded. Sam screamed and dodged as best she could.

She heard Mick straining, grunting in his battle against the other alien, and wasn't sure how much longer he could hold his own. Then again, it wasn't going to matter, because her luck was about to run out.

And suddenly there was an explosive roar of gunfire and Sam was covered with blood—except it wasn't hers. The creature's head had been blown clear off and she heard a defiant Calvin Zapata bellow, *"Smoke that!"*

The headless alien slumped over and Cal shoved it to get it the hell out of the way. He was clutching a smoking shotgun in his hand, the one that Mick had dropped when the alien had attacked him. Cal then whirled in response to a shout of "A little help here!" and fired again. There was a heavy thud and Sam didn't have to see it to know what had happened: the fearsome fury of Calvin Zapata had struck again, decapitating the warrior that Mick had been fighting.

Cal turned back to Sam and looked chagrined. "I don't have a clever quip for killing the second one," he said. "I know I should say something . . ."

"Don't worry about it! Just get me out of here!"

Calvin started working the door frantically and Mick joined him. As they did so, Mick said to Cal, "Actually, I had the thing on the ropes. Just wanted to make you feel good about yourself."

"Well, it worked." Cal grunted as he pulled. "How about you?"

"Better than I have in a long time. And if Sam's fiancé doesn't get un-semied, I'm so hitting on her once all this is done."

Sam didn't bother to tell them that there was a very good chance they were going to be blown to bits by said fiancé. She didn't see where additional pressure was going to be of much use.

I'm going to hell for this. This is it. This is my moment of damnation. And it's not the kind of hell that you wind up in after you're dead. It's the kind of hell where you're living it and you wish you were dead.

As Hopper stood there on the bridge he was sure—absolutely sure—that Sam had been lying to him. It wasn't just the tension in her voice; it was the deliberate attempts at lightness, at making it seem as if everything was going to be just ducky. That, more than anything, told him that the love of his life wasn't in the clear. Yet he knew what she wanted him to do . . . what he *had* to do.

Assuming Admiral Shane had made it through all this, and assuming they themselves survived—neither of which was a sure thing—he hoped that when he told Shane what he'd done, the admiral would simply pull out a gun and shoot him in the head. With Hopper's luck, however, Shane would never do that. It would be too merciful.

Maybe she's telling the truth . . . maybe she's telling the truth . . .

With that infinitesimal shred of hope to cling to, Hopper said hollowly, "Fire forward guns. Whatever we've got left." *And God, if you're listening—which I doubt, but if you are—if she's still too close, find a way to make sure she has time to get clear.*

The front battery of the *Missouri* revolved, elevated. Hopper braced himself, aware that the next sound he would hear might be the one that announced the impending death of his girlfriend.

The gun shook, coughed, sputtered . . . but did not fire.

"Uhm . . . where's the kaboom?" asked Ord. "There's supposed to be an Earth-shattering kaboom."

The alarmed voice of the gunnery mate crackled over

the 1MC. "She misfired, sir. Damned twenty-year-old hydraulic hose . . . can't close the breach. That was our last round. We are fully Winchester, sir."

It was at that moment that Hopper remembered an old quote his brother had mentioned by some French writer. Something about God being a comedian playing to an audience that was too afraid to laugh. He'd been praying that something would occur that would provide Sam sufficient time to get clear. He was thinking more along the lines of someone getting in touch with him and telling him to delay fire. Not a situation that rendered them unable to do anything.

He exchanged worried looks with Ord, Nagata and Driscoll. As he did, he said into the mike, "Mounts two and three, any ordnance left?"

"Second mount tap city, sir," said the second gunner.

"Third mount, one round high explosive remaining," the third gunner reported in.

Hopper breathed a sigh of relief. "Right. Let her go," he said.

"Negative, sir. We took damage, all barrels are down."

"Okay. Tell 'em: have it ready and waiting for us. Engineering? Beast, you still with us?"

"Right here, Captain."

"Get your ass to battery three. We'll meet you there."

"On my way." Beast sounded faintly confused, but he didn't question it.

"Are you—?" Nagata began to ask.

"No time! Everyone except Driscoll, come on! Driscoll, if someone calls, tell 'em what's going on!"

"Okay. Uh, what would that be?" said Driscoll, but Hopper had already exited, Ord and Nagata with him.

Hopper, Ord and Nagata raced down steep ladders into the belly of the ship. As they passed any able-bodied-looking crewman, Hopper would shout, "You! You and you! Come on!" He gathered as many as he could, and as they ran down a series of passageways, he heard the ones in the back asking the ones just in front of them what was going on. None of them knew. That was fine with Hopper. There was no time to explain—only time to get it done.

They clambered down the final ladders to battery three, where the gunnery crew was waiting with the massive 16-inch shell.

Hopper remembered the first time he'd heard his father talking about big guns with their 16-inch shells. Hopper, not more than eight or nine at the time, said that although sixteen inches was kind of big for a bullet, it didn't seem that scary as far as a missile shell was concerned. His father, laughing, had explained that a 16-inch shell was sixteen inches in diameter, stood three feet tall and weighed several hundred pounds. *Unless you've got a few bodybuilders on hand, you're not going to be taking one of those babies anywhere,* his father had told him.

Well, they now had to move one of those shells up to where it could do some good, and aside from Beast—who met them there, as instructed—they didn't have any bodybuilders on hand.

"Four minutes, sir," said Ord, reminding him of their rapidly closing window of opportunity.

"Got it, Ord," said Hopper.

Beast slapped his hands together, squatting like a sumo, getting a grip on the shell. He hoisted, grunted, and the others got in there with him. It took a few moments to sort it out so that they weren't in one another's way. Soon they all had their hands on the shell, grabbing and straining to lift it, wrestling it out of the hold.

They struggled with it through a series of passageways and ladder-like stairs, at one point losing their grip on it completely. It slid down the ladder and nearly crushed Beast, knocking the wind out of him. But he recovered quickly and got his hands back on it, aiding the others as Hopper, through clenched teeth, kept a steady stream of directions going: "Turn here, hold on, slow, together, watch your angle there." He felt like one of those guys who directed a rowing team.

They finally made it to the immediate destination: a single, long passageway that ran the length of the ship. There was a sort of monorail there, like a zip line for moving cargo, with a series of webbing straps hanging down. "Three minutes," said Ord.

"Not helpful, Ord," said Hopper as they slid the shell into the webbing straps and then looped a chain through it. They made damned certain the shell was secure in it—the last thing they needed was for the weapon to slip loose. Then came the trickiest part, the men grunting and screaming with effort as they lifted the shell onto the trolley hoist hook.

"Put your shoulders into it, boys! Let's take it down Broadway!" They proceeded to do exactly that, running like linebackers as they sprinted the length of the ship to get the shell where they needed it to go, so they could fire it where *it* needed to go.

Two minutes later, Hopper, Nagata and the others—drenched in sweat and exhausted—made it to the gun turret and shoved the shell into the loading elevator. As it hauled the missile upward, Hopper and the others scrambled to reach topside.

Meanwhile, the grizzled gunner who was waiting for the shell grinned in relief, smiling, and patted it lovingly as it rose into view. "Come to Papa," he growled as he used a lever to slam it home.

Hopper reached the flying bridge just as Ord said, "Thirty seconds."

Nagata said, "Shut up, Ord." Ord looked as startled as if he'd been smacked across the face. Despite the dire nature of the situation, Hopper allowed himself a brief smile.

"She's hot and ready," said the gunner over the radio.

Hopper summoned an image of Sam to his mind, and thought, *You better be out of there. Because if you die, I'm going with you. Even if I live, I'll be dead. So save both of us, baby.*

His mouth was just in the process of forming the word "fire" when abruptly Ord shouted, *"Shit! Look!"*

Despite his predilection for pronouncements of doom, this time Ord's reaction was fully understandable.

There was movement from the ruins of the flagship. Something was rising from it, some manner of launcher. And poised atop, clearly prepping to be deployed, were two familiar silver metal spheres.

Shredders.

Hopper knew that as bad as the last time had been, this was going to be way worse. The shredders were unstoppable, and this time they very likely wouldn't settle for gutting the ship. This time, with nothing to lose, they'd annihilate everyone in sight. No one and nothing was going to get out alive.

But they hadn't launched yet. If the *Missouri* fired on them before they were airborne, chances were excellent that they would blast the lethal devices to pieces before they could pose a threat.

Except then they'd have nothing to fire at Saddle Ridge.

"We've only got one round left, haven't we," Hopper said, already knowing the answer all too well.

"Yeah," said Nagata.

"Save ourselves . . . or save the world?"

"Not much of a choice, is it."

"Sometimes there's only one choice you can make."

And that's what it comes down to, Sam. Good news. If this missile kills you . . . I'll be along to join you way more quickly than I thought.

"Fire on Saddle Ridge," he said.

Instantly the 16-inch shell leaped out of the launcher. It took off straight to Saddle Ridge, hurtling away at top speed, flying straight and true for the communications beacon.

At that exact moment, the shredders launched . . .

. . . and, turning at a sharp angle, went in pursuit of the shell.

"No!" screamed Hopper. Because now it was a race. The shell had a head start, but there was no way of knowing how fast the shredders were. If they overtook the shell, they could cut it to pieces effortlessly, then turn around and come after the *Missouri.* Hopper and his crew would die on the eve of his planet's destruction being assured.

SADDLE RIDGE

The Land Commander dies inside, even as he finishes putting the last touches on getting the power up and running on the communications grid.

He feels the death of his hatchling mate, the Sea Commander. He senses that, with his last breath, his hatch-

ling mate launched a final retaliation against these . . . these insignificant creatures that have dared to challenge them.

But that retaliation will not be enough. Not in the slightest.

Mere seconds remain for full power to be reached so that the signal can be sent and a full fleet dispatched. Once that has been accomplished, however, the Land Commander will have no more immediate duties. He will have no vessel—the troop transport had returned to the flagship during the night and by now was doubtlessly nothing more than scrap. He will have no warriors at his disposal—they are all dead.

Still, there will be matters to be dealt with.

First and foremost will be pursuing the humans who inflicted this damage that he is attending to. They are racing down the hill on foot. As soon as the signal is broadcast, he will pursue them. He will overtake them. He will destroy them.

Then he will continuously strike from hiding, finding ways to harry and harass the humans, conduct ongoing guerilla warfare to make certain that they—

That is when he hears a sharp, high-pitched whistling that is unfamiliar, and more sounds that are familiar.

He looks up.

He has just enough time to realize three things: a human-launched weapon is about to strike home just before sufficient power has been reached to send the signal; the Regents-launched spheres are not going to stop it in time; humans were really, really not worth this much trouble.

Then the world explodes in white, and his hatchling mates welcome him.

A huge cheer went up from the crew as a great plume of smoke billowed from Saddle Ridge.

"Target down!" Nagata was shouting with joy, proving, somewhat to Hopper's surprise, that he was indeed capable of displays of emotion.

"You sure?"

"Absolutely. I saw the entire tower collapse about two seconds after the missile hit! And the explosion must have taken the shredders with it!"

Hopper stared at his cell phone. *Call me, baby. Just . . . call me. Let me know you're okay. If you were clear of it, you would have seen it hit, and you'd be calling to tell me you're okay. If you aren't . . .*

If you aren't, then you won't answer if I call you. You won't answer and I'll be listening to that ringing, over and over; and worse, I'll hear your voice telling me you can't answer the phone right now, but you'll call me back as soon as—

The phone rang.

He answered it immediately. "Hello?"

"Did you miss me?" came Sam's voice.

He paused, trying to sound as nonchalant as he could. "In what sense?"

"In both, I guess."

"Well, apparently, yes to both." He paused when he heard people coughing in the background. "You were right there, weren't you."

"Well, technically . . ."

"And you say *I'm* crazy? Get your ass down that mountain."

"Roger that. And Hopper . . . I love you."

He didn't answer.

"Hopper?"

He was staring at the horizon, his face going slack. "Gotta go. Love you." And he hung up.

The war whoops of triumph that had been erupting all over the ship turned to cries of alarm. Two small, familiar objects were moving in toward them from a distance.

"Apparently," said Nagata, "I was premature in saying the missile had destroyed them. They must have veered off at the last moment."

"And now they're coming straight for us."

"ETA is ten seconds, I believe."

Slowly Hopper nodded. So instead of being concerned that he was going to have to live without Sam, she was now going to have to live without him. But at least it would be on a world that was safe from alien invaders.

Totally worth it.

He turned and, his back stiff, saluted Nagata. "It's been an honor serving with you."

Nagata returned the salute.

The shredders screamed toward the *Missouri,* and there was absolutely no escape . . .

And then the nearest one exploded, blown out of the air by a Sidewinder missile.

A sonic boom roared through the air and two F-18s whipped down and around, going in rapid pursuit of the second shredder even as pieces of the first one rained down into the ocean and black smoke wafted lazily skyward.

The second shredder banked away from the *Missouri* and then hesitated, faced with too many targets. That single hesitation cost it, as one of the F-18s opened fire on it. The shredder might have been able to avoid another Sidewinder, since it was now aware of the F-18's presence and undistracted. But there was nowhere for it to hide as the plane's nose-mounted 6-barreled Gatling cannon strafed it, pumping two hundred rounds at it

within seconds. The last of the shredders was itself shredded, torn to pieces before the astonished eyes of the *Missouri*'s crew.

The F-18s did one more large circle of the area. Hopper
watched them, and then, in the far, far distance, he saw a
hint of other vessels, with a carrier that he was reasonably
sure was the *Reagan* leading them.

"Gentlemen," he said into the PA, "I think it's safe to
cheer this time."

Which they did, for a very long time.

HARBOR-HICKAM

Hickam Airforce Base had been established in 1948
near Honolulu and served as a key launching point for
operations during World War II. Eventually it had been
folded into a combined base with Pearl Harbor, to become known as the Joint Base Pearl Harbor–Hickam. A
variety of surface ships and subs were homeported there,
including the USS *Missouri* in her heyday.

Now the officers who had most recently, and most un-
expectedly, pressed the Mighty Mo into service against
an enemy that no one could have expected—much less
expected to defeat—were lined up in their dress whites.
Standing at stiff attention in the front row were Alex
Hopper and Yugi Nagata. Ord, Raikes, Hiroki and others were lined up behind them, with Beast naturally
towering over the lot. Even Calvin Zapata was there,
dressed in a crisp, freshly pressed Hawaiian shirt.

The families of those who had survived were seated nearby, including Vera and her kids, Nagata's wife (Hopper had been briefly introduced to her but couldn't remember her name) and Sam, who was smiling but in a measured way. It was wise of her to show restraint, because intermingled with them on this day of both celebration and mourning were many families whose loved ones hadn't survived. They were somber, still looking shell-shocked, many eyes red from crying. Those who had made it through knew they were damned lucky. The families who were bereft of their loved ones kept their attentions focused on Shane, trying not to look at those who hadn't suffered a loss. Because the inevitable question—*Why do we have to suffer and you don't?*—would be reflected in their eyes, and there was no possible answer available.

Shane's voice crackled over the loudspeaker, causing some ear-splitting feedback. As he stepped away while sound technicians rushed to fix the problem, Hopper took a moment to inhale deeply and then let it out. He actually tasted the air as it passed through his lips. It was a typically gorgeous Hawaiian day, the sun bathing them in its rays, the breeze gentle. But there was something about surviving an experience such as what they'd endured—something about living to see another day when the prospects of doing so had seemed terribly unlikely—that just made the air taste better.

Once he received a thumbs-up from the technician, Shane—who had been interrupted by the shrill sounds midsentence—stepped forward and tentatively said, "That the men and women . . ." When no further sound mishaps occurred, he continued with renewed confidence. "That the men and women who gave their lives are heroes is not in doubt. That we owe each and every one of them an unpayable debt of gratitude is undeniable. That we remain united, stronger than ever, with all the great nations of our world, is truer today than it ever has been."

He paused a moment, allowing that to sink in as a sop to those who had endured terrible tragedy. Then he continued, "I can't single out each and every one of you for bravery, so I will instead single out a few for remarkable valor.

"Commander Stone Hopper, deceased, the Medal of Honor."

He held up the framed medal and Hopper felt something catch in his throat. Shane looked right at him, a questioning eyebrow raised. The unspoken question was obvious: did Hopper want to come up there and accept it? Hopper shook his head ever so slightly and mouthed, *Our father.* Without missing a beat, Shane said, "It will be sent to his father, retired Captain Robert Hopper, who could not be here for this presentation." True enough. Alex and Stone's father had recently undergone a triple bypass and had been forbidden to travel. Hopper's mother, taking care of him, had reportedly said, in that undeniable way of hers, that she'd be damned if she'd lose two of her men within days of each other. The ceremony was being broadcast through a naval feed, though, and Hopper had no doubt in his mind that they were watching it back home.

It had been the Navy that had delivered them the news of the loss of their eldest son. When Hopper had finally gotten them on the phone, there was his mother crying, of course, and his father being as stiff-lipped as ever. Hopper had tried to launch into *mea culpa*s, to tell them he wished he could have done more; his father silenced him with ten words: *"You did what we needed you to do. You survived."* He'd barely been able to continue the conversation after that.

Shane was now holding another medal in his hand. Next to him was the admiral of the Japanese fleet. In a formal voice, Shane said, "Captain Yugi Nagata: the Order of the Rising Sun."

Nagata strode forward with brisk, crisp steps. He bowed stiffly at the waist and Shane returned the sign of respect. The Japanese admiral took the medal and carefully pinned it onto Nagata's jacket. Nagata bowed once more to both of them and stepped down from the podium.

Shane shifted his gaze to Hopper and nodded, indicating that he should come forward.

Hopper took a deep breath even as he walked toward Shane. His legs felt numb; he was worried he was going to collapse. *Brace yourself. You know what's coming now. Now Shane is going to say, "As for you, Mr. Hopper, you have a court-martial waiting for you. Take him away, men." And they'll escort you away to your court-martial, where they will, of course, find you guilty and drum you out of the Navy. And they'll have a closed-circuit TV so your folks can be watching and your dad's heart will just stop and your mom will blame you for dad's death for the rest of your life . . .*

He stood in front of Shane, waiting, his back stiff, his eyes not meeting Shane's but instead gazing just over his left shoulder. "Commander Alex Hopper . . ." Shane began, and when Hopper heard the title with his name spoken after it, he actually looked Shane in the eye. Theoretically he'd known this was what was in the offing, but he didn't quite believe it until he heard it spoken aloud. And even now he was braced for Shane suddenly saying, "Psych! Fooled you! Take him away, men!"

As if he could read Hopper's mind—a talent that Hopper wouldn't have put past him—Shane reaffirmed, with a slight smile, "That's right . . . *Commander*—the Navy Cross." He pinned it onto Hopper's jacket. It felt heavy, like the weight of the world was now on his chest.

No. It was the weight of responsibility, something

that—to various degrees—he'd been dodging his entire
life. It felt . . .

. . . good.

"And your own command," said Shane. "You'll take
the USS *Benfold* out to sea." Then he lowered his voice so
that only Hopper could hear him. "Don't screw it up."

"No, sir." Hopper saluted and Shane returned it briskly.
Then they shook hands. It felt odd and Hopper realized
he'd never actually shaken the man's hand before. When
Sam had first introduced them, Shane had been seated at
his desk, going through paperwork. He'd looked Hopper
up and down—seemingly dissecting him with his mind as
he did so, judging him and finding him wanting—and
then said curtly, "I'm busy. This is a bad time." He had
gone back to work. Sam had escorted a shaken Hopper
out the door and assured him in a low voice, "Don't
worry. He'll warm up to you. Everything will work out."

It had only taken an alien invasion to do it. Hopper
reasoned that he'd better not get back on the admiral's
bad side; otherwise he might have to save the entire galaxy
in order to find his way back to the man's good graces.

He returned to his spot and his cell phone buzzed in
his pocket. He extracted it and saw a text message from
Sam: *No better time to ask him.* He glanced toward her
and saw her nodding encouragingly and giving him a
thumbs-up.

Suddenly facing shredders and alien invasions didn't
seem so bad.

Hopper had waited on the parade grounds until Admiral Shane was finally not surrounded by various officials and well-wishers. He'd approached him tentatively,
thanked him once again for this incredible opportunity
and then hemmed and hawed about things that didn't
matter all that much until Shane finally got fed up and
said, "What's your point, Hopper?"

Now or never. Wait: let's consider the many advantages of "never" in the—

"Sir," and he pushed the words out of himself with about the same amount of force a woman used to push out a child, "I want you to know that I love Sam . . ."

Words failed him for an instant. It was the moment when he would normally cut and run, but then he took a deep breath, looked Shane dead in the eye and spoke from his heart.

". . . and I want to ask for your permission to marry her."

He exhaled then. He'd gotten the words out, and that had been the challenge, hadn't it? That had been the toughest part of all this.

"No," said Shane.

"Thank you, sir. I promise I'll . . ." His voice trailed off as Shane's answer sank in. "What?"

As if there was simply no further need for discussion—question asked, question answered, on to the next thing—Shane turned and started to stride away.

"But . . . but I just saved the world!" Hopper called after him.

"The world is one thing, Hopper. My daughter is quite another."

Hopper was in utter shock. "But . . . but . . ."

Shane paused just long enough to say, "No means no, Hopper. Now if you'll excuse me, I'm late for lunch." And as he walked off, he tossed over his shoulder, "Think I'll get a chicken burrito."

Hopper stopped in his tracks as if he'd been hit in the face with a frying pan as the last two words registered. "Wait," he said, slowly realizing, "Are you—*are you messing with me?*"

Shane glanced back at him, and there was a twinkle in his eye that might have been delightful if it wasn't tinged with pure sadism.

"Don't do that!" Hopper cried out. "Why would you do that? Did Sam put you up to this? Oh my God, she did, didn't she!"

Gesturing that he should follow him, Shane said, "Come along, Hopper. Let's discuss the terms of your surrender over lunch." As Hopper ran after him, Shane continued, "And if I'm a little light on cash, I'm sure you could just knock over a convenience store by climbing on the roof, right?" He draped an arm around Hopper's shoulder as they left the parade ground.

SCOTTISH HIGHLANDS

It had taken bloody forever.

The boys had been at it for several days. They had mutually agreed to say nothing of it to anyone, because the moment their parents knew, there were two things of a certainty: they would be told to stay the hell away from it; the authorities would show up and cart it away. When that happened, it meant that the boys would never know what had been in it, and they had far too much time, effort and emotion invested in it to allow that to happen.

So whenever night had been approaching, they had taken care to cover it with branches and brush. It wasn't the world's greatest camouflage job, but it was what they could manage and apparently it had gotten the job done, because no one had found it yet.

Fortunately none of the parents had yet noticed that some of their tools had gone missing. This was something of a problem, because sooner or later Sean's dad was sure to notice that his chain saw was nowhere around. There'd been no point in bringing it back, so Sean had left it where it was: on the ground near the big rock, broken, yet another victim of its seemingly impenetrable surface.

Angus, though, had finally gotten it done. His father's car had blown yet another tire the previous week (the road around them being notoriously wretched) and, in changing it, his dad had thrown out his back. As a result, his mother had insisted that, if the bastards in the local government couldn't be bothered to fix the damned roads, and since no one had invented impenetrable tires, the only remaining option was to make tire changing easier.

By serendipity, Angus had been the only one home when the hydraulic car jack had been delivered. He happily signed for it, then called his pals and—within the hour—they were back at the landing point of their secret stash.

The hydraulic jack had been their last resort. They'd wedged it into the seam in the chamber, and at first it had seemed that the jack's attempts would prove as fruitless as any of the others. But their frustration had turned to utter joy when there was a sharp crack, and a hiss of air. The jack had gotten the job done and, with what was apparently a broken seal, they now had access to it. Angus got to do the honors since he was the one who had obtained the jack, and now he jammed in a crowbar and lifted with all his strength. To his annoyance he wasn't quite strong enough and, through gritted teeth, he said, "A little help . . ."

Immediately the others pitched in and, seconds later, they had the lid clear.

They stared inside.

Their joy turned to shock, and then horror.

And then they ran like hell.

OAHU

The sun was beginning to set on what was easily the best day of Alex Hopper's life.

After handling with aplomb all of the congratulations, Hopper and Sam had slipped off to spend the afternoon enjoying each other's company. They'd hung out at the beach, gotten some surfing in, and were overall celebrating that they were both alive.

Having packed the surfboards onto the back of his truck, Hopper was now driving along a seaside road, with Sam resting her head contentedly on his upper arm. Seagulls were cawing in the distance. He was at total peace and couldn't remember the last time he felt that way.

He wished Stone could see him like this.

Trying to shake off sad thoughts, Hopper glanced down at Sam. "You look hungry," he said.

"Oh, no." She started to laugh. She knew where this was going.

"No, seriously. Tell me you can't go for a chicken burrito right now. 'Cause I'm starving . . ."

"Hopper," she began, but before she could continue, her cell phone rang. She answered it, listened, and then said, "Okay, okay, Dad, slow down. He's right here."

"He come to his senses about my new boat?" Hopper asked, only half joking. Then he took the phone from her and put it to his ear. "Yes, Admiral?"

"Hopper, good news, son," came Shane's voice. "They found one. They found one alive."

Hopper slammed on the brakes, the sudden stop thrusting Sam forward with such force that, had it not been for the seat belt, she'd have cracked her skull open. "*Hopper, what the hell—*"

"Hopper?" The admiral heard that something was going on, but didn't understand. "Hopper, is there a problem—?"

"Sir . . ." Hopper licked his suddenly parched lips. "Did you read the debriefing reports . . . ?"

"There's a lot to wade through, son. I'm about halfway—"

"You're going to want to jump to the other half."

"Why don't you summarize it for me, Commander?"

"No man left behind."

"What? What does that have to—?" He paused and then, because he was an extremely bright man, Shane started to understand. "Are you saying—?"

Hopper nodded even though Shane couldn't see him. "When one of their . . . 'people' . . . fall . . . if they're still alive, then they'll come back for him."

"They'll come back."